TAYLOR BROWN grew up on the Georgia coast. He has lived in Buenos Aires, San Francisco, and the mountains of western North Carolina. His fiction has appeared in more than twenty publications, he is the recipient of the Montana Prize in Fiction, and he was a finalist both in the Machigonne Fiction Contest and for the Doris Betts Fiction Prize. He is the author of *Fallen Land* (2016) and *The River of Kings* (2017); *Gods of Howl Mountain* is his third novel. He lives in Wilmington, North Carolina.

GODS of HOWL MOUNTAIN

TAYLOR BROWN

PICADOR
ST. MARTIN'S PRESS
NEW YORK

GODS OF HOWL MOUNTAIN. Copyright © 2018 by Taylor Brown. All rights reserved. Printed in the United States of America. For information, address Picador, 175 Fifth Avenue, New York, N.Y. 10010.

picadorusa.com • instagram.com/picador
twitter.com/picadorusa • facebook.com/picadorusa

Picador® is a U.S. registered trademark and is used by Macmillan Publishing Group, LLC, under license from Pan Books Limited.

For book club information, please visit facebook.com/picadorbookclub or email marketing@picadorusa.com.

Designed by Jonathan Bennett

The Library of Congress has cataloged the St. Martin's Press edition as follows:

Names: Brown, Taylor, 1982– author.
Title: Gods of Howl Mountain : a novel / Taylor Brown.
Description: First edition. | New York : St. Martin's Press, 2018.
Identifiers: LCCN 2017043677 | ISBN 9781250111777 (hardcover) | ISBN 9781250111784 (ebook)
Subjects: LCSH: Family secrets—Fiction. | Mountain life—Fiction. | Smugglers—Fiction. | Healers—Fiction.
Classification: LCC PS3602.R722894 G63 2018 | DDC 813'.6—dc23
LC record available at https://lccn.loc.gov/2017043677

Picador Paperback ISBN 978-1-250-31158-0

Our books may be purchased in bulk for promotional, educational, or business use. Please contact your local bookseller or the Macmillan Corporate and Premium Sales Department at 1-800-221-7945, extension 5442, or by email at MacmillanSpecialMarkets@macmillan.com.

First published by St. Martin's Press

First Picador Edition: February 2019

To Jason Frye—friend, mentor, and son of Appalachia

I will break the back of this long November night,
Folding it double, cold beneath my spring quilt,
That I may draw out the night, should my love return.

— HWANG JIN-I, OR MYEONG-WOL ("BRIGHT MOON")

And these signs shall follow them that believe; in my name
shall they cast out devils; they shall speak with new tongues;
they shall take up serpents; and if they drink any deadly
thing, it shall not hurt them . . .

— MARK 16:17–18

GODS of
HOWL
MOUNTAIN

CHAPTER 1

The machine started at dusk, headlights slashing their way down the old switchbacks that ribbed the mountain's slopes, thunder and echo of thunder vaulting through the ridges and hollers on every side. The road sawed down out of the high country, angling against valleys welled with darkness, past ridges hewn by dynamite, at times following the pale sinews of logging roads that lashed these hills half a century before. It poured ever east, the motor thrumming long miles through the darkening country of the foothills, the machine leaving in its wake a ghost of dust that settled on mailboxes and ranging cattle and tobacco fields already reaped. The road fell and fell again, surrendering to the speed of the machine, the fire of the engine, while stars wheeled out over the land.

The long bends unwound before the car's nose, the roadside produce stands and billboards and barns big enough to hide the cars of badged men. The road crested a rise and the land lay nearly naked against the sky, vast and blue. The ragged lights of the mill town burned in the distance, borne up on the swells of the Piedmont. The town of Gumtree. Soon the road was humming, paved, plunging through great stands of hardwoods. The mills rose long and hulking on their bluff over the town, pouring black smoke from their many stacks, like ocean liners on a sea of earth. Window after window brightly lit, as if people were having fun in there, a party or a ball. Men and women came down out of the mountains to toil all hours in the heat of those lint-blown rooms, making socks and hose. Second shift ended at ten o'clock. The workers would emerge coughing and white-dusted from those brick bowels like ghost-people, ready for a nip of the hot.

The machine crossed the dam into town. The valley had been flooded for power two decades before; the dam discharged its row of flat white waterfalls under the moon. The car rounded the town square, the big motor rattling the darkened storefronts like man-brought thunder. There was the grocery, the pharmacy, the five-and-dime. The jeweler, the shoe shop, the hardware store. The places where the mill-hands bought on credit, the payments deducted from their wages. The machine drove on, the working neighborhoods assembling before its hood, the low little mill-owned houses huddled close with square, close-cropped yards. Homes so narrow a man could shoot a shotgun and hit every room. Some had. The car drove between them and past them, out into the edges of town where the road descended slowly, gradually, toward the lake.

End-of-the-Road, they called it. The last vestige of town before it was swallowed underwater. Shothouses and bawdyhouses reared out of the bottomland trees, houses for anything a body might want. Their windows a sickly yellow, flickering with shadows. A place for a drink and a fight, a strange bed, strange stars shooting through strange skies if a man dared look. Past that, the road daggered into the depths. Down there was the valley of old, where people had lived so long before the mills came, hungry for power. There were cabins down there, it was said, open-doored to the fishes, their heart-pine floors drowned and cold. There were trees, stunted and lifeless, wavering in the depths as if brushed by slow-motion wind. The bones of land creatures riddled the depths, inhabitants given no warning of the coming flood. The clap of axes and stammer of engines did not carry the weight of thunder or bruised skies. Not yet. Some mean-tempered old tobacco croppers were said to have stayed on their lands when the water came, to spite the government, but most doubted it. It was easy to doubt it all, the lake so flat and calm, a thing whose secrets would never surface.

The first order of the night was a broken-down bungalow with barred windows, the siding curly-cued as if someone had taken a putty knife to it. An indention in the roof housed a dark pool of old rain-water. The lawn was red-churned with tire tracks. Beat-up sedans sat willy-nilly in the grass. Slouching figures stood in line before the kitchen window, their shoulders showered in what looked like flour. Coins glinted in their hands.

Twenty-five cents a shot.

Their eyes were wide when the machine—a Ford coupe— rumbled past them, heading to the back of the house. It parked and the driver climbed out, his face hidden beneath an ancient black bowler hat. He knocked on the door and heard them unbarring it from the inside, the clack after clack of deadbolts unlocked.

The door opened. A white man in a stained apron stepped out. Fat. His face and hair had an unwholesome sheen. The stoop trembled be-neath him as he descended.

"Thought you weren't coming," he said. "Revenuers?"

"None tonight," said Rory.

The man shrugged and handed him a wad of bills. Rory unlocked the trunk.

With each stop the lake drew closer, the road ever sliding toward the blank darkness beyond the trees. With each stop the patrons were drunker, meaner. Some of them who got this deep down the road, they didn't come back.

CHAPTER 2

Granny May held a match to the end of her corncob pipe. Her cheeks hollowed, her chest swelling with smoke. She held a double lungful tickling in her breast. There was no harsh sting, as with tobacco. She rocked back and unhinged her jaw, releasing a blue ghost of smoke into the dawn. The world lay wet before her, dark, carrying the last bruises of night. There were the mountains, ridged like crumbling battlements, and the dewy meadow of her home.

She squinted down her nose, eyeing the tree in the yard. This tree, lone survivor of the blight, stood as centerpiece of all she surveyed from her porch. The others of its kind, chestnuts, had once covered these mountains, the bark of their trunks deeply furrowed, age-twisted like the strands of giant steel cables. Their leaves sawtoothed, golden this time of year, when the falling nuts fattened the beasts of the land, sweetening their meat. That army of hardwoods had fallen, victims of death-black cankers that starved and toppled them. Some exotic fungus had slipped in through wounds in their bark, the work of antlers or claws or penknives. This tree stood alone in the meadow, crowned high against the impending light.

A spirit tree.

Multicolored glass bottles, too many to count, dangled from the branches on tied strings. The evils come skulking over the far hills, out of the lightless hollers and dry wells—the bottles captured such spirits. Contained them. Kept them out of the house, out of her grandson's dreams and heart. When the wind came sawing across the meadow, you could hear them moaning in their bottles, trapped. The spirits were mean, she thought, but they weren't very smart.

The first car came rocking up the drive just after sunup. It was a fancy coupe in green, a low-slung Hudson that chugged in the dawn, sized like something that moved in herds. A girl got out from the passenger side. She had a heavy shawl clutched over her shoulders, piled on like a burden. The boy driving the car sat hunched behind the wheel, scowling. He didn't cut the engine. The girl stood at the bottom of the steps.

"Morning, ma'am. Are you Maybelline Docherty? Granny May?"

"I am. What is it I can do for you?"

The girl looked back at the car smoking in the yard.

"That's Cooley Muldoon," she said. "He's engaged to a girl over in Linville? We, we had us a accident in the car last night."

Granny May squinted at the rumbling machine. The new sun glowed on the glass, shivered on the hood. Not a scratch on the paint.

The girl held out her hands.

"In the . . . backseat of it," she said.

"Ah," said Granny.

"People say you make the moon tea?"

"Come sit a spell, child. I got some already steeping. Seems I knew you were coming."

The girl took a seat in the other rocker and Granny shuffled inside, quiet-footed, as if not to wake the yet-empty house. The pot sat on the woodstove, issuing the faintest curl of steam. Inside, a concoction of pennyroyal and tansy and other herbs, a brew passed down from the wood-witches of old. It could kill if it wasn't mixed right. She got down one of the mugs standing on the shelfboard. She had eyed the girl close, to see what size to pour.

Granny puffed her pipe as the girl drank the tea. The boy was still sitting behind the wheel of the car, now and again raising a pint bottle to his lips.

"Didn't he have a rubber?"

The girl held the mug cupped in her hands, the steam rising into her bent face.

"He won't wear one," she said. "Says it's like eating a beefsteak with a sock over his tongue."

"Is that right?"

"Yes'm. Says he'll have bastards all over these hills before he hides himself under a jimmyhat."

Granny could feel the old ire welling up. She thought of her own daughter in those times long ago. Thought of the fatherless grand-child she kept under her own roof, who slept but fitfully beneath his snarl of blankets, as if his war-lost leg kicked and thumped him in his sleep. She set the shank of the pipe between her teeth and pulled hard.

"Maybe you ought not to ride with him, then."

The girl looked up.

"That's Cooley Muldoon, of the Linville Muldoons. They run more whiskey down from the hills than God does creekwater. He wants you to go with him, you do."

"More whiskey than Eustace Uptree's lot?"

The girl's mug halted halfway to her mouth. She looked around, realizing perhaps where she was. On whose mountain. Her eyes went round.

"No, ma'am, I don't reckon that much."

The boy jammed his elbow out the side of the car, his head follow-ing soon after.

"Hey," he said. "How long's this gonna take? I ain't got all damn day to watch y'all jawing it up."

Granny took the pipe from her mouth.

"It's gonna take the rest of your life, you don't show a old woman some respect."

The boy Cooley got out of the car and slammed the door. He was skinny but hard-made, his flannel shirt rolled up over white long-john sleeves, his suspender loops hanging down like a pair of failed wings. A long stag-handled knife hung from a leather sheath on his belt.

"Listen," he said, "I didn't give twenty dollars to hear the mouth-ing off of some old whore."

He was pointing at her from the yard, just beyond spitting dis-tance, but she could almost feel the long reach of his finger probing her heart. She looked above him, at the bottles in the tree. The wind moved them slightly on their limbs, a hundred tiny mouths whisper-ing their discontent.

"Careful," she said. "You might ought to recollect where you are."

"I know right where I'm got-damn at."

He started across the yard, his arm outstretched to grab the girl from the porch, but he froze at the stoop, snapped as if at the end of a chain. It was a rumble that stopped him, issued as from the mountain itself. A quaking of the ground. Only one motor in the county made a sound like that.

Maybelline.

The coupe rounded the lower bend of the drive, a '40 Ford in black, built like a cannonball. It came clawing its way over the ruts, the big ambulance motor pounding the earth as it climbed. It squeaked to a halt in the yard, stuttering at idle, unaccustomed to so little throttle. The driver killed the engine, the door groaned open. Out stepped Granny May's grandson in his old bomber jacket, his brow hidden be-neath a black bowler that had been his grandfather's. He was short but squarely built, his jaw wide and underbit like a bulldog's. The kind of jaw that once it got hold of something, it didn't let up.

"Rory Docherty," said Cooley. "Heard you was back from over there. Part of you, leastways."

Rory hobbled to the front of his car, favoring his wooden foot. He didn't say anything. Cooley spat in the grass.

"Didn't figure you'd be driving much no more."

Rory pulled a pack of Lucky Strikes from his chest pocket and lit one between his cupped palms. The 5th Marines Zippo snapped closed in his hand.

"Hasn't been a problem," he said, "seeing as it's my clutch foot."

Cooley licked his lips, staring at Rory's left boot.

"That driver, Red Byron, now he's a cripple. Ain't stopped him from racing, I reckon. Course, he still *has* a leg."

Rory blew smoke from his nostrils, a curling blue mustache.

"There some kind of a problem here?"

"We just come for a sip of your granny's tea," said Cooley. "Ella here, she had her a seeding last night."

"Did she," said Rory.

Cooley tugged upward on the front of his britches, grinning.

"Yes, sir. Just needed us a herbal remedy."

The girl gulped down the rest of the tea and stood.

"I'm finished," she said. "We ought to be going. Daddy'll be up soon. I can't have him knowing I ain't been home."

"No," said Cooley, leering at Rory. "We can't have him knowing that."

She came down off the porch and walked to the car, Cooley standing a long moment just where he was. Finally he started back toward the car, bouncing almost on his toes, the fool's grin still twisting his face. He got in the green Hudson and leaned his head out the window.

"Way I hear it, Docherty, they given you a medal just for getting blowed up."

Rory's cheeks darkened as he pulled on the cigarette. The ash flared.

"Yeah," he said.

"Seems awful generous, you ask me."

"Yeah."

"You kilt any slants over there?"

The smoke came blowing again from Rory's nostrils, as if a fire were burning in his gut.

"I believe it's time you got the fuck off my property, boy. Double-quick."

Cooley put the car in reverse, looking at Rory.

"You ought to watch how you talk to me," he said. "Eustace is a long way up that mountain."

Rory limped closer to the car. He rested one hand on the roof, leaning in, the cigarette burning between his fingers.

"Careful," he said, lowering his voice. "They say he's got ears in the trees."

Rory nodded his head at the spirit tree. Cooley's eyes went climbing the branches, like Rory knew they would, and Rory flicked his cigarette into the boy's lap. Cooley yelped, swatting at the shower of sparks, a mob of the red-hot flies assaulting his crotch. The girl sitting shotgun clapped a hand over her mouth, trying not to laugh. Cooley knocked the red cherry of ash to the floorboard and stamped it out. When he looked up, his face was skewed, flushed.

"God damn you, Docherty. You'll be sorry for this."

"There's a lot I'm sorry for," said Rory. "Not this."

He turned and started up toward the house. The Hudson reversed out of the yard, jerking into gear, slinging dirt as it slammed and fishtailed down the drive.

Granny watched her boy come laboring up the steps.

"You don't blow smoke into a snake's den, son."

"Wasn't his den, it was ours." He started inside.

"*Rory.*" He stopped. "You forgetting something?"

He bent, dutifully, and kissed her on the cheek.

"Catheads on the stove," she said. "Gravy in the pot."

"Thank you."

She heard him cross the floor, the cabin trembling under his gait. She heard the springs protest as he crashed onto his bed, his breakfast going cold.

CHAPTER 3

There was the stone pagoda, three-tiered, built on a small hill over a stream that shone like pebbled glass. The platoon had dammed a pool in the stream. They crouched in their skivvies, soaping and scrubbing the August grit from the creases and crannies of their bodies. Howitzers were perched on the hills around them, like guardian monsters. Still, the Marines washed quickly, feeling like prey without their steel helmets and green fatigues, their yellow canvas leggings that laced up at the sides. Their dog tags jingled at their necks, winking under the Korean sun.

Rory stood from the pool, feeling the cool water stream like a cloak from his form. His bare feet stood white-toed on the curved backs of the stones, eon-smoothed, so like the ones on the mountain of his home. He walked up the hill toward the accordion-roofed temple where they were billeted. He passed olive shirts and trousers drying on rocks and bushes, spread like the skins of killed beasts. The air felt full of teeth. Earlier that day, searching an abandoned village, they had taken sniper fire. Their first. They were Marines, but green. The whip-crack of the shots had flayed the outermost layer of courage from their backs; they were closer now to their bones.

A pair of stone lions guarded the entrance to the pagoda, lichen-clad beasts with square heads and heavy paws. "Foo dogs," the Marines called them. There was a nisei in their platoon, Sato, whose older brother had fought with the 442nd Infantry Regiment in World War II. All Japanese Americans.

"*Komainu*," he said. "Lion dogs. They ward off evil spirits."

Someone had thrown his shirt over the head of one of the beasts. Rory pulled the garment away, so the creature could see. He stepped on into the temple. The air felt cool here, ancient, like the breath of a cave. The black ghosts of old fires haunted the sconces. The place smelled of incense and Lucky Strikes and nervous Marines. Their gear lined the walls. He had never been in a place this old. Granny was never one for churches—"godboxes," she called them—and those in the mountains seemed flimsy compared to this. Desperate cobblings of boards, some no more than brush arbors. But standing here alone, nearly naked at the heart of the temple, he felt armored in the stone of generations. Swaddled. No bullet could strike him here. No arrow of fear.

He wanted to remain in this place, so still and quiet amid the hills of guns. But a cold wind came whistling through the temple, lashing his back, and he remembered that fall was coming soon, for leaves and men. Blood so bright upon the sawtooth ranges, and the screaming that never stopped.

He could never forget.

Rory woke into the noon hour, his bedquilt kicked off, his body sweat-glazed despite the October bite. His lost foot throbbing, as if it were still attached to the bruised stump below his knee. He rose and quickly dressed. His bedroom window was fogged, the four panes glowing a faint gold. Paintings, unframed, covered one wall. Beasts of the field, fowls of the air—their bodies flaming with color where the sun touched them. They reminded him what day it was: Sunday.

He scrubbed his armpits and washed his face, slicked his hair back

and dabbed the hollow of his neck with the sting of Granny-made co-
logne. He donned a white shirt that buttoned to the neck, a narrow
black tie, the bowler hat that had been his grandfather Anson's. He
looked at his face in the mirror—it looked so old now, as if a whole
decade had snuck under his skin in the night. The flesh was shiny
beneath his eyes, like he'd been punched.

He was sitting on the porch, carving the mud from his boots, when
Granny came out. She had a pie tin balanced in the crook of one arm.

"I can get that," he said, jumping up.

"I'm fifty-four years old. I ain't a god-damn invalid."

She sat primly in the beast of a car, straight-backed, as if she were
riding atop a wagon. It was no stretch to imagine her riding shotgun
on a Wells Fargo stagecoach, a short-barreled shotgun in her lap. She
looked at him as he slid behind the wheel.

"You had the dreams again?"

"No," he lied.

"You need to take that tincture I made you."

"I have been."

"You been pouring it through that knothole in the floorboard.
That's what you been doing."

Rory fired the engine, wondering how the woman could know the
things she did.

In an hour they were down into tobacco country, square after
square of mildly rolling fields passing on either side of them, the clay
soil red as wounds among the trees. Giant rough-timbered curing
barns floated atop the hills, like weathered arks, holding the bright-
leaf tobacco that would fill the white spears of cigarettes trucked all
over the country. Chesterfields and Camels and Lucky Strikes. Pall
Malls and Viceroys and Old Golds. The highway wound through
Winston-Salem, where the twenty-one-floor Reynolds Building stood
against the sky like a miniature Empire State. It was named after R. J.
Reynolds, who rode into town aback a horse, reading the newspaper,

and went on to invent the packaged cigarette, becoming the richest man in the state.

"They say it's the tallest building in the Carolinas," said Rory.

Granny sucked her teeth, wearing the sneer she always did when forced to come down off the mountain.

"It ain't whale-shit compared to the height of my house, now is it?"

They passed Greensboro and Burlington, assemblies of giant mills, their smokestacks black-belching day and night, while beneath them sprang neat little cities with streetcars and straight-strung telephone lines. They passed Durham, home of Duke Power, which electrified most of the state, and then on into Raleigh, passing along the oak-shadowed roads as they wound upward toward the state asylum at Dix Hill. It was massive, a double-winged mountain of brownstone that overlooked the city, four stories high, the narrow windows stacked like medieval arrow slits. The center building looked like something the Greeks had built, four giant columns holding up a triangular cornice, with a glassed rotunda on top.

They signed the paperwork and sat waiting. When the nurse came to fetch them, Rory went in first. His mother came light-footed across the visiting room floor, hardly a whisper from the soles of her white canvas shoes. She was like that, airy almost, like a breath of wind. She could be in the same room with you and you might not even know it. Her black hair was pulled behind her head, waist-long, shot through with long streaks of silver. Her skin ghost-white, as if she were made of light instead of meat. As if, squinting hard enough, you could see her bones.

"They treating you good?" Rory asked.

She nodded and took his hands. Her eyes shone so bright, seeing him, they ran holes in his heart. She said nothing. Never did. She was always a quiet girl, said Granny, living in a world her own. *Touched*, said some. *Special*. Then came the night of the Gaston killing, and she never spoke again. Rory had never heard her voice. He knew her smell, like coming rain, and the long V-shaped cords that made her neck. He knew the tiny creases at the corners of her eyes, the size of a hummingbird's feet. He knew the feel of her hands, so light and cool. Hands that had scooped out a man's eye with a cat's paw, then hidden the detached orb in the pocket of her dress.

There had been three of them, nightriders, each in a sack hood. The year was 1930. The men had caught her and a mill boss's son in an empty cabin along the river. The place was condemned, destined to be flooded under when the waters rose. They bludgeoned the boy with ax handles, but she fought them, finding a cat's paw from a scatter of tools, an implement split-bladed like a cloven tongue. She took back from them what she could.

An eye.

None of them was ever caught.

The boy they beat to death was named Connor Gaston. He was a strange boy, people said. But smart. He liked birds, played the violin. His father ran the hosiery mill in town. A boy of no small advantage, and she a prostitute's daughter. Probably one herself, the town said. Didn't she live in a whorehouse? Wasn't she of age, with all the wiles and looks? Hadn't she lured the boy there to be beaten, robbed?

She refused to defend herself. Some said a hard blow to the head had struck her mute. Others said God. The doctors weren't sure. She seemed to have one foot in another world. She had passed partly through the veil. The Gastons wanted her gone, buried. Forgotten. This stain on their son's name. The judge declared her a lunatic, committing her to the state. Her belly was showing when they trucked her off. Rory was born in the Dix Hill infirmary. The Gastons were already gone—packed up and returned to Connecticut, with no forwarding address.

Rory and his mother sat a long time at the table, holding hands. Rory asked her questions, and she nodded or shook her head, as if too shy to speak.

"Any new paintings?"

She nodded and brought up the notebook from her lap. They were birds, mainly, chimney swifts and grey shrikes and barn swallows. Nuthatches, bluish with rust bellies, and iron-gray kinglets with ruby crowns. Carolina wrens, chestnut-colored with white thunderbolts over their eyes, and purple-black starlings, spangled white. Wood thrushes with cinnamon wings, their pale breasts speckled brown, and lemon-breasted waxwings with black masks over their eyes. Cardinals, red-bright, carrying sharp crests atop their heads, and red-tailed hawks that wheeled deadly over the earth.

They were not like prints on a wall. These birds were slashed across the paper, each creature angular and violent and bright, their wings trailing ghostly echoes of flight. They were water-colored, slightly translucent, as if she painted not the outer body of the bird but the spirit, each feather like a tongue of flame. Strange fires that burned green and purple, rust and royal blue. Rory knew that eagles could see more colors than men. They could see ultraviolet light, reflected from the wings of butterflies and strings of prey urine, the waxy coatings of berries and fruits. Sometimes he wondered if his mother was like that, if she discerned the world in shades the rest of them couldn't see. As if the wheeling or skittering of a bird's flight were a single shape to her, a poem scrawled in some language the rest of them didn't know.

His heart filled up, like it always did. Tears threatened his eyes.

"They're beautiful," he said.

As always, she sent him home with one. This time it was a single parrot, lime green, with red flushes about the eyes. He would paste it on the wall of his room, part of the ever-growing aviary that kept him company.

It was late afternoon when they started toward home. Rory lit a cigarette, Granny her pipe. Their smoke unraveled into the slipstream. They passed city cars painted swan white or flamingo red, glade green or baby blue—bright as gumballs under the trees. Every yard was neatly trimmed, many staked with small signs that read: WE LIKE IKE. The people they passed looked strangely clean and fresh and of a kind, like members of the same model line.

Soon they were out from beneath the oaks and the traffic thinned, falling away, and the land began to roll and swell, an ocean of earth.

In the old days, Rory would ask Granny to tell him stories of his mother. Of how beautiful she'd been and how kind. Of how she once held a death vigil for a giant grasshopper she found dying on the porch, singing it low lullabies as it lay legging the air on its back, green as a spring leaf. How she buried it behind the house with a little matchstick cross.

"Girl had angel in her blood," Granny used to say. "Where she got it, I don't know. Not from me."

But all those old stories had been told, again and again, save one. The story only his mother could tell.

What really happened that night in the valley.

The land rose before them, growing more broken and steep, the mountains hovering over the horizon like smoke. Howl Mountain was the tallest of those that neighbored it, the fiercest. It rose stout-shouldered and jagged, like the broken canine of some giant beast. On its summit floated a spiked island of spruce and fir, a high-altitude relic of prehistoric times. The wind whipped and tore through those ancient evergreens, whirring like a turbine, and it did strange things. It was said that gravity was suspended at the mountain's peak, and in the falling season the dead leaves would float upward from the ground of their own accord, purring through the woods, as if to reach again those limbs they'd left.

There was a lot of blood in the ground up there, Rory knew. Guerrilla fighters from the Civil War, throat-cut and shot and hanged by rope, and frontiersmen before them, mountain settlers with long rifles who warred with the Cherokee, dying with arrow-flint in their bellies, musket balls in their teeth. And who knew how many rival tribes in centuries past, blood feuds long forgotten before any white man showed his face, the bones of the fallen scattered like broken stories across the mountain. Some said it was all those men's souls, trying to rise, that made the dead leaves lift.

Rory thought of what Eustace had told him, when he was little, of how men in the mountains had made a sport of eye-gouging and nose-biting. How those wild-born woodsmen faced each another inside rings of roaring bettors, their long-curved thumbnails fired hard over candle flames and greased slick with oil, and how Davy Crockett himself once boasted of scooping out another man's eye easy as a gooseberry in a spoon. Back then there was no greater trophy in your pocket than another man's eye, followed closely by the bit-off tip of his nose. A cruel story, like any Eustace told, but designed perhaps to make the boy proud of what his mama had done when cornered.

He was.

He just wished it had not stolen her voice, and he wondered sometimes if there wasn't something wrong with him, that he wasn't himself silenced by what he'd seen in Korea. By what he'd done.

He looked at Granny.

"Is it true you got that eye hid somewhere, stolen by some deputy you had in thrall?"

She sniffed.

"Ain't nothing but trouble in that eye, boy. Some things are best left buried."

"I got a right to see it."

"Sure. And I got a right to tell you to go to hell."

CHAPTER 4

Granny May sat in her rocker on the porch. The hills lay gold-dusted under the autumn sun. Soon the bruises of purpling ash would appear, the bloody stabs of red maple. The colors would peak, flaring from yellow into that momentary gold—all those crowns held kingly and legion to the sun—before the leaves fell browned and crackling to the earth.

This was the best time of year for root-hunting, digging up the raw ingredients for the medicines she made. The teas and tinctures, potions and poultices. In the summer, the plants spent their energy producing leaves and flowers and fruits. In the fall, they drove their nutrients down into the earth, anchoring themselves to survive the hard winter months. When she moved through the forest, she was surrounded by friends. Neighbors. She knew more than their names. She knew the shapes of their leaves, like tiny pennants or knives or hearts, and the size of their bulbs and berries and fruits. She knew the dark gullies where some liked to hide, and the bright patches of forest where others reached for the sun. She knew the scent of their leaves and roots, rubbed between her fingers and lifted to her nose. There were plants that could heal the heart or lungs, the skin or gut or blood. Plants that could stir or settle the body, lift or level the mind. There were roots that could cut you loose from yourself, to skirt the spirit realms, or ground you root-deep in the earth. There were plants that could kill.

There was Solomon's seal, which grew like a spine in the ground, with a perfectly circular vertebra for every year of age. It could soothe the stomach and clear the lungs, slacken excessive bleeding during a woman's time of month. You could draw it from the earth by hand. There was the sassafras tree, whose leaves were often mitten-shaped, chewed into a poultice for poison ivy, the roots dried and steeped for teas to purify the blood and warm the spirit. There was water hemlock, which could cause the most violent of deaths, rife with seizure and convulsion—unlike the poison hemlock of Europe, which shuttled philosophers so gently into the dark. There were these and so many others, a wonder of herbs and plants that ran in green feathers across the mountain, ready to be plucked, and those she grew in hidden plots beneath the trees, whose smoke could soothe pains of the body and spirit, slow time to a crawl, spark giggles from the stoniest hearts.

That morning, she had harvested a seven-leafed perennial known as rabbit's foot or spikeweed, digging and coaxing the long strings of roots from the moist bank of a dry stream, where a bed of mossy green stones tumbled down the mountainside. She would mix the root with honey to make a cough syrup—much needed this time of year—and save the honeyed pieces of root as candy to soothe sore throats. She had washed the moist mountain dirt from the roots, and now they lay drying on a wooden rack in the sun, their pale arms curling like the tentacles of baby krakens.

Granny leaned back in her rocker, packing her pipe, and looked out over the high country of her home. Her blood had been in these mountains a long time, two centuries nearly. Her people had cut timber with axes and crosscut saws, building cabins no bigger than bear dens. They had raised hogs, which they turned loose to fatten on the fallen nuts of the forest, and grown "whiskey trees"—corn—stirring giant copper pots of mash with handmade paddles. They had fought in every war of a young nation, siding with the Union when the state seceded, and they had hunted roots and beasts of every stripe, lining the mountainsides with the iron jaws of traps. They had done whatever they could to keep alive, the same as she had done, and they had died and died and died. They died in the grip of influenza or the hemorrhages of childbirth. They were crushed beneath widowmaker limbs or kicked by mules or burned in stilling accidents. Some walked off into the forest and never came back. Few died of old age.

She was getting older now, sure. Her steps were heavier than they used to be, her feet flatter, her joints more attuned to changes in weather. Her hair, once as black as a crow's wing—the work of rumored Cherokee blood—had lightened to an oaken gray. Those high cheekbones—another gift perhaps of her part-blood—those didn't sag. And her mind was still good. The hell if she would ever let that go.

This time of year, always, she found herself thinking of Anson, her husband, killed so long ago in France. She'd met him just before the first frost. It was one of those harvest dances in the western end of the county, and she'd gone with some of the neighbor girls, one of their older brothers driving the wagon. She wasn't but fourteen. The barn, blue in the night, was warm-lit from within, light like golden whiskey spilling out through doors and busted sheathing. The fiddlers were sawing away, foot-stomping, their songs alive and quick-grieving like the wind.

She was wearing a gingham dress her mother had made her, red and white, and her hair was the color of night, done up in pins. Her mother had spent hours pinning it up, fixing it just-so—this from a woman who never wore her hair in anything fancier than a topknot. Now, years later, Granny knew why. Womanhood had been upon her then, her breasts swelling, shiny black curls sprouting between her legs. Her monthly time coming. And her father, the no-count spawn of an old hard line of mountain people, had begun to look at her funny when he was on the jug. He commonly was. Her mother wanted her out of the house. She wanted her daughter to find a man.

There were boys slumped outside the barn on nail kegs, in the shadows, sipping on something they snickered over, keeping it hidden. Eustace Uptree was the biggest among them. The leader. She paid them no mind, none of them. Anson wasn't with them. She knew who he was already, from a summer dance, and she was looking for him.

He was dancing like she figured he would be. Like she hoped. He was her age, narrow-built but man-tall, long in the leg with tight-cut pants and polished hobnail boots. He had on a chambray shirt buttoned to the throat, and his light hair was tousled rakishly atop his head. He had a big smile, all teeth, that he wore all the time. The dancers were spinning in one big circle, holding hands, and then they split into four groups of four, still spinning, and Anson went hoot-owling between the caged arms of his partners, his long legs bowing and scissoring, his heel-irons pounding the plank floor, his smile big as an upturned half-moon.

When the song ended she went right up to him. She never was afraid, and she was the prettiest there, besides. He looked down at her, smiling.

"I know you?" he asked.

"Nope." She cocked her head, showing the curved line of her neck. "But you ought to."

His smile grew bigger, if that were even possible.

Lord, could she dance. All night if she wanted to, and they did. That music set her feet a-going, her eyes alight. His, too, and his hands were big and dry and warm, his body strong and taut when he touched her. Afterward, they went out under that blade moon to neck in the shadowed lee of the barn. Her blood was singing, hot. She wanted to climb him like a tree and hang in his branches.

When other couples came out to do the same, they retreated up into the woods. The ground was cold but they didn't care, neither of them.

It was her first time. He was like a skillet-handle. He bit her ear as he pushed inside, and he felt like something pulled red-glowing from the coals. It hurt so bad and it didn't. A year later they were married, Bonni on the way, and then he was sent to France with the rest of the boys and delivered home in a pinewood box. There wasn't much way to make a living in the hills as a single woman, and she'd done what she had to for her daughter. Moved into one of the boardinghouse bawdies in Boone, then migrated down into the foothills, Gumtree, when the northern companies started building their textile and furniture mills, drawing cheap labor out of the mountains. A lot of lonely men, then, with a little jingle in their pockets.

She sighed. She hadn't disliked those days as much as she should have. Cash folded thick in her pocket, a razor tucked sharp between her breasts. A line of men hard for the soft country of her flesh. Then there was what happened to Bonni, when she swore off the world below the mountain for all time. Sometimes she wondered how she had birthed a creature so beautiful and kind. So full of light. How she had failed to protect this creature from the evils of the lower world. She had never found the men who did it, never exacted payment from their throats or hearts. Since then, her world had been slightly out of true, a wobbling top. She, with her wiles and witchcraft, had failed to set the balance aright. And now her grandson had come home with war in his blood, and she worried where it might drive him. Down what roads, long sunk beneath the flood. She worried what pain and guilt might come, slithering black through his heart. She knew them so well.

Granny shook her head and pulled hard on the pipe, swelling her lungs with smoke, then exhaled, blowing out this blue host of worries. She let the medicine draw her again into her rocker. The stiff spindles of the chair, the hard boards beneath her feet. The mountain, solid as an army at her back. She was here. Now. She was blood and bone.

She watched a wolf spider creep through a slanted pane of light on the edge of the porch, hunting, and she could almost hear the whisper of its legs over the boards. She heard a brace of grouse explode to flight, startled by some predator, their wings thumping the air as they rose in a storm from the trees. Closer, the bottles sang faintly from the limbs of the golden chestnut, a shifting cascade of light as the breeze nudged them. Below this crouched the old bootlegging coupe, coal-black and mean, the hood opened like a great maw. That big machine-heart gleaming under the sun, full of chambers and valves and unmade song.

The boys scrambled here and there about the car, shirtless, black to the elbow in grease and oil. They had rags dangling from their back pockets, wrenches slung from loops in their dungarees. Their stomachs constricted into a lattice of angular planes when they breathed, their skin gleaming under the fall sun.

Lord, if she were twenty years younger.

Eli leaned across the Ford toward Rory. He had a long beard, bushy as a squirrel's tail, which might or might not have something living in it. In his hand was a glass flask of something that looked like water but wasn't.

"I seen your grandmama eyeing me again," he said. He glanced over his shoulder, licked his lips. "It ain't wholesome."

Rory stood from the motor and looked at him.

"Maybe you ought to give her what she wants."

Eli took his beard in hand, softly, as if to comfort some pet. He cut his eyes back to the porch.

"Shit," he said. "That old chicken hawk?"

Rory held out his hand.

"Hand me those plugs."

Eli belched through his teeth, distracted, handing over a paper box of sparkplugs sitting on a stool beside him. He was not yet thirty, but his hands were ancient, gnarled and hardened and permanently grimed, like the roots of an oak. They had plunged into the innards of nearly every machine that crawled or panted or growled about these mountains. He kept alive a whole fleet of whiskey cars, ass-jacked coupes that sputtered and shook like ticking bombs, that exploded with power when gigged. This 1940 Ford—Maybelline—was his queen of the lot. Powered by a 331-cubic-inch ambulance motor, supercharged.

He watched Rory fit the first plug into his wrench.

"I heard Cooley Muldoon came by here Sunday morning."

Rory didn't look up.

"Where'd you hear that?"

"Oh, you know, it come up the mountain this way or that."

"So?"

"So I heard you about lit his tackle afire."

Rory threaded the plug into the block.

"He brought that on himself."

"You been gone a time. Them Muldoon boys, they ain't like to let these things slide. Not these days."

Rory looked at the V-shaped house of iron beneath his hands. It had eight chambers, fired black, whose songs poured through the stainless organ pipes of the exhaust. This motor had saved him time and again, more surely than any church.

"Fuck the Muldoons," he said.

Eli squeezed his beard, then uncorked the flask again.

"You might not be as quick as you used to," he said. "And I hear the government's sending down some new revenuer from Washington ain't afraid to use his gun."

Rory shrugged.

"Better than a club," he said. "Or a shovel."

Eli cocked his head.

"What?"

Rory shook his head, as if caught by a shiver, and bent again to the motor.

"Nothing," he said.

I. HARVEST MOON

Bonni saw him first in the little town library, where she liked to come during lunch. It was a small brick building, stately. She liked the silence of the place, the smell. The swish of the librarian's skirts between the shelves. She would sit cross-legged in the deepest annals, surrounded by Zola or Yeats, and draw in her notebook, pausing now and again to eat her tomato sandwich. Here she would not be forced to speak to anyone. Instead, she would feel the silent voices of the books, each full of such power, their words floating about her like dust motes.

Connor turned down her aisle. He was carrying three books harnessed in a leather belt, a violin case under his arm. A pair of binoculars dangled from his neck. In his mouth, a fat Magnum Bonum apple, yellow with red flushes. Seeing her, he froze, as if he'd run into a wall. Then he set his shoulders and came on. He set down the violin case on one side and the books on the other and sat between them, taking the apple from his mouth.

Know what Magnum Bonum means?

Bonni shook her head.

Means "great good," he said, holding the fleshy planet before their eyes.

Bonni looked down at her own apple, a hard little Granny Smith. She was not sure what to say. But the boy had already set aside his fruit.

Know where they got the money for this place? The Carnegies. Father says they have more money than God. They've funded more than two thousand libraries, all over the world . . .

He talked and talked.

Bonni soon found herself nodding to his words, as if they were music.

CHAPTER 5

The sky was purple, the mountains dark. The lesser ridges rifled away into the distance, each successive line more ghostly than the last. A pair of headlights, bug-eyed and yellow, came bobbing up the drive, towing a long dark shape in their wake. A truck. A Ford flatbed, which squeaked to a halt before the coupe. The door clicked open and Eustace Uptree climbed down from the cab. Eli's uncle. He was born the same year as Granny—1898—but the man seemed much older, a creature born full-grown and bearded on the mountain. A big man, bald, his beard frost-bright in the dark. Like Santa but uglier, smelling of woodsmoke and sour mash and mule sweat.

The boys wiped their hands on the seats of their trousers as he approached. Eli leaned, whispering from the side of his mouth, "Don't he look cheery tonight."

Rory watched him come, his body rumbling beneath his overalls. People said the old man could disappear in a wink, despite his size, moving sure-footed and silent through the woods like a grandfather bear. Others said it wasn't him that disappeared, it was anyone who went hunting him. They said the mountain had subtracted over the years from the ranks of various law enforcement agencies, and who was behind it but him? They said he had been a machine gunner in the Great War, had mowed down whole companies of the Hun. It was in his eyes, they said, cold and gray as the sea. They said he had ears in the trees, spies in the woods. Every leaf was a tongue, speaking a language only the old man could hear. They said he could tell you where any stranger was at anytime on the mountain down to a foot.

Most all of it was talk, Rory knew, the lies of gummy old men in their rockers, on their nail kegs in front of the feed store. Stories punctuated by black bullets of tobacco juice spat quivering in the dust, attended by ageless hounds that lay tongue-out in the shade like something dead. Only one thing wasn't disputed: Eustace had gone up the mountain the day he got back from France and he hadn't hardly come down. No one knew where he even slept. Some said never in the same place twice.

Rory knew that wasn't strictly true.

The old man stood in front of them, hands on his hips, and spat.

"Maybelline running good?"

"As ever," said Eli.

Eustace looked at his nephew a moment, blinked, then extended his hand to Rory. Rory shook it. The old man's eyes, like always now, lingered a moment on his absent foot.

Eli cleared his throat. "It ain't growed back yet."

Eustace gave Rory a deep nod, then took his nephew's hand. This with pleasure, the knuckles crackling in his grip. Eli grimaced, trying bravely to make himself smile.

He couldn't.

Eustace dropped his hand.

"Show you what I got," he said, turning to the truck.

He unfastened the tie-down straps and pulled back the tarp. Half-gallon glass jars, hundreds of them, packed twelve to a crate. The zinc lids shone like neat little apprentices under the moon.

"Hunnerd gallons of the white stuff," he said. "Doubled and twisted."

He took up a jar and shook it, then held it against the sky. It swelled before them, moon-silver. People called it tiger spit or white dog, panther breath or corn or moon. The three of them watched bubbles the size of frog eyes foam and burst against the glass.

"Good bead on it," said Eustace. "Proof out one-twenty, at least."

Eli reached for a jar of his own. "I might should taste it."

Eustace swatted his hand away. "*Git* them dick-beaters off!"

He pointed his finger at his nephew's chest a long moment, his hand shaped like a gun.

Eli raised his hands to his shoulders, as if this were a holdup.

Rory cleared his throat.

"Best get loading," he said.

Eustace sniffed. He replaced the jar, then jutted his chin toward the house. The porch was empty.

"Granny home?"

"She's home," said Rory. "Been smoking that pipe of hers again."

Eli snapped his suspenders against his chest.

"You're getting too old for her, Eustace. You know she likes them young."

Eustace spat just short of Eli's boots.

"You jealous, nephew?"

"Shit," said Eli, rocking back on his heels.

Eustace turned and walked for the house, flicking his nephew in the balls as he passed. Eli yelped like a kicked dog, bending double.

"Son-bitch," he said. "Son-bitch."

The big man lumbered up the steps, his bulk filling the yellow pane of open door.

Eli waddled to the truck, one hand in his pants, making sure everything was intact. He took up a jar and unscrewed the lid.

"Son-bitch."

The coupe sat ass-high, ready for a load. They set the crates in one after another, and the car squatted down on its haunches like something tame, factory-built. The humped fenders housed oversize blackwalls, good for cornering, and the car had minimal brightwork. The heavy chrome had been removed, the leftover rivet holes lining the body like the work of a machine gun. Here was the car of a feed salesman or Bible-peddler or young man on his way to see about a heifer or sow. Here was the most common car on the road, in the most common color. Everything extra was hidden under the hood or behind the wheel or in the driver's seat.

Rory checked the tires for nails or punctures, the headlights and blinkers for light. He walked around the front of the car. The big engine was ticking from its warm-up, the hood radiating heat. The sides met in a vertical crease up front, like the prow of a U-boat, the whole car leaning into that ramlike nose.

Rory's arms were swelled with blood by the time they finished, jag-veined, and the nub beneath his knee ached against the leather rigging that bound it. He slid under the big steering wheel, the hoop thinly ribbed like a man's knuckles. He looked at his watch. Half past seven. Eli shook his hand through the open window.

"Luck," he said, slapping the sill.

Rory nodded and fired the big motor. It caught straight away, thundering rhythmically under the hood. He looked up at the old four-room house, log-built of ax-hewn oak with dovetailed corner timbers. The porch was sagging a little beneath the tin roof, but holding. The windows burned golden; the clay chinking shone like white stripes in the darkness. Beyond that the single-crib barn, missing a few roof boards, and the hogpen and smokehouse. Everything in its place. Not perfect but neat, the surrounding meadow flushed a deep blue under the moon.

He depressed the clutch with his wooden foot and slid the gearshift into first. He eased the Ford from beneath the big chestnut and started down the rutted drive, wincing as the glass in the trunk protested. He looked up once in his rearview mirror. There was Eli, waving at him from beneath the dappled moon-shadow of the spirit tree. The bottles glowed in the branches above him, as if they housed some luminous substance.

The shadows of the trees played across the road, the interspersed moon-light rippling across the hood like an electrical current. The ridges pressed their case on every side, night-blued, here or there the lone-some flicker of a still-fire. The road spilled down out of the mountains before him like a moonlit creek. He knew it well, as he knew the lesser roads that branched along the ridges and forked down into the hollers, that swung along great walls of blasted stone and through tunnels of black oak and hickory.

He had been driving these roads since he needed a pair of school-books tucked under his butt, his load of sugar or corn or barley thud-ding over the ruts. First there were the local runs, in-county, delivering ingredients here or there for Eustace's still-hands, saving every dollar he could. He bought the Ford the day he turned fifteen, ready for the big runs out of the mountains. The car was bone-stock, unmodified. He and Eli tore the machine down, bolt by bolt, rebuilding it into a thing that roared.

The car sat on heavy-duty springs from a one-ton pickup, with eight-ply truck tires tucked under the fenders. It had a two-speed rear end, a two-ton truck clutch, and the overhead valve motor from a wrecked ambulance. It had a McCulloch supercharger, which spooled like a tiny banshee under the hood, forcing a river of air down the iron throat of the motor. An armor plate protected the radiator. Ex-haust tubing snaked doubled and twinned through the undercar-riage, exiting in a growl. The car would go ninety miles per hour in low gear, booming like a weapon through the hills. There was only one name for such a machine.

Maybelline.

It could haul 120 gallons of whiskey in half-gallon glass jars, with four cases riding shotgun to distribute the weight. There was the rattle and clink of jars in the trunk, the machine balling down out of the mountains, crossing the hill-roads where the revenue men prowled in their unmarked cars. By sixteen, Rory could make a hundred dollars on a Saturday night—more than a week's worth of wages cutting timber or picking lint in a mill. Plenty for a grandmother who raised him, who said she needed nothing but would, and for the mother who wanted to raise him but couldn't.

Then came the war.

Floating on a hospital ship off the Korean coast, surrounded by other half-mummified men, he wondered what he would do in the mountains after the war. The timber outfits wouldn't take a one-legged man, the mills either. He could maybe sweep floors. He came cross-country from Camp Pendleton on the long silver slug of a Greyhound bus, his discharge papers stuffed in the inner pocket of his jacket, his olive duffel riding in storage. His stump still sore, an angry knob that pulsed its hurt.

While crossing the endless plains of West Texas, he read newspaper stories of Red Byron, the champion of stock car racing who had been standing on the catwalk of a high-altitude bomber, twenty thousand feet over the Japanese homeland, when a burst of flak ripped through the belly of the machine. His leg erupted beneath him, as if the very bone had exploded. He rode the six-hundred-mile flight back to their airbase in the Aleutians, losing blood every second, and the surgeons extracted a swarm of shrapnel from the bloody hive of flesh, pinning the fragmented limb back together in a giant steel cage. He spent twenty-seven months in recovery. Two years later, he would enter a stock car race at Seminole Speedway, his leg scarred and twisted like a blackthorn shillelagh. A metal brace still encased the limb, which he bolted to the clutch pedal. He would win at the Daytona Beach and Road Course, sliding from the rough asphalt of highway A1A onto the thrashed sand of the beach again and again, carving a name for himself in black rubber and blue smoke. He would win at Martinsville and Charlotte. He would win and win and win.

Maybelline was waiting at a garage in Raleigh, stored before Rory shipped out. At first he bucked and squalled all over the city, stalling at lights and rear-ending Buicks, scrawling the streets with inadvertent rubber. He stayed in a motorway inn and raced from one side of town to the other, resting only for coffee and cigarettes, sitting in the yellow glow of late-night diners. He hardly slept, hardly ate. He drove in silence, only the raw throat of the machine, his skin coated in the stink of desperation. He drove and drove. The days dying into nights, the nights burning into days. Slowly he became smoother at the controls, surer. The car no longer barked or bucked or stalled. Behind the wheel of such a machine, he was not lame.

Pleasure Island, they called it. His last delivery of the night. It was located in a Quonset hut, a war-surplus hangar of ribbed metal, shaped like a giant roly-poly. Inside, cubicles had been installed, each about the size of single bed, the mattresses laid out on wooden pallets. Sometimes the patrons worked up a thirst.

Rory parked in front of the rear door. Madam Erma had heard him coming. She was waiting on the back stoop beneath a single forty-watt bulb, her eyes raccooned in mascara, her breasts bound in a tight bodice. Her dark-dyed hair a complex nest of pins and bobs. She was lighting a cigarette, her hands bright-knuckled with rings and stones.

"Hey, sugar," she said. "You made it."

"Yes, ma'am," he said.

She pulled the money from the cloven gloom between her breasts. Rory took the bills, moist, and opened the trunk.

"Say, sugar," she said. "My back is acting up tonight. Think you could carry it in for me?"

Her back was always acting up.

"Yes, ma'am," he said. The words were hard in his mouth, like something pickaxed from his throat. He took the crate and followed her up the stoop, into the perfumed cavern of the place. Everything was red-lit, shadow-draped. A hidden Victrola played tinny jazz, a strange accompaniment to the sounds coming from the stalls. A sort of hushed hysteria, like people dying at the bottom of a well. Only the sharpest cries reached him, but he could feel the rest of them, the bass notes, beating at his chest.

The bar was all the way at the front. He limped behind her down the long aisle, the glass jars tinkling in the crate. The girl working the bar smiled at him. She was eighteen or nineteen, with a bloodred mouth, a necklace of flowers hanging from her neck. She seemed to have too many teeth, crowded to fit. Bruises the size of thumbprints dotted her arms. Rory wondered what had made them, those marks, and he could not but think of his mother, the faceless riders that still lurked in the night. The one-eyed man.

Madam Erma touched his shoulder, making him jump.

"You look like you need a drink." She looked at the girl. "Don't he, girl?"

The girl nodded, showing her crowd of teeth.

"Make him one, honey."

Rory set the crate of whiskey on the bar.

"No, I'm good."

Madam Erma's fingers crawled up the back of his neck, talon-sharp, scratching at the roots of his hair.

"Come on now, darling. Sit a spell. Have a drink with us. You're done for the night, ain't you? Time to loosen up."

Rory could hear the sounds coming through the flimsy walls of the place, louder now, yelps and grunts and shrieks. Violent sounds, like love or slaughter. They seemed to pass through his skin, touching his bones. Shame flushed his face, and he spun away from the bar, the outheld drink. He headed back up the aisle, the stall curtains drifting toward him as he passed. They were shower curtains, he realized, covered in palm trees and seashells and dolphins. He did not want to be touched. Ahead, the door stood ajar, a flurry of moths swimming beneath the naked bulb. He was on the stoop when he froze, flat-footed as a beast in headlights. He tried to back up, but the door slammed closed behind him, the bolt sliding home in the lock. The door was metal, cold as a slab against his back.

There were three of them, thin men, leaning against his car. Boys, really. The one on the hood had a shotgun leveled across his knee, a long-barreled double for wingshooting. The other two, flanking him, had their hands in their trouser pockets, each pinning open his coat to show the crosshatched crook of a pistol grip in his waistband. Rory could see they were old pieces, antiques taken from oily rags in Grandpa's bureau drawer. Guns that killed pigs or snakes or stray dogs.

"Those Muldoons put you up to this?"

The boy on the hood smiled. He tapped a cigarette on the butt of his shotgun, then stuck it in his mouth and lit it with the same hand, grinning through the swirl of smoke.

"People say you a war hero."

Rory shifted the weight off his wooden leg.

"I'm not looking for trouble," he said.

The boy on the hood nodded and drew on his cigarette, his cheeks going dark in the light of the single bulb. He pointed the cigarette at Rory.

"Well, you done found it, that there's a given. Only question is how much."

"What is it you want?"

The boy shrugged. "Money. Whiskey. Either's the same."

"I'm out of whiskey."

"Then you know what it is I want."

Rory thought he heard jarflies then. Their throbbing, choral scream. As if in alarm. It was loud to him a moment, and then it wasn't. He felt a warmth in his chest, like the first slug of whiskey.

"It's in my leg," he said. "I hide it there."

The boy laughed, his companions, too. All chuckling. They were standing back on their heels, pushing their bellies against the guns in their belts. Proud.

"In your wooden leg? You got to be shitting me," said the boy. "Ain't that a hoot."

"Yeah," said Rory.

"Well, let's see it then."

Rory came down off the stoop. The low-wattage bulb, screwed into a fixture above the doorframe, made of him a large shadow that swept toward the others. Each of them shifted, uneasy, as if something were spilling toward their feet. Something they shouldn't touch, cold and dark as the mountain hollows, untouched by sun. A dark shape now before them, backlit against the naked light. It bent down and began to roll up its pantleg. One inch, two, revealing the polished black throat of a jungle boot.

The boy stood from the hood, looking at the wooden foot.

"How'd it feel when that thing come off?"

"Bad," said Rory.

"What the girls think about it?"

"I ain't asked them."

The boy was looking down at him now, his head slightly cocked. He was moving the barrel this way, that way, his finger playing across the double triggers.

"Guess that's why God made whores."

Rory had the pantleg just high enough, above the boot, the polished maple gleaming where his flesh should be. There was an old boy in Yelson's Holler Granny used to run with, did woodwork. Mainly duck decoys, he sold them to the rich waterfowlers of the coast. He'd never done much with rock maple until he met Rory. It was a .32 Colt automatic, a Pocket Hammerless, inlaid in the inner calf of the limb. A blued pistol with checkered grips, no hammer to slow the draw. Rory's hand slid beneath the pantleg, unclasping it. In a single motion he stood upright and shot the boy in the shin.

The shotgun leapt from the boy's hands, lifted by his scream, and he fell back against the car. He reached to clutch the dark canker in his trousers but his hands stopped short, the fingers caged over the wound. A ragged red mouth, white-toothed with splintered bone. He stared down at it, his eyes wide and trembling, as if he'd never seen the insides of a man. His friends had bolted, like Rory knew they would. He limped closer. The boy looked up at him, slack-jawed, like some new believer.

The words hiccupped unexpectedly from Rory's mouth.

"I'm sorry," he said.

CHAPTER 6

The boys were gone, their leader piled wailing into the back of a rust-eaten sedan. Rory had called the others out of the dark, told them how to bandage the boy's leg, directed them to the alcoholic veterinarian who treated the nightly victims of End-of-the-Road. He even peeled off the twenty-dollar bill needed for the man to unbar his door. The boys' faces were so pale. They kept thanking him, thanking him. Finally they tore away, their gutted muffler gunning through the trees.

Only after they were gone did Rory realize they had slashed his tires—or someone had—the rubber puddled flat under the moonlike rims. He toed one, gently, like it might rise at the prodding of his boot.

"Hell."

He went and tried the door of the whorehouse. Locked. Hammering brought no one. He wondered what was in the drink they tried to give him. He looked across the street: an old Sinclair filling station, closed for years. The windows were papered over, the Sunday pages making the glass opaque. Green Sinclair dinosaurs bled from the signs. A small place, usually dark, but tonight the windows pulsed, shadows writhing against the illuminated newsprint. The air thumped with sound.

He started walking toward the place. A pair of gas pumps stood out front, gravity-fed, each topped with a glass globe. One was busted, just a jagged bowl. The other was full of something brown. Rainwater, maybe. Not whiskey. Someone would have drunk it.

He crossed the road, the grit crunching beneath his boots. The service doors were down, the papered windows glowing. Shadows leapt against these bars of light, rising and falling, reeling and surging like tongues of flame. The air drummed and cracked. There was something wild in the sound, unhinged. *Electric.* Throttled tambourines stung the air, a whining steel guitar. A mania of twanging metal and screaming chords, of yelps and shrieks, such as the end of the world might make, yet alive and heel-quickening, too. He could almost see the music erupting from the place as he neared, in bolts of rampant light, white and gold, and there were words, too, howled and shrieked and sung. There were some he knew and some he didn't, some sung in an unknown tongue. But he knew what all of them meant. What charged them.

Praise.

"This thing is real!" The preacher's hair was slicked back in a ducktail, jet-black though his face was old, and he wore a shoestring necktie, a button shirt with short sleeves ironed sharp. He held the Book high above his head. The pages were tattered, the cover stained. "It is the Word, and there need be no other."

Amen.

"For whosoever shall call upon the name of the Lord shall be saved."

Amen.

"But we live in a world too silent, do we not? A world of infatuate babble, yet silent, saying nothing. Nothing of his Name. This, friends, this is the very silence of death."

Yes, it is.

"Spiritual death!"

Yes.

He waved the Book high above his head.

"When the saving Word is here, friends! Right here!"

Hallelujah.

"In the ultimate hour, he will separate the wheat from the chaff. The bellies of nations will yawn wide, the unrepentant will be swallowed in seas of fire."

Yes, they will.

"And soon, friends. Soon! It has been nearly two thousand years. His time is coming. The End. Let the world die in ash, sprouting atomic mushrooms that cloud out the sun. In that darkness we will be saved."

Yes, we will.

"For we have the Word. And we call it out, don't we, friends?"

Yes, we do.

"We call out to him! Here in the blackest spot below these mountains. Here in the sinners' very den. We call out his name!"

Yes, brother.

"Not just for ourselves, but for all to be saved in him."

Amen.

The preacher clapped his hand on the shoulder of a man with a guitar.

"Let us sing!"

The guitar had been plugged into a wooden box with a woven-looking face, and the chords crackled through the electric light of the small garage, tinny and strange, buzzing with power. Rory watched with one eye, peeping through a crack in the door. The people were shrieking now and dancing. Rattling tambourines, hammering them against the heels of their hands. They were awash in sweat, their mouths slack like the revenants' of old tales, filled only with crude moans and gasps.

They whirled and stomped, their arms antlered upright like candelabra, their palms cupped as if they held within them holy water or fire. But it was the girl he could not quit watching. She had white skin, milk-smooth, and dark hair that crashed all upon her shoulders, uncut, an avalanche of darkness save for bangs slashed straight above her eyes. That face twisted with pain, or what seemed it, as if she were enduring a great agony, a blade digging into her softest places. Searching them. She swayed at the front of the group, her eyes pinched closed in concentration, her hands held quivering before her as if she cradled a great stone in the crook of her arms.

Then her eyes snapped open, green as jewels, and she looked right at him.

Rory leapt backward as if struck. He tripped over an old tire leaning behind the cash register and crashed into a metal folding chair, hopping across the floor on his good foot and out the door onto the apron, expecting a mob of them to come rushing after him. He hobble-skipped between the gas pumps and across the road, his shadow chasing him crazily down the ribbed side of the whorehouse, flaring and jerking like some hounding goblin. He reached the car and leaned blowing against the door, stump throbbing, fists clenched, waiting for them to come outraged from the darkness with clubs and two-by-fours and ax-handles.

No one did.

Dawn, colorless, crept through the canted trees, the warped dives and cars left derelict in their yards and lots. Rory opened the driver's door with a click. It was quiet, no one about. He got out and stretched and peed in the grass, leaning his forehead against the roof of the Ford. He'd slept but fitfully in the front seat of the car, waking again and again, surprised not to see a flood of faces mashed against the glass, ugly and irate.

He buttoned his fly and started the long walk into town. Behind him the filling station sat dark now, padlocked. An empty husk. End-of-the-Road was a strange place here in daylight, the night's sins left bare as if by outgoing tide. All along the road, casualties lay curled in backseats or mounded against car windows, mouth-breathing, making wet little clouds on the glass. They had passed out fumbling for their keys, for the starter switch or gearshift or headlight knob, their eyelids working in slow motion, their bodies heavy, like men at the bottom of the sea. There were empty bottles in the weeds, glittering bursts of broken glass in the street. A lone boot lay like a roadkilled pet. Shreds of calico and gingham from dresses torn in anger or lust. Footprints on car windows, rubbers left like pale and flattened worms in the road. Blood hardened under the sun, the work of fists or razors or knives. Last night a gun.

His irregular cadence rang out on the hardpack of the road in two-one time, the stump aching every step. He had a special sock he was supposed to wear for the prevention of skin-shear, folliculitis, but he never did. Before long he could feel his skin burning beneath the buckles and straps, angry and raw, the hair follicles risen up in red little hills that itched. Beyond that a deeper hurt. *Distal-end pain.* Too much pressure on the remnant bone and tissue, the stump darkening like a bruised fruit, like something tossed out with the grocer's daily spoil.

Just up the road a truck was pulling out, an old half-ton bloodied with rust. Rory waved and stuck out his thumb for the driver. She was a white woman the color of brick, her flesh clouded with freckles. She stopped at the edge of the road and waved him on. Rory hobbled around the front of the truck and climbed in, pulling home the door three times before it latched.

"Appreciate it," he said.

She had a round face, her arms thick like a man's, wormed and welted with pink and white scars. Rory wouldn't have bet against her in a fistfight with any of the old gunnies he knew. She shoved the truck into gear, a big bulb of muscle rounding out the back of her arm. The transmission scoffed but gave, grating, and the truck lurched onto the road, clattering under the oaks like something that might just fly apart.

The wheels bounding off on their own trajectories, the cab grinding to a halt like a dropped buffalo. Rory looked at her. If the truck was smart, it would keep itself together.

"Where you headed?"

"Garage in town. Needing some tires."

"More than one?"

"Four."

She whistled. "You pissed somebody off. Lady friend?"

"I wish."

She grinned, her teeth dark.

"A boy like you, you ought to have them keying your car every night."

"You run that joint back in there?"

"More like it runs me."

Rory looked out the windshield, cocked his head. The sun was above the trees now, cool and white, the dead leaves chasing one another across the road in fiery loops and scrolls, as if to write some message he couldn't quite read.

"Pretty," she said.

"What?"

"Trees," she said. "Everybody likes the spring, when they're all blooming out." She shrugged. "Not me. Gets like a fucking prison down here, so green, all shadows and pollen so thick you can't hardly breathe. Me, I like when they all fire up, when you know that clean, cold air is coming."

"Yeah," said Rory. "Me, too. Too bad they don't stay this way longer."

"It wouldn't seem so special if they did. Scarce time is worth more. Pure economics, boy."

"I reckon that's true."

"I know it is. Had a boy went overseas." She blinked, gently touching her eyelash. "Every day I had with him was a treasure."

"I'm sorry for your—"

She held up a huge hand, stopping him. The palm was pale, as if bleached, the lines red as cuts. She brought the hand down, slowly, and touched his arm.

"Shhh," she whispered.

Rory felt his eyes burn, silvering, as if she'd transmitted something to him with that touch. With that silence.

CHAPTER 7

Granny sat in her old rocking chair, a black hank of yarn in her lap. The sun was an hour over the eastern ranges, and she was beginning to worry. Her grandson still wasn't home. She tried not to think about it, about all the things that could go wrong. It wasn't much different from the timber crews, she knew. All those tree-cutters with crushed limbs or broken backs, missing fingers or toes or eyes. Or the mills either, the fires that tore through the baled cotton of the blowing rooms like devil-spirits, the linty air that left men hacking up their own dead lungs. Death presided over these lands like an entity itself, a thousand shreds of the same dread spirit just looking for an opening, a wound or weakness of character. Once in, it was tough to get out.

She put down her needles and lit her pipe, the smoke curling warmly into her chest. Eustace was long gone, vanished back into the night out of which he came. He'd given his best, like always. She couldn't say he didn't try. Red-faced, sweating. Gnashing his teeth. So much effort. But there was one thing she'd learned in her years: some had the talent for it, and some simply didn't. His prodigious belly didn't help. It made it so hard to get the angles right. Things had only gotten worse as he grew older, rounder.

She knew if anyone did. The two of them had been at it for years now, ever since Rory was born. Eustace had returned from France without a scratch, none you could see, unlike Anson—her husband—who came home in a box. She always hated Eustace a little for that. In the years after the war, he quickly gained his reputation as a whiskeyman, a hard man. He'd broken loose jaws with those sledgelike fists of his, been chased all through the hills by revenuers and never caught. He'd built his army of stillers. But he never got too rough with her, even drunk. He made sure there was wood ricked along the house, whiskey in the jug. He kept her grandboy under his protection, and employed, with money no other cripple could make. And an old woman had needs. No, it wasn't Eustace's fault he was lucky. She just wished he was blessed with a bit more of certain things. Talent, for one, and at least one other thing besides.

Now that nephew of his: Eli. She wondered about that. Not an ounce of fat on him—all angles and tendons. Not much muscle, but what he had showed. She saw him looking sometimes, after he got into the jar. Sure, it was wicked. That never stopped her before.

She heard the Ford before she saw it. The big motor came growling up the mountain like some new breed of hellhound devised for the very terror of old women on their porches. When it rounded the bottom of the drive and came bumping over the ruts, she made a noise in her throat, squinting up at the sun.

Half past eleven now, if she wasn't mistaken.

She rarely was.

Rory parked under the chestnut tree, killing the engine, and got out. She eyed him as he hobbled up onto the porch, his coat hooked two-fingered over one shoulder. She sucked her teeth.

"Hogs is hungry."

"Yes, ma'am."

"Chickens is, too."

"It couldn't be helped."

She turned her head and spat on the planks.

"You ain't a haint, are ye?"

"No, ma'am."

"Ain't knifed or shot?"

"No."

"Ain't in love?"

He hesitated. She narrowed her eyes at him.

"Some mill town slut? What's her name?"

"It wasn't that," he said. "It was some car trouble is all."

She sniffed. "Out chasing split-tail, more likely."

"I was at church, I'll have you know. Someplace you wouldn't know a thing about."

"Shit," she said. "The hell kind of church in them clothes?"

He didn't say.

"I done told you about them preacher's daughters—"

"Got-dammit!" He stomped toward the door. "Can't a man get some peace?"

"*Rory.*"

He stopped, one hand on the door. She cocked her chin at him. He took a deep breath and blew it loud from his nose, then bent down and kissed her cheek. "You had a good night here, though?"

"I had better."

"With Eustace?"

"With a corncob."

He bolted upright, jaw open, eyes huge.

"Jesus Christ, woman!"

Granny shrugged and held up her yellow cob pipe—just an innocent old woman in a rocking chair. "What?"

"I ain't believing it," he said, pushing through the door. Then again, louder, from inside the house: "I ain't *even*!"

Granny tapped her pipe against the heel of her hand, chuckling to herself.

Dusk he rose from the snarled mess of his bed, maneuvering himself to the edge. He pulled his trousers over his naked white legs, looping the suspenders over his shoulders one after the other. He lifted the booted limb from the floor, hefting the specious flesh in his arms. The little Colt automatic fit perfectly into its hollow, an organ newly implanted into his makeup. He slid his stump into the hollow socket that encased his knee and tightened the leather straps and buckles that secured him flesh to flesh and stood into the dimness of the room. The smears and scrapes of the windowglass glowed against the failing light. The edges of his mother's paintings were curling slightly, as if the birds might lift from the wall, rise into the dark.

The whole house seemed to tremble beneath him as he walked, as if he had gained a hundred pounds in his time abroad. The china plates rattled on the walls; the framed photographs of his mother and grandfather chattered on the mantel. He stuck his head into the kitchen and told Granny he was going down to Eli's. His stump was still sore. He was halfway to the car when he decided to walk. Spite, perhaps, or punishment.

The sky, domed violet, held the first bats, flitting sharp-winged through the ultimate light on their little sorties, and he walked the purpling meadow beneath them, watching them dart and hunt, their trajectories writ crooked and fleeting against the sky. He took the old trails of his youth, maintained in his absence by gray bands of deer, a nearly liquid quickening of power through the woods, and the ambling black bears and the lone remaining she-cat said to live upon the mountain, which would every couple of years climb upon the roof of a cabin and howl like a woman outraged. The trees engulfed him now, clutched against the remnant light, the dying leaves murmuring in their old tongue.

As a boy, seven or eight, he'd come down these trails to get Eli to take him hunting. He had his single-shot squirrel gun yoked over his shoulders, a gift from Eustace for his birthday, but Granny said he could never go hunting alone. He came out of the woods above Eli's daddy's garage, the windowpanes flashing blue and white. Knowing no better, he stood watching through the glass as Eli's father taught his son to weld. The man would point here or there, one hand on the boy's shoulder, and then the two of them would pull down their welding masks in unison, like knights before a joust. Rory watched the small suns birthed staccato at the points of their welding guns.

Soon he knew his mistake. Scars of light glowed in his vision, light-wounds that wormed and pulsed with pain when he closed his eyes. Soon his eyes began to burn, as if some bully had rubbed sand into them, and he could hardly blink for the grit against his eyelids. "Arc-eye," said the doctor. His lenses were flash-burned. For two weeks he had to wear eye patches, lifting them only enough to see his feet as he shuffled about the house. For two weeks he was afraid he would never see clearly again, the squirrels of the mountain forever safe. His vision lost, like his mother's voice.

Rory came out of the woods above the garage like he had all those years before, the windows burning gold in the fallen dark. It was really just an old barn weathered gray, though Eli had had a concrete slab poured flat as a level over the tilted ground. The heavy oak doors hung on iron rollers, above them the hand-painted sign: HOWL MOTORS. Eli was on his creeper, elbow-deep in the underbelly of a '51 Mercury painted the color of butter. Only his boots stuck out. Rory kicked one.

"Who's that?"

"Like you ain't heard me coming."

Eli rolled out from under the car, his hands and face blacked like a man coughed up out of the mines. He wiped his face with a rag that looked even filthier than the rest of him.

"Reach me those cigarettes, would you?"

Rory gave him the pack of Lucky Strikes sitting on a nearby stool, helping himself to one before he handed them over.

"You're welcome," said Eli. He lit his without getting up from the creeper. He pressed his head back and blew smoke. "Heard you run into some trouble last night."

"You're worse for gossip than Granny is."

Eli flicked a little ash from his beard. The dry tangles and snarls looked ripe for a brushfire.

"It's a lot of cars coming in and out of here, each with a flopping mouth aboard. So, you think it was those Muldoons behind it?"

Rory pulled the stool close, the castors squeaking and wobbling across the floor. He ashed his cigarette between his knees with a flick of the thumb.

"I don't suspect they'll be overanxious to admit it."

"Not after how it panned out," said Eli. "Maybe that Cooley boy hired them for it."

"He seems like a real piece of work."

"Not the sharpest," said Eli. "But the little son-bitch makes up for it in meanness, is what I hear. They say he got bit by a copperhead when he was eight. Swelled up like a weather balloon. Ain't been right since. Killed a boy over in Linville last year sold him a lame-dick coon-dog he wanted for breeding. Got off on a self-defense but I don't know. Went and throwed the dog off a bridge is what I'm told." Eli nodded, still flat on his back, watching his smoke curl up toward the ceiling. "There's got to be something bad-wrong with somebody like that, like from birth."

"I knew a few over there. Mean-made."

Eli rolled up on one elbow, looking at him. "In Korea?"

Rory nodded.

"What was it like?" asked Eli.

Rory looked down at the cigarette between his fingers, burning short. He chewed his lip.

"Most I could say is, it was a place where you wanted all those mean-made sons of bitches on your own side, standing behind you. The meanest ones. The sickest. Over there, bad was good."

"Damn," said Eli. "That's heavy."

"Yeah."

"You were scared?"

"All the time."

Eli nodded.

"Well, this Cooley boy, he ain't one to turn your back on. Runs that Hudson in the modified class down at the speedway. Trips it two, three times a week, too. Those Muldoons been in tight with the Sheriff since you were gone."

"What about this new revenue man from Washington?"

Eli's cigarette stuck upright from his mouth, smoking like a tiny chimney.

"Kingman's his name. They say he done a heavy job drying out a couple counties up in Virginia. Ain't too fussy about who gets hurt. Ex-army, some say. Special services and that." Eli shook his head. "Seems you come home at one hell of a time."

Rory dropped his cigarette on the floor, toed it out with his good foot.

"Least I am home," he said. "Mostly."

CHAPTER 8

He ascended the mountain in darkness, no lamplight, a world black and silver and blue. The moon lay scattered through the woods in blades, glowing palely, the wind rising now and again to moan through the trees. The trail scrawled ever upward, toward the looming darkness of the mountain's peak. Above it all the sea of night, the strange ornamentation of stars.

He found Granny on the porch, asleep. Her needles crossed in the little depression between her knees, the ball of yarn partly unspooled between her big man-boots. The pipe lay on the table beside her, a smatter of ash spilled from the fire-bowl. Her chin sat on her chest, rising and falling with her breath. He gathered her up in his arms, light as a girl, and carried her inside to her room. He covered her in her old handed-down quilt. The outer layers were burnished to a luster over decades of sleeping flesh, the inner batting composed of older blankets still. He tucked it under her feet, her elbows and shoulders, and went out into the den and opened the door of the woodstove. A mouth of red coals. He added two lengths of the seasoned white oak they kept stacked on the porch, hot-burning wood for cold nights, and stoked it to a fury before stepping outside.

There was a storm rolling in out of the west. He could hear it on the far side of the mountain, crashing like the ghost of an ocean against the brutal faces of granite. He stepped off the porch and looked up toward the summit. The sky flared silver-white, a momentary brilliance against which the mountain stood jagged and black, a sentinel against the snows and rains borne out of the corduroyed ridges and valleys to the west. The wind came skirling down the mountain, cutting cold across the meadow, and he could not help but remember Korea. The Chosin Reservoir, the fall of 1950. The most brutal landscape you could imagine, just snow and rocks and scorched trees among the frozen ranges, the sharp thrusts of the Toktong and Funchilin passes. A country seemingly made for men to die in.

They did.

A cold front descended from Siberia, thirty-five below, and 67,000 Chinese infantry night-marched from Manchuria. The 1st Marine Division wasn't ready for either. Rory was there for all seventeen days of it. All seventeen nights. When the illumination rounds lit up the sky, you could see the Chinese coming down the hillsides, rising out of the gullies and trenches, swarming like hornets from a ground-nest. Then darkness, flashes, screams. In the morning, the ridges would be weltered black, the blood hard as stone. The Marines built parapets out of the frozen bodies and waited for the coming night. When the cold jammed their weapons, they fought with knives and shovels and rocks. The Chinese infantry were young, and they didn't wear helmets.

Rory's first kill was the one he remembered most, the one that still came to him in his sleep. He and Sato and four others were bunched behind a rocky outcrop at the edge of a small ravine. The companies were blasted to pieces across the hillsides, huddled wherever they could form a defense. It was after midnight and most of their rifles were useless, the gun oil frozen in the bolts, the firing pins stuck. They heard the whistles of the Chinese officers and watched the enemy infantry rise from cover to charge. They came flooding down the far slope, their burp-guns making star-shaped flashes in the night, their ranks bristling with knives and staves and stones. The orange tracer rounds of the heavy machine guns chewed into them, their bodies splitting and bursting in pink clouds and screams. Some of them who tried to retreat back up the slope were gunned down by their own officers, the rest climbing over the dead gathered all strange-struck in the creek bottom, a tangled nest of corpses, then crawling their way up toward the dug-in Marines.

Rory had his entrenching tool ready. He'd spent the day sharpening it against a rock. He rolled onto his back, against the outcrop, with the tool clutched close against his chest. He looked up at Sato, who would give them the sign to attack. All day, sharpening their tools, they'd discussed the vacation they would take after the war. Neither had ever been to the beach. They would go to Daytona, Florida, to watch the stock car races on the Beach and Road Course, where cars thundered down two miles of Highway A1A before sliding sideways onto the beach, blasting back up the sands. They would book a room at the mint-green Streamline Hotel and drink cocktails at the rooftop Ebony Club. The sun would turn them golden; it would warm the marrow of their bones. They would hardly remember what it was like to be cold. They talked and talked, shivering, scraping their shovels into spears.

Sato raised his head over the ledge to check the advance. His forehead split open, his helmet leaping away with a ring. Rory turned and raised up on his knees, the shovel above his head, and looked down. There was a Chinese infantryman on his belly below him, looking up open-mouthed, wide-eyed. A boy, really. Surprised at what he'd done. Rory jammed the pointed shovel into the very top of the boy's skull. He was surprised at how easily it punched through that bony crown, darkening the fur hat with goo. He didn't think it would be that easy. He pulled the boy's burp-gun from underneath him and sprayed it into the others streaming up the slope, praying it wouldn't jam. When the drum magazine was empty, he went back to the shovel.

There were others after that, men or boys killed up close, but he couldn't remember them. Not well. They all looked the same in his mind. He thought of that as a great blessing. He didn't think he could have held them all inside him without busting. He could only remember Sato, his head riven like stone. There was hardly any blood; it froze inside his skull. They wanted to bury him, but the ground was too hard.

Three days later, at dawn, a lone stick grenade came flying over the line, wood-handled like a pepper grinder. It bounced once on the frozen earth, hovering over its own shadow, and Rory hurled himself behind a snowbank. The world shattered, its white-hot fragments screaming through his softest parts. He did not know there was such pain in the world. He thought his leg was gone.

Not yet.

He lay in ringing silence, screaming, and a corpsman appeared white-faced above him, a morphine syrette between his teeth. The corpsmen were storing them under their tongues to prevent them from freezing. The man bobbed over Rory's leg, shaking his head. Rory made the mistake of lifting his head, of looking at the bloodied wreck of meat and leather that used to be his foot. He turned his head, sick at what he'd become.

The corpsman took the syrette from his mouth. He removed the clear plastic hood and punched through the seal with the loop pin. A bulb of liquid stood atop the needle. He opened Rory's overcoat and pulled up the layers of sweaters and shirts to reveal a white sliver of belly. He pinched the skin and slid the needle in sideways, squeezing the soft tube that held the drug. Then he put back Rory's clothes and buttoned his coat and pinned the emptied syrette to his collar. He went about muffling the wound in bandages and gauze, boot and all, shouting it was all he could do.

When the morphine hit, it was a dark wave out of that place. Rory was there and then he wasn't. The pain seemed a long way off, a thing that throbbed its importance thickly, dully, in a world doing the same, filled with muted pops and screams. He could close his eyes and see the stone Buddha sitting cross-legged in the temple by the stream. The figure's right hand was held up, palm facing out, the fingers slightly curved, as if to touch a man's forehead. Sato's voice in the darkness.

Abhaya mudra. The gesture of fearlessness. The Buddha used it to calm the drunken bull elephant Nalagiri, loosed by a jealous monk to kill him.

A pair of dog tags dangled from the Buddha's neck. Rifles leaned against his shoulder. Someone had stuck a half-smoked cigarette through the fingers of his opposite hand. Rory held his gaze on the raised palm, which glowed by candlelight, the fingers flickering like small tongues of flame.

The morphine lasted him two hours, maybe three, and then the pain was back and the cold, which were one and they were everything. The corpsman had sat him against a bank with the other wounded, their collars pinned with empty syrettes. He could hear their moans and whimpers, their stiff silences. The boy next to him had been shot in the gut. It was all in his lap like a treasure he'd lost, frozen black. The boy held his arm, then his hand, until he didn't.

It was getting dark. Rory was in better shape than many of the others. Someone came by and gave him an officer's Colt. He used it that night, then others, the long nights of fear when the Chinese kept coming in wave on wave. He used it again and again. The boys from the line would come by at dusk to give him new magazines for the gun, scavenged from officers killed in the night. Days later reinforcements broke through from the south, and so began the retreat, the long road of ice to the port of Hungnam, the sea. A goat path, really, sunk between ridges that twinkled and popped with enemy fire. Hell Fire Valley. They strapped him to the hood of a jeep alongside men less lucky. Dead. He knew he wasn't one of them. He hurt too much.

II. HALF-MOON, WANING

They ate lunch together each day in the little Carnegie library, flanked by pebbled spines and gold-leafed names. Connor did most of the talking. He was full of knowledge. Words seemed to beat through his blood. His passion was birds.

—Did you know the bee hummingbird weighs less than a penny? Its heart can beat over one thousand times per minute.

—Yesterday I spotted a great grey shrike, rare for this part of the country. Its scientific name means "sentinel butcher." Know why? It impales uneaten prey on thorns!

—Did you know "nuthatch" is a corruption of "nuthack"? Because the birds wedge nuts and seeds in tree bark and hammer them open?

Bonni listened to this strange specimen of boy, feasting on his words. At school, he would lift his binoculars to his eyes, sighting songbirds or kites that came swooping down into the schoolyard. The teachers said nothing, because he could answer any question they might ask.

The loggers' sons snickered and elbowed one another, their faces red-crusted with pimples, but they were careful how they spoke to him. A legend followed in his wake. The first day of high school, when one of the bullies cornered him, Connor's right arm shot expertly into the boy's nose, breaking it. A beard of blood appeared, bright as Christmas.

His father had been a Golden Gloves champion up north, they whispered. He trained the boy in their basement every morning, pushing him through endless rounds of push-ups and punches, the jump rope and speed bag.

After that, Connor wore the cloak of legend. Not even the bullies would touch him.

CHAPTER 9

He had to see her again. It was like a sickness in his blood, some kind of infection planted within him by the green of her eyes. The sun was dawning, the first frost crackling beneath his boots. The little meadow gleamed, the blades of grass iced jagged under the cold hard light. Rory was carrying a pail of chestnuts gathered from beneath the tree in the yard, limping his way to the hog-house. People said there was nothing sweeter than chestnut-fattened hogmeat, so seldom tasted since the blight. The thought seemed ash on Rory's tongue. There could be nothing so sweet as the taste of the girl's mouth, and he did not even know her name.

She was seared in, branded against the backs of his eyelids. He could close his eyes and see her as clearly as someone he'd known a lifetime. He could see her as clearly as he could see his own mother, whose eyes were feathered with faint lines, whose throat would catch, showing its tendons, when she felt something strong, when the words seemed almost to come. He could see her as clearly as he could see Granny, those proud cheeks and razor eyes, those crow's-feet deep as the creeks that ran down the mountain. He could see the girl's face as clearly as all that, clean as crabapple flesh. Her wide mouth and nude lips. The broad thumbprint beneath the slight upturn of her nose. The green eyes, so bright.

The big sow grunted happily at his arrival. She was a crossbred Duroc, rust-colored, with floppy ears and a corkscrewed tail, gentle as a two-barrel Lincoln. Her bulk quivered as he poured the flood of chestnuts into her pen.

"Eat up, sweet girl. Frost on the ground, you know what that means."

The chestnuts disappeared beneath her snout two and three at a time, burrs and all, and the two smaller hogs rooted under and around her legs and mouth. He left them to their meal and headed to the chicken coop on the back side of the house, carrying the feeding pail from the crook of a knuckle. The big bandy-legged Java cock, Commandant, was already marching around on the icy ground, impervious to the cold, having crowed the sun's rise. His feathers were mottled black and white, like a black chicken speckled with snowfall, and he had a cockscomb and wattles of the bloodiest red. He looked to be sizing up Rory for breakfast. Rory grinned.

"Feeling froggy, you old bastard?"

He cast some of the grain before the cock, still grinning, and soon the hens came waddling from the coop. They looked like nothing so much as fat women in overlarge skirts, clucking and gossiping as they pecked the ground. Commandant, king bigamist of the lot, stamped among them, proud-chested like the little general he was.

Rory set the empty pail aside and hobbled back up to the house. The car sat before the porch in a caul of dew-ice, like some gift from the night, and Granny was out in her rocker, smoke curling about her face. Soon a car or mule would show, perhaps someone simply walking, pilgrims come up the mountain for the potions she made. The teas and poultices, the remedies for stiff joints and aching heads, for lax members or empty wombs, for seed spilled in the wrong fields of a whiskey-bent night. How she'd come to know such arts was something of a mystery. It was not handed down simply blood to blood, for the keepers were more often heirless widows or lone hermit-folk foresworn of the outer world. Rory only knew that when he was little Granny had gone deep into the mountains on her own, and she'd come back weeks later with the trove of knowledge she now carried, as if it had been imparted into her very blood or cells. He wondered if she had anything for the forgetting of green-eyed girls, some elixir that burned them right out of you. If she did, he wondered would he willingly drink it. He wasn't so sure he would.

He climbed up onto the porch and sat next to her. She leaned back in her rocker and a blue wisp curled from the corner of her mouth. That smoke had spunk, he knew, and sometimes sitting next to her he could feel it. Problem was, he liked it.

She looked at him.

"Want you some of this?" She held out the pipe.

"You know I don't."

She shrugged. "Might do you some good."

"Good for what?"

"For whatever it is happened the other night."

"Shit."

"I ain't too old to lay a switch on that ass."

Rory shook his head and rolled his eyes, looking up. The smoke was coiling itself toward the blue planks of the overhung roof. Haint blue, to keep the spirits out. They didn't like to cross water, Granny said, and they were none too smart besides. He closed his eyes, opened them. There before him was the chestnut tree, myriad-glinted in the new sun. Another spirit-catcher, or so she said. He lit a Lucky Strike and watched it. The bottles shifted in the wind, the crown sparkled. Trees. You thought they were one shape, a tall stem snaked heavenward for sun, but you forgot what was below the surface, reaching into the dark earth. The cold earth. Reaching.

He shook his head and stood.

"That damn smoke."

Saturday he was rolling down out of the mountains at dusk, night welling up from the slanted earth like a tide. He had a full pack of cigarettes in his pocket and a sandwich in an old poke on the passenger seat. The road scrawled its way through crooked arcades of hardwoods, jagged in some places, sweeping in others. The logging trucks were done for the day and he drove in third gear, the gravel tinny against the undercarriage. The harsh planes of the mountains, the geometric tracings of the ridges slowly gave way to foothills. Gentler, softer. Rolling green balds spotted here or there with shaggy-coated cattle, some horses, all of them circumscribed in palings and fence-wire. Life seemed easier here. The soil deeper, richer. There were scarce hollers or coves to hide in; it didn't seem you had to. He turned onto an unpaved road, then another, angling his way across the darkening countryside, avoiding the little hamlets and yellow-lit farmhouses when he could.

He was running the speed limit, the big motor hardly working, when he crested a small rise and saw at the bottom of the hill a sign that read: DRINK CHEERWINE. He thought of the cherry-flavored pop, the way it bubbled bloodred on your tongue. His flesh felt full of such stuff tonight, a red elation just beneath his skin. A wildness, wanting out. He wondered whether he would see the jade-eyed girl. Whether her eyes could quell him. He wondered if there was something wrong with him. Some madness. His heart felt too big for his ribs, inflamed, as if his blood might jump his skin. He breathed in, deep, thinking of cool air, of silence and stone.

He was exhaling, slowly, when he passed the billboard. A white sedan sat hunkered in the shadows, clean and undented. A government car. The bright ray of a spotlight leapt across the night, filling the coupe. Everything burned the brightest white, exposed, as if lightning-struck, and Rory clenched his jaw, unbreathing. One second, two. Nothing. Then came the cherry-red throb of light in the rearview mirror, the long wail of the siren winding up.

Rory's body leapt to action, as if loosed. He stomped the clutch and downshifted, waking the big motor with his foot. The car shuddered, in awe of itself, then squatted and went. He could hear the tiny scream of the supercharger spooling up, the exhaust racketing through the night. He reached under the dashboard, cutting the taillights with a hidden switch.

He knew this road.

He needed to get off of it.

He crossed the yellow line through a sweeping curve that made the tires howl. He was back up into third now, pushing ninety, when he crossed a flat bridge over a creek, the springs slamming over the joints, and he saw what he was looking for: a red sweep of clay into the road. He had his hands at the bottom of the wheel, palms up, just for this. He braked in hard bursts, to keep the tires from skidding, then hove the big wheel hard over with one hand, downshifting with the other, rotating the car more than ninety degrees back into a firebreak that hit the road at a diagonal.

The road was dry and red. The revenuer's headlights smoked in the whirling dust he made, angry meteors trying to keep up. Failing. They grew smaller, fainter, their powers of illumination weakening under his foot. The road thrust its way through the night, a long red wound in the earth, and Rory slid neatly through the turns, between long stands of unfelled timber, the motor shouting its power through the hickories and oaks. He rounded a curve and stared head-on into a parked logging truck, the big washboard grille glaring madly out of the darkness, big as anything. He cranked the wheel hard, sliding just alongside it. Then the trees broke away, the world opened up. Just stumps in every direction like the aftermath of a bombing run, the night arcing hugely over it all. Earthmoving machines flared out of the headlights to either side, silent as some species of great, angular giants slumbering in the wilderness.

Then trees again, and, behind him, no lights.

———

"I didn't know them boys was out there," she said. "Honest."

Rory upended the crate he was holding, the jars bursting on the floor at Madame Erma's feet. Between the two of them a vicious wreckage of shards and slivers, a hundred gleaming teeth.

"Next time you walk on it."

The money was already in his back pocket. The whiskey-filled air burned like nitro in his lungs, a lighter's click from going boom. He turned to go, his wooden foot prodding the one jar left intact. He bent and picked it up.

He sat at the wheel of the coupe, the jar cozied between his legs, the church pulsing before him. Bodies, backlit, jumped darkly against the glowing windows, shadow-figures thrown as if by cave fire. The walls of the place fairly shook, a gutbucket throb he could feel in his chest. The sandwich was gone, a few crumbs in his lap. He rubbed the ancient poke between his fingers, the brown paper soft-worn as new velvet. Probably Granny May had eaten lunches from this bag, in school. She wouldn't throw out a thing. He set it aside and sipped again from the jar, the whiskey rolling white-hot down his throat. He looked at his hand: the nails hard and square, the day's grime yet unknifed from their quicks. He opened his folding blade with a click.

He sipped as he pared his nails. He could feel the whiskey working in him, in his temples and teeth. A mild roar, like unseen white-water. Distant falls. He was breathing through his mouth. His nails clerk-clean, pale as little moons. He was not very afraid.

He belched through his teeth.

He had to piss.

He got out of the car and set the jar on the roof, the half-drunk whiskey slopping back and forth. He peed in the grass, then started walking toward the church, drawn toward it like a flame.

He peeked through the door. Inside they were dancing, heads tilted back, mouths open. Some of them palsied, seizing, shaken as if by unseen hands. Their arms held in the air before them, twirling, the soles of their broken loafers and pumps thumping on the stained concrete. They sang, or simply said the word again and again: *Jesus, Jesus, Jesus.*

Rory didn't see the girl. He opened the door a fraction wider for a better look. An older woman, standing near, turned and saw him. She reached through the door and took his hand, pulling him into the room, the double-bay garage that held them. The lights seemed to flicker or pulse above him, maybe it was the fluorescents. The people around him were sweating. They shone under the lights—their faces, their chests, their hands—as if glazed in oil. Their eyes were mashed tight or opened wide to worlds he did not know. Their faces so round, like the stone idols of Korea, sitting cross-legged in their thrones of fire. The music charged through them, their bodies jerking as if lightning-struck, the guitar whanging and crackling through the air like raw electricity. He felt his own body livened, his legs moving as if of their own accord. Slow at first then quickening, his blood rising, his body light. His foot there, there, there—banging the floor in time.

Before he knew it he was dancing, his boots stomping and jumping like black-shined pistons, his arm-moves wild and unplanned. The throng leapt and trembled on every side of him, singly and together. A roaring of flesh. A living fire. He was lost among them, weightless. A part of them, inseparate. He saw the girl. She was near the front, her eyes closed. She was speaking a language he'd never heard, to a God he'd never known. He had the sense of being in a shielded chamber, a fortress of gold and light, and everyone was beautiful, and he loved them all. He didn't know what place it was, whether it was inside him or out. He didn't care.

He closed his eyes, opened them.

A little boy, ten, maybe, came in the door and ran down the aisle between folding chairs. His forearm had a big streak of grease on it. The pastor bent down, and the boy cupped a hand to his ear. The man looked up, straight at Rory. Looked with one of his eyes, at least. The other eye stared off in its own direction.

Lazy, perhaps. Or made of glass.

CHAPTER 10

Eustace rose against the ceiling of the bedroom. His weight sent a tremor through the cabin, rattling the bottles and crockery. He looped the galluses of his overalls over the mountains of his shoulders. Granny watched him from the bed, scratching a match for the cigarette she'd just rolled. This was the only time she smoked tobacco.

"What you know about these Muldoons?"

Eustace grunted, putting on his boots.

"Upstarts out of Linville, more balls than cock. Run radiator-whiskey bust your head like a watermelon."

"You got truck with them?"

"What's it to you?"

"The youngest, Cooley, come by for a potion couple weeks back. Snakes crawling through the head, that one."

"Every litter's got one."

"Who was it in yours?"

"Who you think?"

"You got Rory protected when he's down there?"

"He works for me, don't he?"

"You know what I mean. Extra."

"Your stuff pays. But it ain't that good."

Granny let the quilt slip. Her breasts hung heavy as doves from her chest, upturned and pert, the nipples hard as stone pebbles in the slight cold of the house. Breasts men had come from counties all around to see. To touch, if they had the means.

"Ain't it?"

Eustace's nose twitched slightly, seeing them, and then he turned on his heel.

"You should of tried that a hour ago," he said. "When I would of gave a shit."

He clomped through the door, out of the house. Granny lay back on the bed, blowing smoke as the door of his truck slammed home.

"Hour? If three minutes is a hour, I'm old as Christ."

A tap on the window. Rory bolted upright. He'd had his head on the ribbed knuckles of the steering wheel, trying to will away a steel knot of headache, some irregular clash of whiskey and Jesus in the front part of his brain. When he saw it was the girl, his body jumped as if electroshocked. He rolled down the window, pulling off his hat.

"Didn't mean to make you jump," she said. "It's just I seen you in there."

Rory swallowed.

"Seen me?"

She nodded. "Last week, too. You're new."

"I am."

"You dance pretty good," she said.

His stump throbbed.

"Considering," he said.

She cocked her head, as if she did not understand, then thrust her hand through the window.

"Christine," she said.

"Rory."

They shook. Her skin felt charged—the thinnest envelope, holding air or spirit or light.

"Pleasure," he said.

She pulled a lock of hair across her mouth and crossed her feet, twisting shyly in place.

"You gonna be here next week?" she asked.

Rory swallowed.

"Are you?"

He did not notice the gauges at first, thinking as he was of the girl's face. The touch of her hand. The way he could still feel her fingers on his arm, as if she left traces of herself on whatever she touched. The way her body moved inside her dress. How badly he wanted to examine its workings, the genius of its engineering. To move the limbs, gently, through their range of motion. To test the suppleness of her calves and feet, her hands and arms, and taste the sting of her skin, the red dart of her tongue. To set his ear against her belly, listening to the growl of her insides.

White bolts of vapor erupted from the hood.

"Shit."

He hit the brakes.

The hood was hot to the touch. He lifted it and batted through the steam, twisting off the radiator cap with the help of a rag. His flashlight showed it was at least a gallon low. He traced the coolant hoses and found a neat gash in one, made possibly with a blade. He got a roll of duct tape from the tool kit in the trunk and banded the hose, then refilled the radiator from the canteen he kept in the glove box.

All the time he was thinking of the girl, so bold. There was the way she thrust out her hand in introduction, speaking through her shyness, the mask of her hair. She seemed fearless in comparison to him. He could hardly even remember his own name.

"I come every week," she'd told him. "I'd go crazy otherwise."

"Crazy?"

"It gets it all out, the fears and worries. The week's demons. Burns you clean."

Rory felt tears sting behind his eyes. He didn't know why.

"You work in town?"

She nodded.

"Up at the hosiery mill. A looper. I sew the toes on socks all day."

Rory thought of the rows of women sitting in ladder-back chairs, bent in front of sewing machines. It hurt him to think of her there.

"But that ain't my passion," she said. "Of course it isn't. I'm not content to be sewing toes the rest of my life."

"What's your passion?"

"Hats."

"Hats?"

"Hats," she said. "Like the ones that cover your head. I make pill-boxes and jockeys, cloches, calots, fascinators. Mainly from old ties and coats and dresses. Look, I made them all."

She swept her hand, and Rory saw the ladies' hats floating in the night, decked with feathers and orchids. They sat rakish and fine upon the heads of these working ladies in their plain dresses, their bangs curled wetly against their foreheads from the heat of dancing.

"I got a good little industry going," she said.

"Looks like it."

"They ain't the only ones. I got the fancy ladies in town lining up. I done a custom one this year for a lady going to the Kentucky Derby at Churchill Downs. She was wearing it when Hill Gail beat out Sub Fleet by two lengths."

Rory rubbed the tatty brim of the black bowler that had been his grandfather Anson's. The crown was scarred by decades of use, lashed by the low-hanging branches of horse paths and carriage rides.

"I never thought much of my cover," he said. "Maybe I ought."

"You know hatmakers used to use mercury vapor to size the felt of their hats. Caused all kinds of problems. Amnesia, shyness, even red noses and toes. That's why they say 'mad as a hatter.' Did you know that?"

"I didn't. You don't use mercury, do you?"

"Why, you think I'm mad?"

"No, ma'am. I, I just—"

Her hand touched his arm.

"I was just kidding." She'd looked up, into the dark, as if her name had been called. "You should come back next week," she'd said. Then she was gone.

Rory closed the hood of the Ford, wiped his hands, slid behind the wheel. The car shuddered back to life, and he continued on down the road. The trees shone a stony white in the headlights, an irregular colonnade leading toward the drowned world of the lake. The moon hung halved in the black sky, the stars made as if by shotgun blast.

There had been harsh times, he knew, when the government came to flood the valley in '31. People did not want to give up their land, the homes their great-grands had built, nor have their ancestors exhumed, their bones trucked to alien soil. They did want to lose their copper pots, which lined every cool creek. The whole valley once smoked like a vent in the earth, people said, the blue smoke of a hundred still-fires spread dusky and ragged across the sky. Whiskey was life. It fed and clothed. A single mule, which could carry only four bushels of corn out of the valley, could carry twenty-four bushels' worth of corn whiskey to market.

The valley people fought. There had been government trucks turned over and set alight, and trees spiked against the loggers' saws, and dozers and tractors driven into the river, where they sat strange and fossil-like as the waters frothed over their wheels and buckets and blades. Loggers had to be brought in from out of state to clear the land, and they were jumped and beaten when they moseyed down side-trails for a piss or left their worksites for the night, in the parking lots of the honky-tonks and nip-joints that edged the valley. They were beaten with hickory clubs and ax-handles, with stones and bricks and steel-toed boots.

There was talk of this becoming a second Whiskey Rebellion, like the one of the 1790s, when George Washington trotted out a federal militia of fifteen thousand men to suppress insurrectionists in western Pennsylvania. There was talk of the national guard being brought in, as they were for the Battle of Blair Mountain in '21, when an army of miners in red neckerchiefs rose up against strikebreakers in West Virginia. *Rednecks.* When war-surplus bombs were dropped by hand from hired aircraft and air corps bombers out of Maryland flew reconnaissance patrols up and down the hollers. But in the end it was not the army that poured into this valley but nightriders with hoods and torches, dark wings of them that swept through the trees like some herald of the coming flood. They fired homesteads and hanged rousers, dynamited stills and threatened women and girls. In a matter of days, the will of the valley was broken. The clearing crews worked unabated, and the river rose bubbling through the land like a flood of old, dark and inexorable as blood from a wound. The valley was drowned.

The road led into the water now, knifing pale into the shallows, and a man who didn't know better could drive right on into the lake at speed. A number of drunks, out-of-towners mainly, had done just that, more than one of them found still upright in the driver's seat, hands on the wheel as if driving themselves straight into another world. Just before water's edge stood a lone mailbox, watched always from the woods, where the county's cut was left. This money kept whiskey coupes passing freely through the tangle of local prowl cars, kept the federal men on the hill-roads outside of town.

He rounded the last bend before the lake and felt a cold stone drop into the pit of his stomach. There was Sheriff Win Adderholt's Oldsmobile 88 parked slantwise in the road, a white coupe rumored to be as built as any blockader's. The pale body glowed against the trees, the chrome mouth grimaced in threat. Some strange whale beached from the lake depths. The sheriff was leaning on the hood, one foot on the bumper, smoking a cigarette.

"Shit."

Rory rolled to a stop, the two cars parked nose-to-nose, black and white, as if to fight. He left the motor idling and hit the parking brake before stepping out. Sheriff Adderholt wore a gray suit, tailor-cut, with a gray felt hat on his knee. He rubbed the brim with his thumb. He looked like a lawyer or big-city businessman but for the star pinned in his lapel, the leather of his face.

"Evening, Sheriff."

"Mr. Docherty." The Sheriff nodded. "Running a little late, aren't you?"

Rory leaned back on his own hood and crossed his arms.

"Little car trouble is all, sir. Seems somebody poked a hole in one of my coolant hoses."

"Is that so?" The Sheriff threw down his cigarette and stood from the hood of his Olds. The pearl butt of his service revolver peeked from behind a lapel. "Seems you been running into a lot of trouble down here of late."

"Now, Sheriff—"

The Sheriff held up a hand. "I'm not saying it's just you, Mr. Docherty. We had other boys with tires slashed. One boy had sugar poured in his tank. Another found a snake in his car."

"A snake?"

The Sheriff nodded. "These issues, son, it's the kind of a thing that attracts *attention*."

Rory felt the big engine thumping beneath him, like something trying to beat its way out of the hood. The Sheriff looked up at the sky. The half-moon, twinned, floated in his horn-rimmed glasses. He held his hat almost over his heart.

"I been mulling it over, son, and I come to a conclusion on the matter. The house-to-house deliveries are over at the End-of-the-Road. I'm forbidding them."

"Say what?"

"From now on, you're going to run a tank, emptied at a single location."

Rory was standing from the hood.

"You want us to build a tanker? We might as well be running wet every second. Revenuers don't got to catch you but with a drop. Intent to sell."

The Sheriff nodded, sucking his teeth.

"I hear your concerns, son. But the thing is, I ain't asking you this. I'm telling you."

"Telling me or what?"

Adderholt's face hardened.

"Or you won't sell a god-damn drop in my county again."

Rory was starting to see the shape of this thing.

"What about payment?" he asked.

"On delivery."

"Ten a gallon."

The Sheriff whistled. "See now, those are retail prices. We're talking wholesale now. Seven-fifty. But you won't have to go door-to-door."

"Eustace won't like it."

The Sheriff leaned back on the hood and crossed his arms, holding his hat.

"I don't hardly give a shit what Eustace likes, son."

"I'll have to talk to him."

The Sheriff leaned forward, arms crossed.

"You do that. You go and tell him you'll be here this Saturday with a wholesale tank."

"Will I?"

"You will." The Sheriff nodded up the road. "Old repair shop, out behind the old filling station."

"The church?"

"Gone before the service starts. It's all been arranged."

Rory looked back up the road, thinking of the place. Someone had recently hung a handwritten sign in between the garage bay doors: CHURCH OF THE NEW LIGHT.

The Sheriff was watching him.

"You ain't hanging around those people, are you?"

Rory shrugged. "I could be."

The Sheriff was standing close to him now.

"Don't. They're trouble, the lot of them. That pastor especially."

Rory looked into the dark shape of his reflection, twinned in the man's glasses.

"If he's trouble, what are you?"

The Sheriff put on his hat, straightened it.

"I'm his brother."

CHAPTER 11

Granny was awake before the cock's first crow, the windows yet dark, the eastern ridges scarcely dawn-edged against the night sky. Something wasn't right. She'd been waked. She set her feet on the floor, the planks ice-cold, the window of the woodstove glowing the dullest red. There it was again: the sound of the roof-timbers groaning. There was something up there, heavier than a squirrel or raccoon or opossum, creeping spider-slow across the cedar shakes, and she thought: *panther-cat*. She crossed to the mantel and took down her single-barreled shotgun, loaded with triple-aught buck, the gun she'd had since she was ten. She slung the leather belt of shells over her shoulder and cocked the hammer with her thumb. She checked that the door was barred, and she was stepping back across the floor, gun in hand, when a scream rent the air like a woman murdered, a blood-scream so high and terrible it seemed her very own, and she raised the shotgun toward the point in the roof where she judged the creature to be crouched. The scream died in what sounded almost like a snigger, a stifled chuckle, and she was already pulling the trigger.

The sound was deafening in the enclosed space, the house trembling, her ears ringing in sustained alarm, and she felt the cedar splinters and dust on her upturned face before she heard or felt the thump of something hitting the ground outside. The spent shotshell zipped smoking from the chamber as she breeched the gun, and she took a new shell from the leather belt slung across her shoulder and slid it home and snapped the gun straight and headed for the door. She slid the heavy oak plank from the iron locks and pushed open the door, the pre-dawn cold stinging her through the thin shift she wore, the rock-salted steps clapping beneath her bare feet. She wheeled around the near side of the house, finding nothing, the ridges limned in now greater light, and then she was around the back of the house, the mountain high and dark before her. At the edge of the meadow she saw the understory swaying and let loose with a second spray of shot, chasing whatever it was into the woods.

She stood breathing hard in the paling light, suddenly cold. She searched for signs near the house, her breath smoking, and found no spatter of blood bright in the meadow-grass nor any tracks, neither hoof nor paw nor boot. When she finished, the peak above her was burning white-gold under the new sun, torrents of dawn-light breaking down its slopes and ridges, seeping into its clefts, spreading in broken shields down the mountain and into the meadow like something liquid. Commandant, the big speckled Java cock, hopped down the chicken ladder. His chest was puffed out, his wings tucked behind him like a pair of clasped hands. He looked sideways at her with one beady eye before lengthening his neck and crowing over his dominion.

Granny spat in the grass.

"Little late for all that, now ain't it?"

The sun sat perched upon the serrated blade of the eastern ranges, chasing night out of the hollows and ravines, when Rory's coupe came rumbling up the drive. Granny sucked her teeth as he came up the steps.

"You feed them hogs?"

"No, ma'am."

"You feed them chickens?"

"No, ma'am."

He stooped and gave her a kiss, then walked through the door.

"Christ, woman! The hell happened in here?"

She could picture him standing there in the main room, his face peppered in light, then standing aside to see the sun-shafts lancing down from the constellation she'd blown in the roof. She lit her pipe.

"She-cat, likely. Though I never heard tell of one that amuses itself."

Rory was back on the porch.

"How you know it was a panther?"

"Boy, you think I never heard a panther-cat scream of a night?"

"And you shot at it?"

"I wasn't gonna lullaby it to death."

"You blowed a hole in the got-damn roof, you know that? Big enough to fill a number-nine washtub when it rains."

"I guess you best get to patching it, then."

"Hellfire, were there even tracks?"

She sniffed. "Don't leave much sign in that oat grass."

"You sure you weren't dreaming?"

"Dreaming? Listen here, son, I known what it was I heard. They was something on that roof and it wasn't no damn squirrel or raccoon like you think. It was man-sized, at least, yowling bloody murder across the mountain. A cat or someone playing at one, 'less you think a woman got stabbed to death on that roof. You might of heard it, too, you wasn't out hunting split the whole damn night."

"Split—? God, I don't have to listen to this."

He tromped back in the house, and she could hear him banging around in the kitchen.

"Or was you at church again?" She cocked her head toward the open door. "Getting you' cock hard for one them Holiness Christers?"

He came back out on the porch with a biscuit in his teeth. He was putting on his jacket. He fought to get one of his arms in right. He took the biscuit out of his mouth. His face was red.

"Why don't you just calm it the hell down," he told her. "I got places to go."

He rumbled down the porch steps and made for the car.

Granny sucked her teeth again.

"You best not of lost that old poke of mine," she called out. "I used to eat school lunch out that bag."

"Yeah, yeah."

He got in the car, slamming the door, and fired the big engine. He turned a circle in the yard and tore off down the drive.

Granny watched him go. She leaned back again in her rocker, smiling despite herself.

That grandboy of hers. If he wasn't in love, he was close.

Eli was riding shotgun, stroking the gnarled mass of his beard. Rory looked over at him.

"You do that long enough you think it'll purr?"

Eli spat out the window.

"Your dick purr for you, all that handiwork you given it?"

"I got hope just yet."

They were headed up the mountain to deliver the Sheriff's news, the road forking and forking again, Eli squinting as if to read signs at each juncture, then pointing them this way or that. They wound higher and higher, the leaves darkening on the trees as they climbed, the risen sun slanting down through the branches in heatless planes of light. The tires churned through muddy slogs and bounced over knotty clutches of roots, the big motor roaring against the feathered clutch. The air grew colder, scarcer, and the car-roads petered out into old wagon-trails that branched again and again in ever-steepening runoffs, some of them just the ghosts of roads through overgrown woods. Who knew what histories lay up or down those paths, what births and murders and madness high on the mountain? So many stories jumped mouth to mouth down the slopes and across the hollers, across the years, and so many did not. There were broken-down cabins scattered across the ridges, some more than two centuries old, their roofs imploded by decades of snow burden or crushed beneath storm-felled oaks. Some mere foundation stones, fire-scorched, razed by lightning or oil-lamp or trouble-seeking boys.

"Up here," said Eli. "Yonder's his truck."

The big flatbed sat parked at the edge of a small clearing, covered in camouflage netting like they used in the war. They parked alongside it and got out. Three separate footpaths struck off into the woods.

"Which one?" asked Rory.

"The middle," said Eli, pointing. "I think."

"What's up the others?"

"I don't think we want to know."

The track itself was rocky, but Rory could discern cart tracks in the softer places, hoofprints between them. The signs of a workway, a still-path. The trees were gray on either side of them, naked already of leaves, their antlered crowns clattering in the wind.

"Airish up here," said Eli. He shivered.

Rory didn't say anything. The air felt a cooling salve against his flesh, as if he were running a few degrees too hot. Eli shrugged and produced his hip flask.

"Least my belly's warm."

Eustace had stills scattered all across the mountain, in gullies and coves and laurel slicks. They were run by a small army of old men with gnarled hands and bent backs, many disfigured by war or logging accidents or lovers' squabbles. Their silence was legendary. They'd farmed rock-ridden hillsides, or tried, and fought Germans with bayonets and trench guns in hells of mud. They'd cut whole mountains to stumps for Northern timber barons, blasted rock and driven spikes for narrow-gauge lines. Then in the 1920s the timber ran scarce and the camps folded. Dry flumes laced the mountains like abandoned amusement rides, and there was no work. They would have to move west to work in the coal mines, scurrying underground like the Welsh sappers they knew in the war, carting out the black rubble of prehistoric swamps to fuel cities they would never see. That or down into the brick prisons of the mills, the heat and lint and machine-gun rattle. A choice of black lung or white, each contracted beneath the shoddy suns of electric bulbs. Then came Eustace, who gave them the moon.

The trees opened onto a grassy bald, a sward of oat grass cut by a crooked black stream that ran tripping and fleeing from the mountain heights. They climbed toward where the stream broke from the upper tree line. A thousand green spires of spruce and fir, untouched by ax or saw. The evergreen cathedral, cloud-rung, which Eustace called home. Rory looked back before stepping into the cold shadows of these giants. They were close now to the summit of the mountain, and the land lay all crinkled and ridged beneath them, studded by lesser peaks the color of woodsmoke. The world seemed unreal from this height, the work of someone's imagining.

Eli held out the flask to Rory.

"Tell me about this girl you're all knotted up over."

Rory took the flask.

"What girl?"

"Don't give me that shit. You been brooding."

"I haven't."

"What's her name?"

Rory sipped from the flask; lightning struck down his throat.

"Christine," he said.

"She cute?"

"More than."

"What's she do?"

"Makes hats."

"They built a hat factory down there?"

"No, she does them herself."

"Well, damn. A entrepreneur. She gonna make you something smart to replace that ancient piece of shit on your head?"

"This was my granddaddy's."

"Let me tell you something: your granddaddy wouldn't never have caught a woman like Granny wearing that thing. Not like it is. Looks like something went and died on your head."

"You thought about that a lot—catching Granny?"

Eli grabbed the flask back.

"Gimme that."

They stepped into the trees and followed the stream. They found the still first, an eight-hundred-gallon pot shaped like a submarine. Thin blue feathers of flame tickled the base, dancing from lengths of drilled one-inch pipe. There was a sustained hiss of burning gas, like a distant jet. The still was enclosed by a three-walled house of rough-hewn timbers, mud-daubed at the chinks. There was a folding cot against one wall, a burlap flap on the open side pulled back like a curtain. It was a structure that could be built in a day. Probably had been. One of many shelters rumored on the mountain, set in caves and groves and uprooted trees. Several feet away stood an old gray mule, worn nearly dead from packing in sugar and meal, then packing it out again as whiskey. As they stood there the wind came up through the trees. Rory waited for the leaves to rise hovering from the ground, as legend had them.

"The hell y'all doing up here?"

They wheeled. Eustace stood behind them, frowning, eating from a can of beans. They hadn't heard a thing.

"We had to talk to you," said Eli.

Eustace squinted at them. He was chewing a mouthful. He swallowed and licked clean his spoon, a little thing with tines like a fork. A souvenir from the war in France, the homemade utensil of a dead German. Rory had never seen him eat with anything else.

"Talk, then."

Eli looked at Rory, waiting. Rory shifted on his wooden leg. There were stumps scattered about. Eustace didn't ask them to sit.

"I talked to the Sheriff last night."

"And?"

"He said no more milk-runs. Said he's forbidding them."

Eustace stiffened. He set down the can of beans.

"Forbidding them."

"Yes, sir. Says we got to run a tank. Sell wholesale."

Eustace sucked clean his teeth.

"Wholesale."

"Yes, sir," said Rory.

"For how much?"

"Seven-fifty a gallon."

The old man tugged his beard, hard, twisting the hair between his fingers. Rory could feel him, his great pressurized bulk, his body seeming to tremble like the cap on a mash boiler—the kind you had to keep down with a big rock or length of chain. He cleared his throat.

"He say what come him to this?"

"He said there's been too much trouble," said Rory. "Cars sabotaged and such. Said we'll have a single location for off-load."

"Where at?"

"This filling station, down at End-of-the-Road. Lately a church."

Eustace growled, crossing his hands over his chest, thumbs up.

"His daddy's old place. Mite convenient, that. Payment on delivery?"

"He said."

The old man growled again. His great belly shook.

"He's lording," he said. "It ain't a thing I'm like to brook."

"What you want us to do?"

Eustace leaned, arms crossed, and spat. A clot quivered on a nearby rock.

"Do it," he said. "For now."

————

Granny leaned against the trunk of a red oak to catch her breath. The sun shafted cold and white through the shattered roof of the forest. She adjusted the sling of shells over her shoulder and kept on, tracking the direction she thought the creature had run. She had found no blood-spoor drying on the leaves, no prints in the windblown piles upon the ground. She had found twigs and branches broken as by passing beast, and this she followed, her big man-boots crackling beneath her, her shotgun cradled in the crook of her arm. She was old, she knew, but she wasn't crazy yet.

The wind soughed through the trees, kicking up swirls of leaves, and that lonesome sound put her in mind of her past. So much of her life had happened in the falling season. She could see that now. It was a fall day when she set out to learn a way of making a living for the little boy that had become her warrant. Her old life had been swallowed in the rising of the lake; her Bonni had been sent away. She would have no more of towns with their kept little women, soft-skinned in houses of brick and stone, bitter when their men followed strange bents in the night. Shapes to which they themselves would never deign kink. Women who whispered that her daughter had asked for what she got. That God had struck her dumb. She who should never have been consorting with a boy of high birth, when she wasn't but a whore's daughter. Perhaps it was her own mother at fault, for sin will out.

Granny had needed a new way of living for the boy, and she sought it out herself. She went deep into the mountains with only a mule, toward the Cherokee lands, the leaves coming down in a whispering storm, blood-colored and gold. The first frost came with her asleep in the crater of a wind-felled oak, waking to find herself clutched in the icy talons of the tree's exposed roots. Three days later she found the woman she sought, a white healer living in a one-room cabin near the Tennessee border. People said she'd been widowed in 1865, her husband hanged by secessionist guerrillas from a black oak in the front yard. According to Granny's calculations, that made her something more than eighty years old.

She waited three days beneath that tree for the old woman to open the door. The first snow fell, ledging itself upon the brim of her slouch hat, in the creases and folds of her shawl. She sat cross-legged on the ground, shaking, and she knew somehow that building a fire would only keep the door barred against her. Will must be proven. Wisdom earned. She waited, eating dried pork from her sack, drinking snow she melted in the cup of her hands. After three days, the door opened, a pane of rectilinear yellow light giving unto a whole other world. Granny rose and struggled toward it, stoving blue holes in the snow, stunned at the woman she met at the door. A woman so like herself, twice-distanced down the same hard road.

"Welcome," said the old woman, as if she were expected.

Granny bent to the ground before a deadfall of graying timber and brushed at the wind-piled leaves. In the earth an indention, vaguely angular, such as the edge of a boot sole might make. She kept on, climbing over fallen limbs moldering slowly back into the earth, their bark sloughing away to reveal the pale flesh beneath. She searched for claw-slashes in the softened wood, or the strike of heels, finding neither for certain. She went on. The wind rose again, the woods murmuring in a low ocean of voices. A hare exploded in a fire of reddish leaves, a streak of brown fur shooting up the nearest rise. She reached a creek that ran nearly straight across her path, the black sluice speckled with fallen leaves, tiny ships in fleet.

She searched the soft earth of the banks, finding nothing, and thought of turning back. Instead she clung to a sapling grown aslant the creek, her arm shaking slightly as she stepped nearly across. Her boot sank into the soft mud at the edge of the creek bed, the water bubbling at the throat of her boot, and she climbed the far side, the shotgun still tucked in her arm. She was a little ways farther on, rounding the mountain toward the south, when she stepped through a broken tangle of brambles and found a boot print in a soft patch, perfect as a mold. She knelt. It was a number-ten shoe size, or thereabouts, and the toe-strike was deeper than the heel, as of a man in flight. She sniffed and spat on the ground beside it. A few yards on, the trees broke onto the skinniest excuse for a road, such as the kind teenagers favored high on the mountain for necking and carrying-on. She cocked her head. Tire tracks, unmarked by paws or hooves or feet.

"Got you, you son of a bitch."

CHAPTER 12

It was near hog-killing time and the feed store had plenty of barrels in stock. The clerk led them out back of the place. Fifty-five-gallon steel drums stood in ranks along the fence. All through the hills, the barrels were buried at a diagonal in the ground and filled with scalding water. Bled-out hogs were dunked long enough to loosen their coarse winter hair, then hauled smoking onto wooden pallets, their scalded hides scraped hairless with dull knives.

Rory scratched his chin.

"I heard the steel gives the whiskey a tang."

"Not our department," said Eli. He looked at the clerk. "You got a dolly?"

They wheeled the barrel out to the car, and Rory paid the man from the sheaf of bills stashed in his back pocket.

"You been selling more of these than regular?"

The clerk made change from the canvas apron he wore, then cocked his head toward the car.

"Seems boys in V8 Fords got a special taste for pork chops this season."

"You sell to any of them Muldoons?"

The clerk grimaced like someone had elbowed him in the ribs.

"I really couldn't speak to that, young fella."

Rory peeled off a ten-dollar bill.

"What if Alexander Hamilton was asking?"

The clerk looked Rory in the face.

"I'd tell him to duck next time."

They sat in the singed air of the garage, the doors open. Dusk was falling over the mountain, the sky purpling over the jagged black trees. The ribbed drum lay sideways in the trunk of the coupe, set on a plywood cradle and secured with leather straps. Eli had welded on a filling spout. A long snake of garden hose looped from the spout and slithered out of the garage. There was the hollow, distant rumble of water filling the tank, like someone drawing a bath in a claw-foot tub.

Eli sipped from his hip flask and smacked his lips.

"Who you think is behind all this trouble the Sheriff was talking about?"

Rory leaned back on his stool and held the jar of water he was sipping to the light. He could have told it wasn't whiskey just by feel. It was too heavy in the glass, rolling and muscling its way around.

"I'm not for sure."

"Could be it's the Sheriff himself behind it."

"I thought of that." He sipped from the jar. The water was cold, from deep in the mountain, and tasted almost sweet. "You know that preacher down there, his brother? He's only got one eye."

"So?"

"So you know my mother carved out the eye of one of those nightriders."

Eli set down his jar.

"Lot of people lost a eye around here. Half the mountain's caught a splinter cutting timber, seems like."

Rory nodded.

"I know," he said. "But I'll always be a little prejudiced against one-eyed sons of bitches, thinking they might could be the one."

"It isn't something you'll ever know. Not unless you had an eye to match it with, and you don't. You got to make peace with that."

Rory stood.

"Come on, tank's about full. Time for a shakedown run."

Highway 321 sped through the high country, clutching blasted rock faces striated by dynamite grooves, crooking in hairpins sheered against the stars. Guardrails zagged in the headlights like endless bolts of lightning, striking ever deeper into the night. The blacktop heaved beneath the car, cresting, then dropped quickly away, the two of them floating against their lap-belts as the road sang beneath a ridge that put Rory in mind of ambush. He glanced up as he drove, half-expecting to see men on horseback silhouetted against the sky.

Eli was sliding side to side in his seat, sipping from his jar, casual as an old woman riding a buckboard wagon to church.

"Tell you what, I'd eat the crust off a heifer's teats about this moment."

Rory skewed his mouth toward his friend, keeping his eyes on the road.

"You ate an apple not two hours ago."

"Mushy as mule shit."

"You'd bitch if they hung you with a new rope."

Eli touched his neck with the blackened tips of his fingers, squinting with thought.

"Hell," he said. "I might."

The tires bawled into the belly of the curve, the motor exploding off the stony wall of the ridge. The car jostled through the sharpening curves, a mighty hulk prompted in one direction, then another, roaring as it went. The wheel was light in Rory's fingers, the accelerator a mighty button beneath his foot. He was letting the machine do the work, his arms rowing through the gears, his feet dancing among gas and brake and clutch, his heart calm, not racing the throttled engine.

"Yonder's the spot," said Eli.

"I know where it is."

Rory let off the gas coming down toward the roadhouse, the exhaust popping and crackling as the car decelerated. They rolled crunching into the graveled lot and Rory cut the engine and they got out.

"What you think?" Eli patted the trunk.

"She's solid. And you don't got to worry about busting any glass."

"Just don't tell Eustace you like it."

"I'm not as dumb as you."

The roadhouse was a two-story clapboard built on the very edge of a ravine. There was a shared porch running the length of the second floor. A couple of girls, underdressed for the cold, leaned on the railing, smoking cigarettes. Out back a cedar deck hung far out over the edge of the abyss on a skeleton of thin stilts that looked ever-so-slightly out of plumb. More than one man had been thrown or pushed or kicked over the side during a brawl, his body broken on the rocky crags far below. Still more drunks had managed to fall over the waist-high railing while relieving themselves, enthralled perhaps by the sight of their golden banners streaming out into the void. There were notices plastered all over the place warning against the practice, mostly ignored, and hammered to one of the porch supports a hand-painted sign: THIS AIN'T HELL.

People called the place Hell for short.

The screen door slammed behind them and they sat at the counter and ordered cheeseburgers and spuds and beers. It was Falstaff in white cans, taken from an icebox below the bar. The bartender punched them open with a church key and set them pooling on the bar. Eli took his up and turned to survey the place, his elbows resting on the back of his high chair. There was a small square-dance floor with nobody on it. A few people smoking in the surrounding booths, their eyes half shut, and an old man trying to work a coin into the nickelodeon, his hand shaking.

Rory sipped his beer.

"Granny blowed a hole in the roof last night."

"Say what?"

"Said she heard a panther up there."

"Good hell," said Eli. "You think she was hearing things?"

"That woman, I don't know. She don't spook easy. I'm figuring something must of been up there. Panther, I doubt it."

Eli squinted one eye and crossed his arms.

"What time was this?"

"Along about dawn or a little before."

Eli nodded, thumbing his beard.

"I was up early this morning, finishing a head-job on that '51 Merc? Heard a built motor out on the road. Thought it was you coming home till I realized it was going down the mountain and not up."

"Could of been one of Eustace's other boys."

"Sure, but it wasn't a V8. It was a straight-six."

"You sure?"

Eli's beer froze halfway to his mouth.

"You think I can't tell the difference?"

"I wasn't saying that."

"Sure you weren't." Eli took a long pull from his beer, belching through his teeth. "You know those Muldoon boys favor the Hudson, that high-compression six."

"Could you tell if you heard it again?"

"Can a pig eat shit? I know where to find them, too."

"Where?"

Eli grinned.

"Gumtree Speedway, Friday night."

Rory cursed himself. It had begun to rain, a staccato clapping on the body of the car, marbly and hard. He hadn't yet patched the cabin roof. He could imagine the rain streaming down in narrow-gauge shafts, tinkling into an old spittoon or chamber pot. Granny just watching, sucking her teeth. He'd already dropped Eli back at the garage.

"Tell Granny May not to shoot me next time I come to visit," Eli had said.

"Just stay off the roof."

"That, I intend to."

Rory drove slowly now, in low gear, climbing the mountain toward home. The edges of the road were swelling, a pair of small rivers tumbling down the mountain. Beyond that the world was slanted and white-blown with rain. The tires spun on the rocks, in the mud, and he squinted for washouts and mudslides and wind-felled trees along his path. He wondered if it was storming down in the valleys, in the foothills and mill towns. In the place where she—Christine—lived. He wondered if it was raining over in Raleigh, on the roof of the ward where they housed his mother. He wondered what it sounded like, there inside her room.

When he got home there was an iron stew pot below the leak, half full, and the door to Granny's room was closed. No light flickered at the threshold. He dumped out the pot and set it back in place, then fed the stove. He went to his room and pulled off his boot and sock and his wooden leg, which he stood on the floor beside the bed. He peeled off his sodden clothes and hung them to dry and lay on the bed a long few minutes before he realized he was shivering with cold. He got up to warm himself by the stove but realized he'd have to hop, waking Granny, or else crawl along the floor. He lay back down and curled himself in the covers, still shivering, hoping not to dream.

The paintings watched him from the wall, hanging upon their silent flames of wing.

CHAPTER 13

Gumtree Speedway roared on the edge of town, a red crater in the earth, smoking and quaking with the mania of throttled engines. Gum lumber grandstands stood along the front straight, shivering before the onslaught, the terraced benches filled with spectators huddled in scarves and woolen hats. Stadium lights shone in white-eyed barrage, their black wires bellying pole to pole. The racers wheeled beneath the lights, a tornado of gutted-out coupes with giant motors, each knifing sideways through the red clay of the track. They were machines salvaged from wrecking yards and cobwebbed garages, reborn at the hands of speed-crazed farmboys and mill-hands.

Rory and Eli parked on the hill above the track. The spectators' cars were parked in formation, long ranks of them close-huddled like an armored division, ticking as they cooled. Among them a number of V8 Fords, squatty coupes or sedans sitting high-tailed on bootlegging springs. Cars that could be heard on the hill-roads night after night, paying for themselves.

They walked down the hill toward the gate. Rory had patched the roof earlier that week, kneeling on the cedar shakes with nails stuck from his mouth like awkward fangs while Granny, unseen in her rocker on the porch, assaulted him with gossip. He wasn't sure where

she got so much of it. It was like she pulled the rumors straight out of
the air, like a radio would. He figured people must come by when he
wasn't there. She said one of Milly McMann's goats had been taken by
a neighbor-dog. She said poor Linney Wallace's son had come home
from the knitting mill with a case of the white-lung. She said there
was this crazy little church that had sprung up down there in town,
in a filling station. She said it was full of crazies, the kind that ought to
be avoided—same's that Cooley boy with the snakes in his head. Try
as he might to shut her out, Rory's hammer kept ringing down as if in
punctuation to what she told.

They bought their tickets from a fat lady sitting behind a folding
card table, a dollar for the two of them. Rory paid. They handed their
tickets to a skinny man working the gate—the fat lady's husband—
and walked down in front of the stands to look for seats. They didn't
know the faces in the crowd. These were mill-hands, mainly, people
who'd come down out of the mountains for "public work." Wages. A
thing almost unheard of in the hills. Now they worked in the mills
six days a week. They were sweepers or loopers or oilers. Some worked
in the card room, preparing the cotton. They were pale and soft-
looking, with sickly creases underneath their eyes, like they lived underground. To hear it told, they subsisted on Double-Cola and Goody's
Headache Powder from the dope-wagons, wheeled pushcarts that cir-
culated the mill, peddling sugary cakes and sodas and tonics. Tonight
they had other remedies: jars of white whiskey secreted between their
knees, their faces jolly-red in the autumn dark.

Rory and Eli found seats in the top row, up among the snickering
teens and early drunks, and they excused themselves past people already seated, Rory trying not to smash anyone's foot. As soon as they
sat, Eli drew his big glass flask from the throat of his boot and pulled
the stopper with his teeth, the clear liquid beading under the light.
Rory swallowed open-jawed, exhaling through his teeth.

"That's whiskey."

The cars were lining up for the feature race, twenty of them staggered in motley pairs. They squatted on meaty rubber, their bodies
humped and raked, their grilles glaring in the spotlights. Some of
them had fancy, two-tone paint schemes, with the names of filling sta-
tions or wrecking yards or hardware stores painted on the doors. Most
of them didn't. Most of them had mismatched fenders and hoods,
their brightwork stripped for speed, their bodies ugly and cruel as
junkyard dogs. At the front of the pack crouched one low-slung
Hudson Hornet, dark green, that looked like a road-going car with a
number taped on the door.

Cooley Muldoon.

The cars rumbled and smoked as they awaited the green flag, a herd
of steel hulks twitching beneath the lights. Their hoods torqued ever so
slightly as the drivers raced their engines. The sound of the motors tore
through the night, snarling and snapping, each fighting to be loudest.
Children slapped their hands over their ears, muffling the noise, their
daddies watching stone-faced and open-eared as if they took a grim
pleasure in going deaf. The race official, clad in a set of gleaming white
coveralls, stood in the flag stand, a rickety platform that looked built by
treehouse boys. He slashed the green flag through the air like a battle
standard.

The night exploded, every motor wailing at once. A stampede of
crazed metal, of hard bright edges slashing through smoke and dust,
like sabers or lances, and then a car speared ahead of the storm, stretching for the first turn, and the others crowded quick upon its heels. The
drivers hurled their cars sideways into the corner, their tails kicked out,
skittering for traction on the bank. Some went high, some low, the
drivers in their white helmets fighting the wheel, steering the skinny
front tires counter to the turn, angling them this way and that, each car
riding the edge of control. Their tails wagged with power, threatening
to spin them back into oncoming traffic.

The cars strung out down the backstretch, two wide at full song, then bunched again in turns three and four, fenders clashing, paint scuffed away or banged newly in place. Then out again from the corner, throttled sideways for speed. Coming down the front straight, past the grandstands, they sounded like warplanes, the gull-winged Corsairs that strafed hillsides and ridgelines. The gum lumber trembled as they passed, as if in fear of being struck, the deadwood singing beneath the spectators' clenched rumps.

Eli pointed out the cars as they boomed down the straight. Who built this one, who drove that one. Cars rumored to be running cheater heads and racing cams, oversize pistons and triple carburetors. High-performance parts mail-ordered from speed shops in Charlotte or Atlanta or Chattanooga, sprung from whiskey money. He banged Rory on the knee.

"This is what *we* should be doing."

"We're here, aren't we?"

"I mean *in it*. Out there."

Rory spat between his boots.

"Expensive."

Eli huffed.

"Ain't nothing worth doing that don't cost you."

A maroon coupe ran too high in turn one, too fast, and the car slid straight instead of turning, the canted wheels tearing across the clay like plow blades. The machine ran straight over the top of the track, tumbling out of sight, and the spectators leapt upright, hands thrown to mouths or hearts. *There were trees down there.* They waited for an explosion, a balloon of fire to rise from the pines beyond the track. The seconds stretched out until the driver surfaced at the top of the berm, waving his helmet. Everyone let out their breath at once. Relief, it sounded like, or disappointment. The gum lumber groaned when they sat.

Later a cream sedan tangled with the Hudson coming out of turn two. The Hudson bumped the machine in the quarter panel, hard, and the sedan tipped sideways, the rear wheels coming off the ground, the car rolling barrel-like across the track, pieces flying off in every direction. The car came to rest on its roof, undercarriage turned up to the sky. Two yellow flags came out, waved frantically by the white-coated man in the stand. The racers slowed, filing into a single line, snaking around the wrecked car.

Safety workers ran out onto the track, pulling the driver through the crushed window. The man looked limp, dead. The workers huddled all around him, kneeling and squatting, jumping back as he came awake. The rest of the crew was gathered up against the side of the car, trying to right it. The driver leapt up and joined them, the bunch of them heaving against the running boards, rocking the car until it rolled over, righting with a bounce. Neither door would open. The driver crawled back through the window and cranked the motor. A blue-black cough from the tailpipe. He drove the crumpled machine down off the track and into the pits.

"That's why we aren't out there," said Rory.

"Shit," said Eli. He took a big pull off the flask.

Cooley's Hudson leapt ahead after the restart, outpacing the others into the first turn. It was one of the new step-down models, built low and sledlike, green as the money spent to keep it so handsome and quick.

"Got that Twin-H 308," said Eli. "Jump out them corners like a scorched jackrabbit."

Rory grunted.

The cars kept carving into the clay, rutting it dark with shadow and rubber. They dove screaming into the corners, angled high on their outer wheels, bumping and clanging the cars on either side. Machines careened off the track, slung like breakneck satellites from orbit, spewing dust and smoke and shrapnel as they rolled. Cooley, winning, turned any car that crossed him. On the second-to-last lap he ran a blue Ford into a light post. The transformer exploded, a burst of showered light, like the white bloom of a phosphorus bomb, and the track went sudden-dark. The cars raced on undaunted, a vortex of screaming shadows, their headlights ripping haloes in the night.

Rory and Eli sat in their seats afterward, sipping whiskey as the stands emptied out. The track was still dark, the infield crawling with headlights, double-set like the glowing eyes of creatures of the night. Bears, perhaps, or wolves or panther-cats.

"So what you think? Was it Cooley's Hudson you heard the other night?"

Eli tugged on a grip of beard.

"Hard to say."

Rory ground his teeth.

"I thought you were the damn expert. The motor-witch."

Eli looked at him a long moment, like watching something behind a wall of glass. He shook his head, sipped from the flask.

"Lot of other racket out there."

"What if you had to guess?"

"I wouldn't want to guess about a thing like that."

"Dammit," said Rory, standing up. "Let's go."

Outside the gate they waited for a jet-black Lincoln Capri, long as a hearse, to slide rumbling past them. The fat lady was riding shotgun, a pile of cash stacked in her lap. On the dashboard in front of her rested a long-nosed revolver, nickeled to catch the moon. They were headed to the infield to pay the winnings.

Cars were all over the place, reversing or pulling forward from their parking spots. A long line of ruby lights snaked its way over the hilled fairground and into the trees. They disappeared east, toward town. The drivers would go out to End-of-the-Road, most of them, to keep the party going. Others down to the lake, to scream and swim naked in the too-cold water, clinging to the nearest warm body. Some would go on home to belch and grunt, to wrestle in bed and pound the walls until the whiskey put them out.

Rory stood in front of the coupe's door to unlock it. Over the roof, he watched a group of boys come walking toward a rust-patched car a few rows away. They slapped and cursed and shadowboxed one another as they came, big grins on their faces. All but the boy in front, who was on crutches. He wore a big plaster cast on his leg, his foot sticking out the bottom, the flesh swollen and discolored around the toes. He had a buddy on either side of him, more serious than the others, flanking him like guards. Rory recognized them from the other night.

The boy looked up in Rory's direction, then cut his eyes away, quick, like he hadn't seen him. He looked at the ground.

Rory waited for something to well up in him. Sympathy, maybe. Or regret.

"What is it?" asked Eli.

Rory shook his head and unlocked the door.

"Nothing."

III. SICKLE MOON, WANING

Connor hardly even touched his lunches, which seemed treasures to Bonni. He brought pimento cheese sandwiches on triangles of bread so white and neat they looked like cake. He brought wormless apples that cracked like falling trees in his mouth and corn muffins peppered with poppy seeds and whole shingles of store-bought peanut brittle.

Why won't you let me see your drawings? he asked.

Bonni clutched her sketchbook tight, as if it might open on its own.

They're dumb, she said.

They are not. Let me see.

Why was it so hard to show him her work? Why did it feel like cracking open some door in her chest, revealing her raw, beating heart?

She set the sketchbook on the floor, pushed it across to him. He was gentle, opening the book with the edge of his thumb. He began turning through the pages, slowly at first, then faster. They were animals, mainly, a compendium of those she loved. There were grasshoppers and finches, field mice and gamecocks and barnyard cats. Antlered stags and bandit-masked raccoons and barred owls on the wing. They seemed to trail echoes of their own feathers and in their wake, ghosts of movement, as if they were caught not in a single moment but several.

Connor looked up at her, bits of apple stuck on his tongue.

My God, these are beautiful.

She leaned across to him, kissed him on the mouth. She could taste the great good apple on his tongue.

CHAPTER 14

Granny trudged up a small branch that zagged down the eastern slope of the mountain, the current dashing white-knotted from rock to rock, hastened by the recent storm. It was Saturday, early, and it had rained again in the night. Her shotgun lay across her back, the hemp sling slashed between her breasts, and she had a denim pouch slung from the opposite shoulder. In this she carried the roots she gathered. In her hand was the grubbing tool handed down by her father, an ancient mattock with a three-foot hickory handle. It looked like a pickax in miniature, with a hoe blade and spike.

She was hunting ginseng, the potent root that loved the moist darknesses of the east-facing slopes, the earth kept rich and black by the thick canopy of crisscrossed branches that stood like veins against the sky, lacing the ground in shadow. It was a root she used in teas and tonics, in vialed liquor potions for all manner of ills: digestion and appetite and lethargy, fainting and blood troubles and masculine vigor. She combined it for various uses with yellowroot and black cherry, with parsley or corn silk or whiskey.

Her father had been bad to drink, a whiskey-breathed man of strange bents, but he could find ginseng better than anyone on the mountain. So good, people got to calling him a sang-witch. As a girl, she thought it was a sixth sense of some kind, a nose for the elusive root that grew pale and fleshy as a man's organ beneath the ground. Only later would the old granny woman teach her to read the earth and signs. She would learn to search for sang on east- and north-facing slopes, in the company of bloodroot and goldenseal and other companions, in patches of light understory that would not overshade the small leaflets.

The old woman said that, in the Far East, the tiger was lord and protector of the ginseng, and the ancient people of Manchuria once kept patches of the holy root hidden high in the mountains, ever guarded by their god-beast of fire and ink. There were no tigers in these mountains, but perhaps a panther still roamed. Granny stopped, listening, and moved on.

The woods were wet about her, the dying leaves slick and heavy and dark. Tiny beads of moisture hovered in the fuzz of the sweater she wore, and fugitive streaks of wet-dark hair fell from the bun cinched atop her head. They clung to her face. She stepped gently through a clutch of thorny briars and found a patch of yellowed leaves of the sort she sought. She bent to the earth and began to remove the woodsy litter from the base of a three-leafed plant, creating a one-foot halo of bare earth about the sprout. Then, gently, she began to dig away the dirt with her bare hands, revealing the neck of the root. She counted seven bud-scars there, from the seasonal death of the leaves, making the plant at least six years old. She dug further, seeing which way the main root grew into the earth. Finally she brought forth the mattock, chipping and picking at the soil, careful not to damage the fibrous offshoots of the main root, fine as hairs in the churned-up ground. She harvested what she could, filling her pouch, and squeezed the seeds from the berries back into the holes she'd dug.

Done, she carried on, stepping through the slick undergrowth, her footfalls muffled on the sodden leaves. She crossed the same creek she had the week before, in pursuit of her panther-cat, and continued on until she arrived at the old side road. Just the rumor of a drive to some disappeared homestead farther up the mountain. Perhaps a jumble of foundation stones lorded over by weeds and snakes. The previous Sunday's tire tracks were pocked now with mountain traffic, the marks of hooves and paws and bird feet. She dug in the deep pocket of her skirt, bringing up one of the crude iron caltrops she'd stowed there. It rested upon her palm like a piece from the childhood game of jacks, only spiked, shaped to blow any tire that rolled over it. Rory and Eli had installed a pouch of the mean little stars beneath the trunk of the Ford, the release actuated by a string that ran up through the floorboard between the driver's legs. In a drawer in the toolshed, she'd found the extras.

She bent to her knees and began to dig at the earth with the mattock, chipping and picking until she opened a small hollow in one of the wheel ruts. Here she planted the caltrop, an evil seed of things to come. Then she moved farther down the rut, opening a second small hollow, sowing her irons along the road.

Saturday Rory started his run without supper. Eustace had already gone inside by the time they finished filling the tank, and the door was closed, and neither he nor Eli wanted to chance a sight of what those old bodies were doing in there. He knew there was a roast in a pot on the stove, waiting for him, and pork gravy besides. Gravy that slowed the blood, thickened it, made you less worried about revenuers waiting around every bend, about hard beds and iron bars in places like Chillicothe, Ohio, where federal violators were sent. It made you less worried about the green eyes of a girl, and what they saw when they looked at you, at your broken body and worshipful face.

He lit a Lucky Strike and watched the smoke go sliding into the slipstream beyond the cracked window, hurried to its own unraveling. The days were shortening, only a keen edge of light over the dusky ranges to the west, the land growing softer as he descended, less angular. The roads reddening, cut from that long scar of clay that ran diagonal across the Carolinas, parallel to the mountains. The lifeblood of tobacco and cotton fields, the accumulated death of prehistoric ranges. The sky darkened. A thin blade of moon rose.

He pulled off on a side road and got out, leaving the car idling. He had an idea how those revenue men had pegged him last week: dust. The pale dust of mountain roads, when the foothills were red. He opened the trunk and removed an oil tin filled with water and a towel and doused the roof from the can's metal spigot, watching the water cut through the chalklike dust that coated the doors and fenders. The water streaked down the body in crooked arcs, spreading like the skeletal underpinnings of a broken umbrella. He watched a long moment before beginning to wipe the body clean, the night-black paint flecked with stars.

The filling station stood lightless at the end of the road. It looked abandoned, a place that might well be sitting in the shadows at the bottom of the lake, fishes gliding past the pumps instead of cars. Rory wheeled the Ford around back of the place, bumping over the grass, toward the old double-bay repair shop set back under the trees. The roof was bloodied tin, the weeds uncut around the base of the structure. It was flanked by the giant cylinder of the gasoline storage tank, like a paint-flaked submarine. Written on the side: SINCLAIR H-C. The place looked a home for rats and snakes and squatters. The walls, once white, wore an eerie green film. The doors of the nearest bay swung out as he approached, pushed open from within, a man-size shadow fading back into the darkness.

Rory pulled the car into a square black maw. The loping idle of the engine grew loud in the confined space, and the doors swung closed behind him. Someone lit a lantern. Rory could make out the form of a man perched wide-kneed on a stool, thin as a vulture, the lantern dangling between his legs. The floor was spotted beneath him, stained from leaking oil pans and differentials.

The man turned up the flame, the orb of light swelling toward the corners of the room, and Rory saw it was an attendant from the service station in town. He wore a pair of oil-streaked coveralls. His chin was pointed, his face pocked and whiskered, his Adam's apple bulbous and white. He left the lantern on the stool and approached the driver's side window, grinning a hatchet grin, his mouth crowded with yellow teeth.

"Evening," he said.

"Evening," said Rory, cutting the engine.

The man pulled a red bandanna from his back pocket and wiped his hands.

"Fill her up?"

Rory clicked open his door. The man stepped back so he could step out.

"The opposite, I reckon."

Rory opened the trunk. The man retrieved a hose and ran it into the tank, then knelt before a pump set in the corner. He primed the carburetor and yanked the pull-starter. The little motor rapped to life, loud and smoky in the small space. The hose had an inline flowmeter. The man clicked a flashlight at it and made a note in a small spiral notebook.

The hose climbed the wall and left the building through a window cracked just enough to let it through. A long snake of whiskey.

"Where's it end up?"

The man scratched his head.

"Old gasoline tank, where you think?"

"That safe?"

"For who?"

"For the people drinking it."

The man shrugged. "Ain't my department."

"What's the idea, serve whiskey through the gas pumps?"

The man pushed out his bottom lip, coylike.

"You're shitting me," said Rory.

"Hey," said the man, "I ain't paid to have opinions. But if it works, you gonna have trip boys from all over—Charlotte, Winston, Raleigh— coming here to buy wholesale, filling their tanks with the stuff."

"The Sheriff masterminding all this?"

The man sniffed. "I ain't paid to name names, neither."

"I ought to known," said Rory. "I'm going out to smoke."

The man shrugged. "Suit yourself."

Rory walked out through the side door. It was full dark. The wind was going, the moon dancing in silvery shards through the trees. He could hear the dull pounding of whiskey inside the great hollows of the tank. He pulled out his pack of Lucky Strikes and started across the grass, toward the filling station up at the side of the road, stepping around old tires crowned in weeds, lengths of chain and beached engine blocks. He leaned in the shadow of the building, resting his shoulder against the wall, and shielded the flame in the cup of his palms, lighting his cigarette.

He looked at Pleasure Island across the street. The place was quiet at this hour, the people just making their way out into the dark. By midnight you would be able to put your hand on the metal siding and feel the throbbing hollows within, the walls corrugated beneath your hand like the rib cage of some prehistoric beast. Madam Erma there inside, directing her girls. He wondered, if he weren't born, would it be Granny running that place. Granny with blood buried in her rings, money tucked between her breasts. Her girls beneath her, working in the honeycomb of stalls, each a daughter on a bed in the dark.

He heard the loping throb of a built motor, saw the twin stars of headlights rise flickering through the tunneled trees that led to the lake. The car slowed to a halt in the road. The Sheriff's Oldsmobile, the paint glistening like poured milk under the moon. The car had a grumpy idle, restless, like it couldn't wait to do something wicked. The shotgun window began to roll down.

Rory threw down his cigarette—they must have seen the red cherry of ash—and pushed himself from the wall. He walked toward the open window. It was too dark to see inside, and as he walked between the old fuel pumps he had the sudden feeling that he was about to be shot. A long barrel through a dark window, a bright flash, a lead hammer through the belly. Over quick if you were lucky. He flexed, as if that might help.

No shot.

The Sheriff was riding shotgun. He wore a rabbit-felt trilby with a feather in the hatband, the hat slightly cocked as he worked his gums with a toothpick. His jaw muscles danced beneath the thin flesh of his face. Hard to imagine what he might have eaten down there at the lake. Rory pictured the granite riprap that armored the shoreline, pale-shouldered in darkness, and beyond that the black surface of the lake, a liquid cavern rumored to hold all manner of secrets and beasts and bodies.

"Mr. Docherty."

"Sheriff."

"Enjoying the fresh air?"

"I was." *Until you showed up.*

"Good," he said. "I knew you'd come to your senses."

"It wasn't really up to me."

"No," said the Sheriff. "I reckon it wasn't."

Rory leaned forward, placing one hand on the domed hood of the Oldsmobile.

"Tell me something. Is it true what they say?"

The Sheriff looked at Rory's hand resting there on the hood.

"What's that?"

"That you got a built motor in here will run any tripper's?"

The Sheriff dug the toothpick against his canine.

"What do you think?"

Rory smiled. "I know one it won't."

"The thing is, Mr. Docherty, I don't need it to."

"No?"

"If I ever want you, Mr. Docherty, you'll come to me."

He tapped the dash. The deputy pulled the column shift down into gear. Rory stepped back as the car pulled away from him, the rear tire crackling just past his foot. He listened as the big motor rumbled away between the trees.

"Pricks."

The diner shone like a beacon in the good part of town, a gleaming fixture of steel and glass and light. The people looked flawless through the picture windows, like display models of the species. The waitresses moved back and forth above them in pink uniforms and perky white hats. They carried steaming pots of coffee and milkshakes in steel cups, thick china plates of mounded roasts and mashed potatoes. Rory felt the hot rush of saliva under his tongue. He slid the thumping Ford into an empty space and got out.

The place went quiet as the bell rang at the door, a river of faces turning to look. Rory felt the stained overalls he was wearing, the battered leather jacket, the prewar car in the lot. Still he stared straight back at their soft round faces—faces soft as eggs—until they fell back to their plates. There they whispered, as if praying over their meatloaves and milkshakes. Rory took a seat at the near end of the counter, closest to the door, and the oldest waitress came over. Up close, her face looked like a sheet of newsprint wadded up and flattened out, crosshatched with wrinkles. You could tell she used to be pretty.

"Want to see a menu, sugar?"

Her voice rasped hard from her throat, and Rory could hear the years of smoke and shouting.

"No, ma'am. I'll just have a burger, fries, and a coffee, please."

"Cheese on your burger?"

"No, ma'am."

She stepped back to the kitchen window.

"One patty!"

Rory saw a black man working the kitchen, sweating amid banks of stainless equipment. New meat hissed on the griddle. The waitress set a mug in front of Rory and poured the coffee steaming from the pot, one hand on her hip.

"You from around here?"

"Not really."

Her eyes flicked out at the parking lot, seeing the car, and she might have smiled, just one corner of her crinkled mouth.

"Cream and sugar?"

"No, ma'am, thank you."

She nodded and took the pot back to the warmer.

Rory got out his pack of Luckies and slapped them against his palm. He lit one and set the pack and lighter on the counter in front of him, one atop the other. The bell jingled and in walked a wide man in a ragged tweed coat, such as a schoolteacher or newspaperman might wear. He clomped down the aisle and mounted a stool two down from Rory's, swinging his leg over the top like it was a horse. He wore little wire eyeglasses, lenses the size of quarters, and a black glove over one hand. A waitress crossed behind him. He followed the plumlike swing of her bottom, entranced, and then he looked toward Rory. His eyes fell on the lighter—the eagle, globe, and anchor soldered to the front. He lifted the gloved hand, pointing.

"Dubya-Two?"

"Korea."

"Who with?"

"Marines, Three-Five."

The man leaned back and whistled.

"Chosin Few?"

Rory nodded, then caught himself looking at the glove. The man saw this and held his hand an inch off the counter, fingers spread, considering it like something he might buy at the store.

"Ilu River," he said. "Pacific." He closed the hand, opened it. "You wouldn't want to see it without the glove. Not before you ate your dinner. But I got to keep it, at least."

Rory didn't say anything about what he'd gotten to keep or hadn't. The waitress came by and refilled his coffee, then poured one for the man.

"You want your regular, Harmon?"

He smiled up at her.

"By God, Darlene, you done something with your hair?"

The woman stood slightly taller, blushing. She palmed the bun crowning her head.

"I might of."

"Hell, I like it. And yes'm, my regular would be just wonderful."

She turned and walked down toward the other end of the counter, refilling mugs, a little extra bounce in her step. The man poured an avalanche of sugar into his coffee, stirred it viciously. He looked up at Rory.

"Tell me, son. What you think about the Hell Bomb?"

"The what?"

"The H-bomb, man. Hydrogen."

Rory shook his head.

"Don't know much about it, to be honest."

"Rumor is they're gonna blow one before the year is out. Eniwetok Atoll. Don't you read the papers?"

"Not that often."

"They say it'll make the A-bomb look like a runt. Thousand times more powerful. Big enough to end the world." The man leaned toward him. "They say the Russians aren't far behind. We might should of done like Patton said, driven the fuckers out of Berlin and not stopped till Moscow."

"You say they're testing it in the Pacific, this H-bomb?"

"That's the word." The man shrugged, gulped down half his coffee before setting it back on the counter. "Least they found something to do with all those fucking islands."

Just then Rory's burger arrived. The waitress leaned in close as she set it down.

"You might should of ordered to go."

She cut her eyes toward the parking lot, and Rory followed the look. A white Ford had pulled into the lot and two men in ties emerged. Their faces were shaved clean, their spines regiment-straight. Revenuers. They might as well have square heads.

Already Rory's coupe had caught their attention. They moseyed toward it, fingers perched on their waistbands.

"They eat here?"

"Couple nights a week."

Rory stood from his stool.

"Is there a back way out of here?"

She nodded. "On through the kitchen."

He started down the counter, then stopped.

"My bill."

"I got it," said the old Marine. "Best get."

"Thank you," said Rory. He clopped around the counter and the waitress led him through the kitchen and the cook opened the door for him. Rory turned and looked up at them from the back stoop.

"Thank y'all."

The waitress only winked, disappearing, and the black man held up a finger. He reached behind the door and handed Rory a brown paper bag, grease-spotted and warm.

"One to go."

"Who was it for?"

"Don't matter. I can make another one."

"Thank you."

The man nodded and pulled closed the door with the gentlest click.

Rory crept to the corner of the restaurant and leaned to look. The two men were standing around his car. One was scribbling in a small notebook with a pencil nub, taking down the plate number, probably. The other stood idly by, white-shirted, his hair gleaming like an eight ball. His trousers were tweed, tucked into the high throats of jump boots.

Agent Kingman.

Rory pulled the burger from the bag and took a bite, chewing and watching. He couldn't tell what they were saying. Finally the man worked the notebook back inside the inner pocket of his coat and the two of them headed inside. Rory could no longer see them around the corner, but he heard the bell ring as they walked in the door. He wadded the empty bag and stuck it in the pocket of his jacket, then got out his key. He refused the impulse to run. He simply walked to his car, got in, and reversed slowly out of his space, as any man would, easing into the street with hardly a touch of the throttle. He was around the first turn before he stepped into the gas.

CHAPTER 15

Pastor Adderholt stood in front of the worshipers, no pulpit. His face shone, the Book held high before him in both hands. He was staring at it.

"Glory be to God," he said.

Amen.

"Because there ain't but One."

Hallelujah.

"The Lord Victorious."

Yes, brother.

"He that confirms the Word with signs following."

Yes, he does.

"I read you from the Gospel of Mark, chapter sixteen, verse fifteen: 'He that believeth and is baptized shall be saved. But he that believeth not shall be damned.'"

Yes, Lord.

"'And these signs shall follow them that believe. In my name shall they cast out devils. They shall speak with new tongues.'"

Yes, Lord.

"'They shall take up serpents. And if they drink any deadly thing, it shall not hurt them. They shall lay hands on the sick, and they shall recover.'"

Hallelujah.

"Have we not witnessed these signs?"

Yes, brother.

"I wouldn't back up on the Lord for nobody. Not for the whole world."

No, brother.

"For he is the world."

Amen.

"He is Lord in every corner of the earth. The King of every nation."

Praise him.

"And he made all of us of the one blood."

He did.

"In his image. No matter age nor color. No matter male nor female. We were made to praise him."

Glory be.

"To receive the Spirit."

Yes, Lord.

"That quickening power of the Holy Ghost, come down in a whirlwind."

Yes.

"Shouting of victory in tongues."

A woman, stout with steel-gray hair, bolted upright from her chair. She began to pray aloud, a stream of praise that wound in and around the preacher's words, shoring them, swelling them with greater power, like a wind. Then a boy in white shirtsleeves stood too, speaking of high kings and glory, of worlds without end. Then others stood. Beseeching, praising, singing. The prayers pouring out of them in unbroken concatenates, words whirling together in greater torrent, a single voice that flooded the room, crashed against the walls, thundered in the chest and lungs. The steel-haired woman began to jerk and spasm, her arms flung high above her head.

"*Shon-dama-ha-sai!*" she said. "*Holla-mo-shalla-ah-sai!*"

A steel guitar stung the air, crazed, and tambourines sounded their rattling tattoo. The people were dancing now, whirling and stomping, so many flaming tongues of flesh, and Rory was drawn into the fire, pulled by hands he did not see, his world set spinning, his body weightless as a cinder. Here an old man bounced up and down, his bald pate shining under the lights. There a fat woman shrieked as if stabbed. Rory wheeled and crashed into the girl, her breasts pushed against his chest, her eyes so green and bright. They seemed to flash at him, as if she could control their brightness. He felt them inside him like searchlights, finding him out, and it seemed it was only them here, their own room, and there was no one else. The hollow at the base of her white neck was full of sweat, asking for his tongue, her nipples button-hard against the fabric of her dress. But when he looked again to her eyes, they were directed above him, captive, in awe of the light.

Just then the pastor came scooting down the aisle with a wooden box the size of an encyclopedia. The bodies parted before him, a great many cries thrust up at the sight. The box had a cane-weaved panel in the lid and brass hinges, and he handed it to one of the other men. The box began to pass around the room, hand to hand, slowly at first then faster, so fast it soon seemed to flutter above the floor of its own power, rising and falling with the flitting mania of a butterfly. When it got to Rory he felt it vibrate in his hand, as if there were a tiny motor inside, and when it got to the steel-haired woman she opened it.

Out it came, unfurling into her arms. A black-phase timber rattler, a single slick-skinned muscle with a head like a weapon, an arrowlike point. Dark chevrons lined its back. She held it aloft, at the front of the room, as if in offering. It was coiled partly around her arm, the rest sliding high across the tips of her fingers, calm despite the mania, the forked tongue testing what new world was this. The rattle erect and vibrating, one more instrument in all that glory.

"Did you get an anointing?"

"A what?"

"When you receive the Holy Ghost. It's called an anointing."

They were leaning on the side of Rory's car. Whenever he looked at Christine's eyes, his thoughts seemed to run aground, forgotten, his words gone stony on his tongue. Her hair tumbled from beneath a black felt cloche. Her bangs were cut straight across her brow, two long blades of hair loosed to frame her face. She looked like pictures of French girls he'd seen.

"I don't know," he said. "I never been one for church. But I felt something, I think. It's like . . ." He paused.

"What?"

"I don't know." He looked at his boots. "I felt it once before. Overseas. Like a place you can't be touched."

"Touched?"

"Hurt."

She took his hand.

"Come on, I want to show you something."

She led him out of the yard of parked cars, past people dabbing the sweat from their brows and talking worldly matters now, workplace shifts and casseroles and the price of milk. Whether Eisenhower would be elected president next month. They passed a giant of a man, clad in mill clothes and sawdust, who'd taken the serpent from the steel-haired lady during the service and worn it writhing upon his head like a crown. Christine held fast to Rory's hand, careless, it seemed, of what anyone thought. No one seemed to notice them. Their faces were buzzing, bright as spotlights. The Bunyan-size man waved. Rory saw a twin pair of bubbles in the web of his hand. Scars, as from the strike of fangs.

Christine led them out back of the place, and they passed the very tank that now held whiskey. Rory thought of the deadly drink that Mark had spoken of. *It shall not hurt them.* He'd heard rumors of people testing that verse, too. Drinking poison. Strychnine.

Christine led him past the rust-scabbed tank and onto a trail in the woods, an open corridor he never would have noticed on his own. Her feet were still bare from dancing, whispering along the path. Rory could feel the earth descending under his own heavy footfalls, the hard beat of his wooden foot. He felt he was being led into the dark by some secret being of the woods, some sylvan creature more perfect than man. The trail kept on and on, the pain in his leg hardly felt, until finally the trees broke onto a clearing of broomsedge, silver-gold under the moon, and in this little sea of grass lay a fleet of shored and abandoned rowboats.

They were oriented in the same direction, canted ever so slightly on their keels. Their oars still sat in the locks, their hulls mossy with age. There were no signs of them being dragged, and Rory saw no path wide enough for such conveyance. They looked like a lost expedition, the flotilla of Louis and Clark run aground.

"How'd they get here?"

"That's not the start of it."

She took his hand and led him into the field. Nearer, he saw they were full of water, strange mirrors turned up to the moon. He stood before one and saw dark shapes moving beneath the glassy surface, darting and curling, creatures thriving in these manmade ponds some quarter-mile from the lake. Christine pulled a glassine envelope the size of a playing card from the pocket of her dress and began sprinkling a yellow-gold dust on the surface of the pool, black petals of fins rising to surround the little islands of feed.

"Maybe a tornado lifted them out of the lake and dropped them here," he said. "I've heard of tornados raining fish."

"True," she said. "Though unlikely."

"Maybe a eagle dropped a fish he caught."

She looked up at him; her green eyes glowed.

"Well, he must of dropped a pair of them, don't you think?" She winked, and Rory felt it in his chest like a sledge. He licked his lips.

"You got a point there, I reckon."

"Anyhow, there's fish in more than just this one, so it would take a clumsy bird." She turned and leaned her butt against the edge of the boat, resting on her hands, and looked out across the field. "You got a smoke?"

Rory lit a Lucky Strike for her, the small flame throbbing in the night.

She sucked on the cigarette, holding one arm across her stomach.

"Thing is," she said, "I don't even think I want to know how these boats got here. I think I'd rather be free to wonder, you know? It's the mystery that gets me. The not-knowing."

There was a flower in the band of her hat, colored the bloodiest red. A scarlet begonia, perhaps. A tiny heart. Rory felt the urge to touch it, to test whether it was real or not.

"Is that how you feel in there?" He cocked his head back in the direction of the church.

"No. In there I'm sure. I know. It's the other ninety-nine percent of the time I don't."

"So you keep going back?"

She nodded. "It's the wanting to reach it again. That certainty. When I know we're more than just blood and meat. That we have spirits inside us that don't die. You can't take up a serpent without believing that, without *knowing* it."

She sucked on the cigarette, her cheeks going dark. Rory watched her, his eyes tracing the pale blue veins in her arm.

"Have you ever taken one up?"

She nodded.

"Once. The Spirit moved me to it."

Rory felt the burn of jealousy in his gut, hot as whiskey. He wanted to be the thing that moved her, the beast sliding through her fingers.

"Has anyone ever been bit?"

"Sure. If nobody ever got bit, what would be the point? If you can know everything, there's no need for faith."

Rory leaned over the gunwale of the boat, staring into the mirror of water.

"I don't know. There's some things I'd like to know."

"Like what?"

He started to tell her of his mother, but the words wouldn't come. His throat seemed too small, the things he would say too large and sharp-cornered to come out. They stayed stuck in his chest, embedded like shrapnel in a wound. All that came was a heavy breath whistling through his teeth. She took his arm and sidled closer, so close he could smell the sweet reek of her, of sweat and woman and cedar, a scent dabbed at the base of her throat or exuded from her skin.

He could feel one of her breasts against his arm, pert as a bird, and he could feel something else. He looked down, surprised to see her leg crossed toward him, her toes set over the laces of his boot. His wooden foot. He couldn't look away. Her foot was pale and clean in the moonlight, slightly curved, tiny crescent moons capping the nails. She slid the foot fully atop his boot now, crosswise. Her sole was arched, hugging.

He swallowed hard.

Her toes curled against him. A small gesture, big as anything. When he looked up she was waiting to be kissed. A short wait.

CHAPTER 16

The pastor was standing near Rory's car when they emerged from the woods. His head was slightly cocked, his eyes grazing the swells and contours of the vehicle's body. He looked like a Sunday tire-kicker at the car lot.

"She ain't for sale," said Rory.

The man looked up. He had on the same white shirt he always wore, short-sleeved and starched, and a straight black necktie with a winking tie pin. A thin silver watch looked almost effeminate on his wrist.

"Evening," he said. He looked to Christine. "I don't believe you've introduced me to our new friend."

Rory felt her stiffen slightly beside him.

"Rory, this is Pastor Asa Adderholt. My daddy."

Rory's spine snapped to attention.

The man reached out to shake. "Rory . . . ?"

"Docherty."

The preacher's hand was dry and coarse, strong, and he held Rory's hand a moment before letting go, as if taking his pulse. Rory tried not to look at the one eye staring off into its own place, seeming to see things outside his ken.

"Docherty," he said. "I know that name."

Rory nodded, his chest swelling up.

"There was an incident, in 1930, down in the valley before they flooded it. It involved Bonni Docherty. My mother."

Pastor Adderholt stiffened.

"I'm sorry, son. I remember that. I always heard she was a sweet girl."

"So did I," said Rory.

The man nodded and took a step sideways from them, toward the door of the Ford, his gaze lingering a long moment on the tail of the car. He had that black hair, too black for his age, for the battled lines of his face. Vanity, perhaps, or something else.

"And you live in the mountains now?"

"Yes, sir."

"And what is it you do there?"

Rory rubbed his tongue against the back of his teeth.

"Little of this," he said. "Little of that."

The pastor cut an eye at him.

"Tough business to make a living in."

"Sometimes."

"Lot of sinner-work up there."

"Daddy," said Christine.

"Yes, sir," said Rory. "There's a lot of people hungry, too."

The pastor nodded. Nobody was arguing that.

"We come up out of the valley in thirty-one," he said. "Just after I lost my eye. Timber-cutting accident." He cleared his throat. "That loss was a gift. Best I ever got, save Christine." He touched her arm a moment. "It woke me up to the Lord. Sometimes he takes something from you to make you see."

Just then a little boy ran up. The pastor bent down, the boy cupping his hands to the man's ear. Adderholt nodded, then stood again.

"This is my son, Clyde, Christine's little brother. He wants to be introduced."

The boy had a pie-shaped face, pinched, with narrow eyes. He was maybe ten, dressed like a miniature of his father: white shirt, black tie, hair slicked in a gleaming ducktail.

"Pleasure to meet you," said Rory.

The boy stepped forward to take his hand, nodded, then stepped back in line with his father. He had the most concentrated look about him. Suspicious of the world, perhaps. Certainly of Rory. Like it was his duty to sort it all out.

Rory looked to the pastor.

"What was it you did in the valley?" he said. "Before they flooded it?"

The man shifted his head, settling his one good eye on Rory's face.

"Little of this," he said. "Little of that."

That eye: an old stone well, mossy and black with depth, that must hold all manner of secrets at its bottom. Rory wondered whether he would have to put it out.

He had just crossed the dam out of town when he picked up a set of headlights in his rearview mirror, a pair of stars growing quickly brighter. He was running the speed limit, the motor drumming along in top gear, and he waited for the car to pass. Instead the machine ran right up on his bumper, riding him close, and the high-beams burst into the cabin. Rory downshifted into second gear, raising the motor to a growl. There was no siren. Perhaps town boys bored on a Saturday night, or some tripper trying to pull his chain. Rory let them hover close, then floored the accelerator. The motor exploded with power, squawking the tires and shoving him into the seat, but the headlights stayed right on his tail.

Not town boys, then.

Soon the land began to undulate, the black pavement rising and dropping through forests of oak and hickory, understories of dogwood and gum, the outlying timber that fed the big furniture mills of the state.

He knew an old farm road was coming up, which formed a crossroads with a logging road after half a mile. Both roads were unpaved, and he could blind his pursuers in a cloud of dust. He rounded a bend, the roadside breaking onto a wide expanse of reaped tobacco fields, furrows of red clay shooting off to either side. Far in the distance, the dull gleam of the tin-roofed curing barns.

Ahead was the turn-in. He would slow, then heel the wheel hard over and go screaming between the fields, past the barns and onto the logging road in a storm of dust, his pursuers blinded and lost. But in the last moment before the turn, he thought better of the idea. He couldn't say why. He coasted past the road, peering a long moment into its darkness, then short-shifted into third, settling to legal speed. Soon the fields ended, the hardwoods again pressed close, and the lights began to fall away, dimming, the car finally making a U-turn at a gravel turnout in the road. The driver seemed to lose interest when he didn't take the old tobacco road.

CHAPTER 17

Granny May sat beneath the white sickle of moon, smoking her pipe. She did not plan on going to sleep this night. Eustace was already gone, disappeared into the mountain's upper heights, and Rory would not be home until the hour before dawn. She had her shotgun laid on the side table, loaded with triple-aught buck, and her sling of shells lay across her shoulder, the rows of paper shells nestled between her breasts. If that panther-man came calling again for blood, it would be tonight. The moon was mainly in shadow, the menfolk all gone. A good night for panthers and haints, for shape-shifters, for murderers of old women. It wasn't dying that she feared, it was dying bad: leaving her grandboy alone in the world, unprotected, his wounds unhealed. Death, which walked ever through these mountains, knew she would not go down easy. If some dark upstart came prowling out of the shadows, thinking she had not a world of fight in her heart, they would be informed from the throat of her scattergun.

She swallowed a yawn before it could even start. Her day had been long despite the shortness of light. People were catching cold in the wake of the first frost, a wildfire of red-raw throats tearing along the ridges. People in the hollers were hacking up a yellow-green phlegm. They came to see her in cars, by horse, on foot. She handed out lumps of sugar soaked ruddy in bloodroot juice for the taming of coughs, and vials of the cough syrup she made from rabbit's foot. She boiled pine needles for a tea that thwarted colds. She roasted more onions that morning than she could count, hammering them into spun-wool rags for mothers to drape upon the chests of their younguns, saving others for people to wear tied round their necks to draw the sickness out. She had them gargle salt and vinegar for their throats or rub pine-oil into their Adam's apples, and she boiled wild ginger for the flu.

The kitchen was filling up. People paid in paper money, sometimes, but more often in eggs or milk or lard. Sometimes in jarred honey or good dark bread, in wild roots that were hard to gather, in promises of painting outbuildings or fixing roofs. Other times—more often than Rory knew—they didn't pay at all. But she, like all of the granny-women before her, knew that what you gave into the world came back to you in kind, and you could wear what you were owed like an armor into the darker times. She could have called on fifty good men to stand with her this night—men she'd delivered from sickness, from the terror of virginity or their mother's own stricken wombs. But she didn't. This was a night she could handle well enough alone.

She drew again from her pipe, the wind speaking to her through the trees. It spoke of cold in the months to come, of forests laid naked to the bone, and she let it fill her nose with the hard bite of woodsmoke. The folds of the hills glinted here or there, secret fires sparking through the leaf-thinned trees. It was a dangerous time for stilling. Sound carried farther through the trees, and light, and mash took twice as long in the cold. Still they carried on, Eustace among them, for men grew only thirstier as the days turned dark and cold.

Just then she caught movement at the edge of the meadow, a form that seemed to detach itself bodily from the trees, emerging onto open ground. She brought the shotgun into her lap. She looked not directly at the phantom but slightly askance, in that old hunter's trick to better her sight, and the figure seemed to waver in and out of visibility, collected sometimes into the greater backdrop of night only to be thrust out again, closer each time, its limbs silvering under the moon. She laid the barrel in its path. Only closer did she see it was lurching and weaving, slinging its arms like a man wading a creek, and she did not think death would come drunk to her porch this night—not unless it wanted to be sent home with a heart full of shot. She leaned forward, shouldering the gun, steadying her elbows on the bony caps of her knees.

"You," she said down the barrel. "One more step, there's gonna be two of you, each flopping round in the dark for the other'n."

He jerked to a stop, his upper half rebounding over his planted feet.

"Granny? Is, is Eli."

She felt something leap inside her at his voice, a tickle at the backs of her legs. She let down the hammer on the gun.

"Well hell, son, how come you didn't say?"

He stepped closer, tottering slightly in the angled panes of light thrown from the windows.

"I was waiting—" He hiccupped. "I was waiting to see if you was asleep or not."

"Sleep ain't a thing I'm doing tonight."

He straightened a little.

"You ain't?"

She set the shotgun back on the side table.

"Bad night for panthers," she said. "And they ilk. What brings you?"

He took his beard in hand, the veins standing out in his fist. He looked at the ground.

"I, I just come for a remedy."

"Come sit a spell," she said. "Tell me what it is ails you."

He nodded, still holding on to his beard, and dutifully climbed the porch steps, setting himself in the rocker next to hers. His head was down.

"Well?" she said.

He put a fist to his mouth, coughed.

"I got this little cough crept up on me," he said. "I was thinking some that rock-candy syrup you got—"

She held up a hand.

"Son, twenty-some years I had boys feigning coughs for a taste of that liquor-medicine. You ain't fooling me for a damn second."

Eli scratched the top of his thigh.

"Well, there is this other thing."

She squinted at him.

"You got the clap?"

He bolted upright.

"Hell no, I ain't got the clap."

"Crabs? You got them crabs?"

"No, it ain't anything like that." He pulled on the inner seam of his trousers. "Well, maybe a little like it."

Granny waited. "It ain't nothing I never heard before, I can tell you that." She reached out, touched his knee. "Just let it out, son."

Eli leaned forward, setting his elbows on his thighs. He had one fist on top of the other, gripping his beard.

"It being Saturday night, I had me a few nips of the white stuff down at the garage. The days is getting shorter, reckon I was feeling a little"—he hiccupped—"little lonely. Figured I'd go on down to Hell, see if I might could find some company for the night."

"The roadhouse?"

"Yes'm. It's not too difficult to find some company there, long's you got twenty dollars in your pocket. This girl, Edna-Lynn, I gone with her a couple times before. She makes you feel like—I don't know— like she's your girl or something. Acts excited to see you, like you're just the one she's been hoping would turn up. I might be a little sweet on her. Hard not to be, she acts like that. So I give her my money, and we start to fooling around, but I keep on thinking of this son-bitch I seen coming out her door, tucking in his shirt. I can't help but wondering if he gets the same treatment as me. And I'm thinking all that and I start going soft." He cleared his throat. "Down there. She starts to tugging and everything, even using her mouth on it, and it's nothing happening. When we try and get down to it, it's no better than a roll of bread dough." He shook his head. "I never had something like this happen before." He looked at Granny, silver welling in his eyes. "You think it's broke?"

"Hell no, it ain't broke, son. You just got too up in your head. Your big head." She set her hand on his knee again, squeezed. "Sit right here, I got just the thing."

She rose and pushed through the door and into the house. Behind the kitchen was a small pantry shelved floor to ceiling, populated with motley ranks of jars and jugs and bottles and flasks. Vials stood together like ammunition, and there sat fishbowls jumbled full of roots and herbs. There were powders of every color, meant to be smelled or snorted or blown into the back of the throat with a goose-quill, and oils and essences and spirits of various strength and provenance. There was jimsonweed for asthma and mayapple for constipation, catnip and ground ivy for the bold hives, burdock to purify the blood. There was stumpwater and bug-dust and brimstone, breath-killers like wintergreen leaves and birch twigs, and even a bucket of switches for a cure she called peach-limb tea—otherwise known as a good ass-whipping.

She slid sideways between the shelves and unscrewed the zinc lid of a large jar, removing one of the ginseng roots she'd gathered that morning, then took down a vial from the upper shelf. When she walked back onto the porch, the organlike root lay across the open flat of her hand, glistening with oil. She sat and proffered it.

"Your remedy."

Eli's eyes grew big. He picked it daintily from the palm of her hand by the stem, holding it dangling between the two of them in his pinched fingers. He twisted it back and forth in the light.

"What's that coating it?"

She cleared her throat.

"Holy oil. Off that priest from the church in Boone, trades it for saltpeter to curb his urges." She paused a moment. "You anoint yourself with it."

"Anoint . . . yourself?"

"You rub your pecker with it."

He looked down at his crotch, then up at her. His eyes were wide. "Here, now?"

Granny breathed in, a slight shudder on her outbreath. She licked her lips.

"No, son. You best take it on home, do it there."

He swallowed, his shoulders sinking slightly from his collarbones. "Oh." He sat a minute longer, as if hesitant to rise, and when he began to stand she stayed him a moment, her fingertips light on his knee.

"That don't work, son, you just come on back. That ain't the only remedy an old woman's got."

He stared a long moment at her hand.

"Yes'm, I surely will."

Granny drew her fingers from beneath the blanket that covered her lap when she heard the big ambulance motor come grumbling up the mountain. The eastern ridges were cut jagged against the light of an impending sun, a whitish glow that promised clear weather this day, skies a cold blue. She was thankful for the hot-dark visions that had kept her awake through the night. She stood and removed the sling of shells, draping it over the coatrack just inside the door, and she set the shotgun back in its rack above the mantel, as if it had never come down. She was sitting again in her rocker, her blood cooling, as Rory's coupe turned the curve at the bottom of the drive.

The spirit-bottles were just beginning to catch the light, a faint twinkling in the fall-darkened crown of the tree, like the electric bulbs townspeople weaved through firs in their windows at Christmastime. A pretty sight, even as the wind came tumbling down off the mountain, rocking the bottles on their strings, and she thought how easy for one to fall, bursting in a hundred glassy teeth, and what spirits would out.

Rory hauled himself from the car and came up the steps. He stooped to kiss her on the cheek and frowned.

"You ain't got a fever, have you?"

"Fever . . . why?"

"You look a little flushed."

She jerked her chin.

"Where you been? Church?"

He leaned on the doorframe and crossed his arms.

"You say it like it's a bad thing."

"Them Holy Ghost people, I don't know." She blew smoke from her nose. "They know what it is you do for a living?"

"I think that preacher has an inkling."

"Asa Adderholt? He ought to."

Rory squinted.

"What does that mean?"

"He wasn't always no preacher, I can tell you that."

"What was he?"

"Whiskeyman, like the rest of them. Rumor was, him and his brother was the ones leading them valley people that fought the government."

Rory's arms crossed tighter against his chest.

"He's only got one eye."

"So?"

"So he might could be the one," said Rory.

"The one that what?"

"Don't act like you don't know what I'm talking about. I got a right to see that eye."

"How come you care so much all the sudden?"

"It don't matter why. I just do."

"It's too late, son. I popped it in my hand one time, so mad I couldn't help it. Run through my fingers like an egg yolk."

"Bullshit."

"Ah." She pointed to him with the shank of her pipe. "Good you can see that. You gonna need a real good bullshit-detector, you spend any time down in that godbox. Now tell me this, what's got all this pop in your step? The Spirit, or this girl?"

"What girl?"

"Bullshit."

He couldn't help but smile. He rubbed his shoulder against the doorframe.

"Little of both, I reckon."

She set the pipe shank between her teeth and scratched a match to life, inhaling as the weedy ball glowed red. She spoke from the back of her throat, exhaling.

"Ain't a thing to get confused, son."

"I'm not confused."

"Your age, maybe you ought to be."

He pushed his hands into his trouser pockets.

"I seen a few things."

She nodded.

"I know you have, honey. I know." She tapped the ashes out of the pipe. "But you ain't seen everything."

Rory's hands balled up inside his pockets.

"I haven't, now have I?"

CHAPTER 18

Rory had just fallen asleep that morning when he heard a motorbike throbbing in the yard. The twin hammers of the pistons beat like a heart: *thump-thump, thump-thump, thump-thump.* He'd been riding such a machine across the landscape of his dreams, a great snowfield cut by a long dark road, cobbled lead-gray under a white sky. The bike was slamming and wobbling over the giant cobblestones, each the size of an infantryman's helmet, and he knew there would be blood soon, come guttering across the snow in crooked scrawls or welling up from the road itself. He came hard awake, as if to escape. He sat up in bed and pulled on his leg.

The machine sat chugging in a white cloud of itself, the fenders and tanks gleaming night-black under the sun, the rider clad likewise in that color: leather jerkin and knee-high jackboots, a scarf around his neck, a pair of leather-padded goggles pulled up on his forehead. He was leaning between the wide handlebars of the machine, smoking a cigarette, chatting with Granny. The rear tire wore a gleaming chain for traction on the rough mountain roads.

Rory stepped onto the porch.

"Sleeping it off?" asked the carrier.

"Till you showed up. Don't Eustace know it's Sunday? Even God rested the seventh day."

"Rest? That man would tell God himself to quit his skylarking." The rider dabbed something from his tongue with the tip of his thumb, the cigarette smoking in the crux of two fingers. "Anyhow, he says there's a sugar shipment coming in today. Wants you and Eli to pick up a thousand pounds." He zipped open the asymmetric flap of his jacket and tossed Rory a folded envelope of bills. Rory thumbed through the money.

"Who we buying from this time?"

"Some bomber pilot."

"Bomber pilot?"

"Flying into a little farm-strip over in Wilkes County. You're supposed to be there at noon. Directions in the envelope."

"A whole planeload coming in, huh? Who's gonna buy what we don't?"

"Every bootlegger and whiskeyman around, I imagine."

Rory folded over the envelope and stuffed it in his back pocket.

"Well, shit."

They drove east toward Wilkes County, Rory at the wheel. The road glittered before them, a hard thin river rushing down out of the mountains, dropping now and again through dynamited swallows of rock where the air was suddenly cooler and darker, then breaking open again to the light, thrust along sheer ridges over a model-trainman's world of tiny square fields and toy houses, herds of cattle positioned just so in their valley pastures. The silver-barked trees at the higher altitudes looked almost brittle, like skinny-limbed old men reaching for the sky, the leaves already browned and fallen from their upthrust hands. But soon the road descended into greater cover, the late-peaking hillsides clouded in honey and rust, here or there a smoky patch of purpled ash.

They were chewing Bazooka bubble gum, their jaws pulsing. Eli had a look on his face like he was chewing on a wad of cud.

"How come you to forget a new carton last night?"

Rory bought them a carton of Lucky Strikes each week from a shothouse at End-of-the-Road. The cartons sold at a heavy discount, rumored to be gleaned from a tractor-trailer that slewed off a mountain road some time back.

Rory blew a bubble.

"I don't know how. Just forgot."

Eli squinted at him.

"You never forgot before. You were distracted is what it was."

"Could be."

"You were thinking with your wrong head. Your little one. It's this girl, what's-her-name."

"Christine."

"Christine, hell. Sabotager of the heart, is what she is."

"Saboteur."

"Don't be a snob."

"Least the car hasn't been sabotaged again."

"Till that one-eyed preacher wants otherwise. You said yourself that boy of his come in the church that time with a streak of grease down his arm."

"So?"

"So that was the same night your coolant hose was cut. Pretty damning, you ask me."

Rory looked at him. "I didn't ask you, now did I?" He turned and spat his gum out the window. "Could be he's waging some kind of righteous war against the whiskey business."

"This preacher?"

"Yeah."

Eli shrugged. "Sure, that's a theory. Another is he's in cahoots with his brother, taking down trippers to end the milk-runs, making the both of them a little something extra on the side."

Rory's thumb tapped on the wheel.

"Yeah, I thought of that, too."

At the county line they passed a prowl car decked in flashers and spot-lights, a golden seal emblazoned on the door. GREAT STATE OF WILKES, IMPERIUM INTRA IMPERIO. The deputy gave them a hard frown as they passed, one elbow perched on the door. The black reflection of their machine flitted across his mirrored sunglasses.

"'State within a state,'" said Rory, quoting the county's motto.

"This damn place."

Blue ranges, jagged, dominated the horizon in three directions, walling off the county like a fortress. A magazine had dubbed it the "Moonshine Capital of the World."

They arrived just after noon, navigating a bewildering set of red farm roads, none of them marked or named. The airstrip was bulldozed into a string of harvested tobacco fields down in the lower part of the county, where the land flattened out. The earthmovers were parked a little ways from their handiwork, a couple of three-wheeled tractors, red as fire engines with tires treaded like paddlewheels. One was mounted with a dozer blade, the other a road scraper, their seats surrounded by a motley crop of levers and pedals. They looked tired, still dirty from the work.

Liquor cars lined the airstrip, plain-Jane coupes that anyone might drive, clerks or foremen or shopkeepers. But they seemed fatter than their civil kin, meaner. Their tires were wider, their rumps higher. Large-bore pipes snaked through their undercarriages, exiting like gun barrels beneath their tails. There were armor plates in their doors, their trunks hulled out for space. All of them had their hoods already up, displaying motors built as carefully as giant hearts. Men milled around them, hands in their pockets, nodding and spitting tobacco juice in the dirt when they liked something or didn't.

Rory pulled bumping over the field and parked at the end of the line. Eli jumped out to pop the hood. Men began to shuffle toward them, drawn to the supercharged motor like cows to a feeder. Rory stood away, letting them talk. He found himself next to the driver of the neighboring car, a towering man with a boyish face.

"Rory," said Rory, extending his hand.

"Junior," said the man. The name rolled from his tongue, soft and gentle. *June-yuh.* They shook, and Rory could feel the calloused strength of the man's bear-size hand.

"Wait," he said. "Is your daddy Glen Johnson, from up at Ingle Hollow?"

The man nodded. "Yes, sir."

In the thirties, revenuers had seized more than seven thousand gallons of white liquor from the man's home—one of the biggest busts in history.

"Junior Johnson," said Rory. "People say you can drive a car."

Junior shrugged. His hands were in his pockets now, his eyes scouting the hills.

"I better."

Out of the corner of his eye, Rory saw Cooley Muldoon detach himself from his green Hudson, heading their way. He was wearing a white longjohn shirt under a red flannel with rolled sleeves, his suspenders down. A knife the size of a small sword flopped against his leg as he walked. Two or three others followed behind him, big men, his brothers or kin.

Junior watched them come.

"Looks like they got eyes on you."

"Damn pop-skullers," said Rory.

"So I hear."

Cooley carried a jar high against his chest. All his power was up in his face, his smirking mouth, like a spring tree with the sap running. He looked at Rory the whole way, but turned his attention to Maybelline once he got close. He circled the car, bending to its every detail, clucking and poking. Eli became distracted, watching him.

"See something you like?"

Cooley straightened, shrugged.

"Looks like a right pig to me."

Eli spat.

"Ain't how it looks that matters, now is it?"

"Some old whore tell you that?"

Rory's blood ran hot, rising against his skin. He held his breath quivering in his chest, loosing it slowly through his nose. The iron of the pistol throbbed in his calf.

Eli pointed below Cooley's belt.

"You got some holes there in your britches," he said. "Drop some ashes in you' lap?"

The other men laughed. Even the kinsmen cracked grins, and a crazed look came into the Muldoon boy's face. One eye seemed to grow higher and larger than the other, as if his face had been glued from dissimilar halves. "Fifty bucks says you two sons of bitches can't beat me into the mountains with a half-ton of sugar."

Rory could feel every eye turned upon him. Junior stood beside him, tall and strong as a tree, his blue eyes judgeless.

Rory spat.

"It ain't a game, Cooley. All this. Someday you'll learn that."

Junior nodded, and Rory was turning from the conversation, digging his pockets for his missing cigarettes, when Cooley let out a scream, high and curdling, like a panther in the night. Rory stopped dead, as if his name had been called, then turned slowly on his heel. The world was white and cold beneath his eyes.

"Make it a yard, motherfucker."

One hundred dollars.

Cooley hawked and spat an enormous gob into his palm, extending his hand with a grin.

They heard it first, a tiny drone that warbled in and out of earshot. They searched for it, squinting beneath the flat of their hands, grown men each wanting to see it first. There it was: just a wink in the far sky, like a daytime star, growing over the jagged spine of the Brushy Mountains. It seemed to sprout wings as it neared them, resolving to shape. A cargo plane skinned in naked aluminum, the twin radial motors humming in their cannonlike nacelles, spitting oil down the wings.

"Gooney Bird," said somebody.

The craft circled the field once, silver-struck under the sun, so bright it hurt the eyes. The pilot, they said, was a local boy by the name of Caruthers, who had flown a Flying Fortress in the Mighty Eighth. Obviously, he was enterprising.

One-room holler stores once sold more than a million pounds of sugar per year, more annually than the entire cities of Richmond and Raleigh, until the government came in, throwing up barricades of paperwork. Now any sale over one hundred pounds had to be reported with a special form. The stillers were forced to buy their sugar from black-market profiteers, corrupt army quartermasters, sea captains sailing ten-thousand-ton loads straight out of Cuba. From ex–bomber pilots.

The lumbering transport turned upwind for final approach. It fell lazily from the sky, shimmering like something molten, only to flare its wings at the last moment, the tires blooming twin spirals of dust as they touched. Just in front of them, the tail wheel kicked out and the big plane rotated in place, streaking the world red, blasting the drivers with a stinging barrage of dust and seeds and debris. It settled, pointed back down the runway, ready for takeoff. The prop blades were still winding down as the cargo doors opened and two men stepped down on a retractable ladder. They both wore high-altitude bomber jackets and aviator sunglasses with green lenses. Everyone started toward them in a single movement, like a herd of cattle, but the shorter crewman held up a gloved palm.

"Stop."

They did. He was scarcely taller than five feet, with a voice that seemed to come from his nose rather than his mouth. But he had a submachine gun strapped across his chest, a mean-looking piece known as a grease gun.

"Who's this little pinch-a-turd?" asked somebody.

"Caruthers's old tailgunner," said somebody else.

The tailgunner raised his voice.

"We're gonna do this orderly, one at a time."

"How much is they?"

"Eleven a sack."

Somebody whistled. "Steep." Others muttered their assent.

"You don't like it, don't buy it." He pointed to the first car in line. "Bring her up."

They were hundred-pound sacks, burlap, which read: TRUCANE, PRODUCT OF CUBA. The pilot took the money, making change from a cashbox, while the tailgunner supervised the loading, one hand always on his weapon. It was little more than a metal tube, barrel, and magazine fitted with a wire stock. He looked like he might just enjoy plugging a couple of hillbillies with it.

Rory bought one thousand pounds of sugar from the envelope of cash that Eustace's courier had delivered. Eight of the sacks fit in the trunk, with the whiskey tank removed, and they tucked the last pair behind the front seats, covering them in a wool blanket.

Afterward, they sat on Maybelline's hood, wishing for smokes. Their nerves were up, buzzing under their skin. Junior appeared, holding out a soft pack of cigarettes, a pair of butts sticking up just for them.

"Thank you much."

"Careful out there," said Junior. "I wouldn't trust a Muldoon farther than I could throw him." With that he walked back to his own machine.

They lit the cigarettes and inhaled, squinting at the line of boot-legging cars. The trip boys were hanging around despite their loaded trunks; no one wanted to miss the show.

Eli ashed his cigarette with a flick of the thumb.

"You ought not to done this."

"Done what?"

"You gave that crazy son-bitch just what he wanted."

"What's that?"

"A crack at you. That's all he wants."

Cooley was leaning on his flashy green Hudson, waiting while a bigger man slung his trunk full of sugar. The boy turned and looked at them, his arms crossed, and smiled at them, as if they were friends. Rory smiled back, speaking through his teeth.

"Sometimes when you get what you want, you don't like it so much."

"Sure," said Eli. "And sometimes you do."

The cars crouched side by side, each rattling and smoking like a bomb ready to blow. Liquor cars lined the road on either side, chugging at idle, ready to run if the law showed up. Trippers sat on the hoods, warmed by their engines, their eyes bright with anticipation. They were watching the starter, a sprite-size beauty in a red gingham dress. Somebody's sweetheart. She cocked one hand against her hip and raised a red handkerchief high overhead. Every eye followed that red scrap of cotton, waiting, waiting.

The handkerchief floated free of her hand. The Hornet leapt, torqued sideways with power, and the two machines roared in eche-lon past the girl, each a side, the bandanna swept tumbling in their slipstream. Great balls of dust billowed from the rear of Cooley's coupe, like it was on fire, and Rory powered through the wake, blinded, squinting to see the gleaming blade of the bumper. First gear, second, third, topping a hundred miles per hour along the length of the airstrip, the two machines tearing a red storm of dust from the earth, and then they were braking, downshifting for the coming turn. The Cooley boy whipped the Hudson hard into the corner, kicking the tail wide, and Rory followed close, his tires breaking loose as he cocked the wheel opposite the turn, using the throttle to steer. Maybelline rolled well onto her side, sliding sideways as Rory gassed them onto the next stretch of road. Eli rode with both hands on the dashboard, bracing himself.

The car hounded down the next long straight, every surface singing with power. Rory stayed right on the Hudson's bumper as they tore between reaped tobacco fields, waiting for the boy to make a mistake. Cooley went too fast into a turn, plowing deep into the belly of a deserted crossroads, and Rory goosed past on the inside. Eli howled in delight. Soon they were flying down a narrow road cut through a sea of unharvested corn, the stalks slashing past their windows in a liquid green rush, and then they were sliding in a squall of rubber onto the paved highway that went snaking up into the mountains.

Rory's eyes flicked to the rearview mirror. There was the silver grille of the Hudson, shaped like an enormous frown, and Cooley himself, hunched over the wheel, grinning like a fiend. Rory knew he would spin them if he could, send them into the trees or through the guardrail. He yanked the shifter into third. The tires barked, the dual exhausts racketing between the trees like a machine gun.

The turns were sweeping here, and long, and steep ridges rose to either side so that it was like running through a channel cut into the mountains. He'd never liked this road for that. It seemed like there was nowhere to go, no way to stop what was coming. Still he stepped deeper into the accelerator, the motor surging between ridge and road and sky, mindless, willing to die. Soon the Hudson was shrinking in the mirrors, its power fading, and Rory didn't let up. He used both lanes when he could, the machine flattening itself to the road as they charged higher and higher into the hills, the mountains rising blue-toothed before them.

They were nearing the town limit of Boone—the finish line—when the road rose to meet the stone bridge of the Parkway overpass, white as a monument in the sun. They flashed through its arched hollows, a blast of sound as if through a chute, and Eli turned to look through the back window.

"Showed that son of a bitch," he said.

Rory's eyes flicked to the mirror a moment, the Hudson but a toy in their wake. When his gaze fell again to the road he was stunned to see a doe struck rigid on the pavement before him, ill-propped on a set of splayed and delicate limbs, her ears wide and white-tufted as little wings. She was on that alien river again, so hard beneath her hooves, and this time she could feel it vibrating, speaking through the very meat of her, seizing her heart with a terrible knowledge: she would die.

Rory swerved, flashing past her, and looked to the mirror.

"Move," he said. "Move!"

She didn't. The Hudson came straight on, never turning, and struck her square in the hindquarters, slamming her spinning and tumbling across the pavement in a flailing wreck of herself. Her legs thrashed at obscene angles, her neck curling under her body as she rolled. She slid crumpled onto the shoulder and lay there in a whelm of dust, still as a sack of feed.

Rory downshifted.

"The hell?" said Eli.

The Hudson flashed past them, one headlight mangled and bloody, blowing its horn in celebration or spite. Rory wheeled the Ford around in the road, heading back the way they'd come.

"Rory," said Eli. "Rory!"

He pulled in behind the doe and left the motor running as he stepped out.

She was moving now, or trying to. Her hindquarters lay in ruin, her once-tawny hide stretched over the broken miscellany of what had made her fast and strong. A purple wreckage of crushed bone and meat. Her legs lay wrongly angled, connected only by red strings of remnant tissue. Jags of bone stabbed through the wounds, pooling blood. She smelled already, the flap of her tail tucked tightly between her legs, as if to keep her insides from spilling out. It didn't. The white tuft had darkened with ooze. Her forelegs were moving, making walking motions though she lay on her side. Her cracked hooves scratched against the pavement.

Rory knelt beside her. One eye looked up at him. It was huge and dark, a brown almost black, round as a world. She had a long neck, slender, with white patches under her chin and around her eyes. He held up his right hand, palm out, like the stone god of the temple. He touched her on the head, gently, between her ears. The meat of his thumb lay in the furrow between her eyes. He tried to give her something in that touch. He wasn't sure what. Whatever he had.

When he stood he had the pistol in his right hand. He shot her where he had touched her, between the eyes. He didn't want to look but did. He didn't want to miss.

The high country town of Boone. Narrow storefronts lined the street, tall and brick-faced, each a different color. A few cars were parked along the curb for the places open on a Sunday. The movie theater, the pool hall, the soda fountain. The places the people in the teachers' college went.

The Hudson was parked in front of the drugstore, as agreed. Cooley Muldoon was leaning on one of the posts that held up the sloped roof of the building. Sunken windows stared out of the hand-split shingles above him. Rory made a U-turn in the street and pulled in behind the Hudson. He left the motor running and got out. The hundred-dollar bill was in his hand. What he owed. He had folded the bill into a neat square the size of a postage stamp, pressed tight under his thumb.

Cooley dropped his cigarette and ground it under his toe.

"Got showed, did you?"

The big kinsman behind him chuckled, crossing a pair of ham-size arms.

Rory lifted his free hand in front of Cooley's face and snapped his fingers. The boy opened his mouth, confused, like Rory knew he would. Rory grabbed the scruff of the boy's neck and yanked back his head, jamming the bill into his mouth and clamping it shut under the vise of his hand. Cooley grabbed his wrist in both hands and tried to scream but couldn't. Rory watched the boy's throat work, pumping down the bill so as not to choke. A stifled scream tickled his palm.

The kinsman was coming at him now. A crude blackjack dangled from his hand, a heavy object stuffed into the end of a long woolen sock. A padlock, maybe, or a fistful of ball bearings. Rory shoved Cooley to the sidewalk and raised his arms to protect his head.

"Drop it!"

The big Muldoon froze, the heavy end of the blackjack sagging limply from his raised hand. It fell to the sidewalk without a bounce, as if magnetized. Behind him stood a giant of a man in uniform, a white napkin hanging from the front of his shirt: Big Carling, sheriff of the high country. He had a belly the size of a pie-safe, hard as a punching bag. A face as square and grim as a stone jug. The blue steel of a Smith & Wesson revolver dangled at his side, sized like a popgun in his over-large hand.

The man belched through his teeth and stepped off the sidewalk, peering through the windows of the cars. He opened the door of the Ford and pulled back a corner of the blanket that covered the two sacks of sugar there. He walked up to Rory, the pistol tapping against his leg. He was the opposite of Sheriff Adderholt. Carling wore his uniform all the time, the buttons aligned just so, the belt buckle polished bright. He had been a tank commander in Europe. Some said he kept a war-surplus howitzer in his backyard, oiled and polished like a giant pet.

"You a baker, boy?"

"A baker, sir?"

"A baker, got-damnit."

"No, sir."

"You wear you a apron at home, tie it in a pretty bow over your bare-naked ass?"

"No, sir."

"Two hundred pounds of sugar in your backseat, I figure you must be baking me a cake. A cake big as a got-damn house. Otherwise, I might think you was putting that sugar to nefarious ends."

"Nefarious? No, sir."

"I might think you was a degenerate. I might think you was the kind too often found at the bottom of a ravine out on the edge of my county. Slipped his footing, too drunk on his own medicine."

Eli was standing behind Rory. He cleared his throat.

"Sheriff? If I might—?"

Carling cut him off.

"Don't feed me your bull, Uptree. I know who your uncle is."

Eli sidled closer, lowered his voice.

"No, sir, Sheriff. But I was just thinking, what if we *was* baking for you?"

The man's napkin, gravy-speckled, still hung from his throat.

"You blind? I'm already eating. You interrupted my got-damned lunch."

"You ain't eating *stackcake*."

Carling straightened. He cut his eyes up the street, down, then back at Eli.

"Talk."

"See, Sheriff, this here is Granny May's grandson."

Carling stood still taller, looking down at Rory.

"Maybelline Docherty?"

"Yes, sir," said Rory.

Carling worked his tongue around the inside of his mouth, as if he'd lost something in there. He squinted into the distance, possibly the future. His free hand toyed the edge of his napkin.

"Tell you what," he said. "You bring me one them stackcakes your Granny used to make. You bring it to Sunday-night service. That's to-night. You do that, I might could believe you're transporting that sugar for your granny."

"Yes, sir," said Eli. "We can do that."

The man holstered his pistol. "You can and you will." He turned to Cooley and his kinsman, his big hand still resting on the butt of his gun. "As for you two, you and none of your rotgut kin is even sup-posed to be in my county. I advise you to get the hell back to Linville before I finish my lunch." He turned and took in this whole scene on his Sunday street, a sneer of disgust on his face. "Ball-hootin' black-guards." He stepped over the makeshift bludgeon lying there on the sidewalk and back into the café.

Cooley watched him go, then turned to Rory. His face twisted per-versely, a dread asymmetry of halves.

"You're one lucky son-bitch, Docherty. Weren't for him, they'd be mopping you from this here sidewalk."

Rory walked back to the car, Eli behind him.

"Big talk from a boy ate himself a hundred-dollar lunch."

The boy's eyes skewed vertical, as if they might arrange themselves in totem, one atop the other, and Rory noticed for the first time the two fleshy bubbles on the boy's neck—the serpent's bite.

"You ought to put that smart mouth on the track, Docherty."

Rory opened the driver's door of the Ford, speaking across the roof. "Why's that?"

"Because dying's better than wishing you had."

Rory tapped the roof with his fist, thinking of the deer in the road.

"You might be smarter than I thought, Cooley. You just might."

IV. NEW MOON

They were sitting side-by-side between the shelves, cross-legged. Connor wore short sleeves, his veins branching down his thin, golden arms. Bonni wanted to trace those rivers of blood, climbing her fingers under his shirt, searching for their source. Connor was looking at her newest piece, painted in the high turret of her room the previous night.

Wait, did you see these yourself?

Bonni nodded. It was a pair of small green parrots, yellow-headed, with a flush of orange about the eyes. She'd seen them as a girl.

Where?

Down in the valley along the river. Came out of a sycamore hollow.

These are Carolina parakeets, said to be extinct. The last known specimen died in the Cincinnati Zoo in 1918.

He took her hand.

Come on, we have to go see.

Mama says it's not safe in the valley no more.

For us it is.

They descended into the valley on the chestnut mare that Connor rode to school each day. His violin case and books were lashed over the beast's rump. Bonni's hands rested on the boy's hips. His waist was so taut. She leaned to his ear, her words light as bees' wings.

Is it true what they say about your daddy teaching you to box?

The boy's back straightened, as if he'd been stung.

Two hours each morning, he said. Or I'm not allowed my binoculars or violin.

CHAPTER 19

Granny had her sleeve rolled up, her arm working a mixing bowl tucked against her hip. Rory came into the kitchen with a finger in the air, his cheeks bulged with words, and she told him to get the hell out. She'd baked him out of trouble before—schoolteachers and deputies and wardens, a dime-store shopkeeper who caught him lifting a pack of dirty picture cards—but she'd never baked for any Presbyterians before. She did not like to start. She knew them: walking so chin-high through town, looking down their noses if they looked at all. Most simply turned their heads the other way when they passed, like they didn't see her. The women, at least. The men, they had their own looks, some of them. Animal eyes that made her feel naked and small, at least in daylight.

In that first bawdyhouse, the one in Boone, they would come climbing the stairs in the midnight hours, seeking what cures her body had to give. The biggest men made suckling boys, groping so madly for something in the dark. Medicine she had to give and would. Now it was their wives who came, their stately sedans rocking up the mountain, the women stepping out in their heeled shoes, as far from the earth as they could get. The look on their faces, you'd think they were stepping into a feedlot.

They wanted the old cures the town-doctors couldn't give them, and the ailment they sought most to remedy came as no surprise. They wanted the powders they could slip into their husband's coffee or whiskey, that might make him stand tall again through his trousers, or perhaps a little dose of something for themselves, for those days when the neighbor-boy came to cut the grass or clean the gutters—when the last thing you wanted was a dry spell.

She knew they suspected her cures were something not quite Christian, even witchcraft, for faith in the old ways was slipping. Still they came, paying always in paper money, and when they looked long down their noses she stared right back at them, as she had in town long ago, on the sidewalks and in the stores. The women and men both. She never once lowered her head. It wasn't in her to. She'd fed Bonni every day of her life, no matter the sin it took, until the state took her away, and then she fed Rory. She hung the bottles in the tree to keep him safe. She prayed while he was in Korea. Prayed and prayed. Not to the church-god, exactly. To her own. One that lived closer, up on the mountain, perhaps. For here was a place fit for a god to live, not in any building or book. Here she was understood. She was wicked, sure, but no hypocrite. She had fought every day of her life, same as the beasts of the field. The bloody Christ nailed naked and roaring to the cross—his bones iron-split, his body whip-flayed to the meat—he was hard as they come. Surely he prized grit, a game heart. Same as she did.

The rest of it, she could give a fuck.

Rory stepped again into the kitchen, hungry probably, and she drove him out with the wooden spoon, dripping spots of batter on the floor. She didn't care. The floors and counters were covered in flour and sugar already, the apples and cider simmering on the stove. Eggshells sat in the slop bucket, fated for the pigs, and jars of cinnamon and ginger and nutmeg stood open-topped by the sink. She was making an eight-layer stackcake like the one they had the day she got married in 1913. Back then they were too poor for a store-bought cake, so each family in attendance baked a single layer, the thin cakes stacked one atop the other like the stories of a house, each mortared with sweet apple filling. That was how people did then on the mountain. Years later the old stackcake became fashionable again, this time among people who could afford any cake they wanted, and when she returned to the mountains with Rory as a baby, she sold her stackcakes through a bakery in Boone until someone—some nosy Presbyterian, probably—discovered who made them, and that was the end of that.

She poured the batter into a pair of hoecake pans she'd buttered, then lowered the hot jaw of the oven, hinges groaning, and set them side-by-side on the rack. She closed the oven and wiped her hands on the old apron she wore, blowing the fallen hair from her eyes. She'd always hated to bake, more so even than lying on her back for a living. Perhaps the anti-cake campaign of the Presbyterians those years ago had been a blessing in disguise. She figured one blessing warranted another, and the old wicked light came into her eyes. She went hunting through the shelves and drawers of her pantry, the roots and powders and potions, searching for just the thing. She found it in an old coffee tin, cuttings from the secret garden she kept in the trees beyond the house.

She was bent over a seething pot, chuckling to herself, when she felt the floor pulse again with footsteps. Rory launching a third offensive, she figured, and she raised the wooden spoon over her head, advancing toward the door.

"Boy, I done told you twice now—"

She stopped. It was Eli standing in the threshold, his eyes wide with terror, glued to the spoon like it was an ax. She made no move to lower it from skull-cleaving height.

"Rory sent me in, hoping to get him a biscuit. Said you was less likely to give me a paddling."

Granny eyed him up, down.

"Don't be so sure."

The Presbyterian church was in the middle of town, a rich-looking behemoth of red brick with four white columns holding up the front, an arrow-point bell tower that looked ideal for a sharpshooter. Stained-glass windows lined the sides, luminescent in the last rays of the day's sun, and there was an annex jutting out from the rear. Rory parked down the street and got out. He never felt comfortable in Boone. He knew the people down here were suspicious of Granny, this witch-woman on the mountain who read auguries and concocted potions. This once-whore, rumored to set hexes and speak with spirits. Of course, such prejudices didn't stop them coming up the mountain when the medicines of the lower world fell short.

He walked up the sidewalk, holding the cake. It looked like a pet ghost, covered as it was in a white cloth. The big doors of the church hummed with organ music, and he thought better of a straight-on approach. A walkway ran down the side of the building, and down this he tromped, the shards of stained glass catching the light above him. Flaring, fracturing. He wondered what would happen if he slung a rock through one. He imagined an angry mob issuing red-faced from every door of the place to beat him down or string him up.

He'd slicked back his hair and put on one of the shirts he wore to see his mother, and he walked up the steps to the back door of the place and knocked. A woman in a peach-colored suit opened the door. Her hair was balled high atop her head, and her face was round and bright, bearing the slightest extra chin. She grabbed his wrist in one hand, her nails varnished.

"Oh, a cake! Now aren't you the sweetest? Come now." She tugged him along. "I have just the place for it." She led him into a fellowship hall and there to the dessert table, where she shifted a plate of cookies an inch this way, a dish of brownies an inch that. She took the cake from him and pulled off the cloth with a gasp of delight. She looked over her shoulder at him. "Now whose boy are you? I need to know who I have to thank for this fabulous cake."

Rory shifted his weight to his good foot.

"Maybelline Docherty, ma'am."

"I'm not sure I know her—"

Rory cleared his throat.

"Granny May," he said.

The woman straightened. "Oh." She folded the white cloth that had covered the cake and handed it back to him, her eyes walled off. "How nice." She turned and walked away, and he saw her whispering to another woman in front of the punch bowl.

"Bitches."

Sometimes he wondered if it was more than just Granny that rattled these people. If it was his mother, too. These brickhouse Christians, they feared misfortune like a curse, like something they could catch by touch or word or tongue.

He leaned one shoulder against the wall and looked away from them, waiting for Sheriff Carling and the others to come flooding into the hall. He was starving, subsisting on the single biscuit that Granny had allowed him. As long as he had to be here, he intended to take full advantage of the long tables of food. There was chicken baked and fried, pulled pork, greens drowned in yellow ponds of butter. Baked beans and mashed potatoes, bowls of dark gravy, layered casseroles of every color and description. But first: the stackcake.

Granny had grasped his hand on the way out the door.

"Don't you go eating none of that cake, hear? It's for the congregation, not you."

"I won't," he lied.

He could feel the organ music more than he could hear it, an energy surging through the walls, building in ever-greater mountains of power, rising into a long, sustained plateau before stopping. Soon the parishioners came filing in, dressed in their Sunday finest. The men were carrying their hats, the women a-chatter, missalettes flittering in their hands like white little birds. They crowded the food table like trough-feeders, and Rory made for the table of sweets. He cut himself a handsome slice of the stackcake and found an empty table and sat himself in a folding chair to eat.

He was surprised when the chair next to him groaned: Sheriff Carling sat down with a mounded plate of food. A cake wedge the size of a garden shovel sat on its own plate.

"Eight layers." He prodded the cake with the flat side of his knife. "She's went and outdid herself."

Rory forked himself a bite.

"Didn't know if anybody would eat it, seeing who made it."

Carling chewed a hunk of pork in the side of his mouth. He nodded.

"Oh, these people is mainly schoolteachers and professors, clerks and bankers and lawyers and accountants. Hardly venture out of town. They're afraid of anything outside the city limit."

"What about you?"

Carling quit chewing.

"I don't make trouble for the mountains as long as they don't make trouble for me." He pointed his fork at Rory, lowered his voice. "But I got you here for a reason. Seems shit's been starting to flow downhill here of late, and I don't like it. You can tell Eustace that."

"I'm sorry about the sugar, sir—"

Carling leaned forward, looking left and right.

"It ain't about the *got-damn* sugar," he hissed. "I had some federal man come sniffing around last week, asking questions I don't like to answer. I told him as little as I could, but it ain't the same as it was when my daddy was sheriff twenty-five years back, when Eustace and the rest of them had their little county trades." Carling sat upright, smiled hello to an old lady walking past, then bent again to Rory. "Now it's ugly. Worse than Prohibition ever was. You got pop-skullers like them Muldoons running what amounts to poison, making more money than God, sprouting up like weeds I can't even begin to trample down. This federal man said they caught one of them Muldoons the other week had him a Thompson submachine gun on the floorboard."

"Cooley?"

"Hell, no. You think he'd still be walking free?"

"Where'd he get it from?"

"I don't know. Point is the son of a bitch had it, and that's the kind of thing the government can't ignore. It's never been the same since they flooded that valley in thirty-one. Whiskey's got to run down out the mountains now to feed the mills, and the money runs up. And you know who we can thank for that."

"Who?"

The old tanker eyed him balefully, then grunted.

"Who you think?"

Rory excused himself to the restroom. He was feeling strange. He had the feeling as he walked across the room that everyone was watching him over their food, suspicious of his blood or history. He walked a straight line to spite them, forcing the standing rings of people to part, their eyes cutting against him. The door to the men's room was narrow and groaned. Inside he bent over the sink and washed his hands and splashed cold water on his face. The light was dim, a single weak bulb, and in the mirror he thought for a moment that he saw not his own face reflected but that of his grandfather, Anson Docherty, killed in 1918. Rory's age. Cut down in a French wheat field by German teenagers in spiked helmets. A man seen only in the one photograph Granny kept of him on the fireboard, square-jawed and tall in his dress blues, his cap set jaunty over one eye. A vision slightly blurred, made as if with ash and charcoal instead of light.

He shook his head and dried his hands, patted his cheeks with a hand towel. Two men had come and gone while he stood before the mirror. He opened the door and stepped again into the room; it was different than before. The voices were purling like water, gushing invisibly over the tables, and the bulbs looked of a lower wattage. They hummed with yellow light. The food table had elongated, a long tongue glistening with feast. A metallic ditty rose from the scrape and rattle of silverware.

Rory simply stood there, in thrall to the scene. He was breathing through his mouth, as if to inhale the voices, the light and food. How hungry he was, and it seemed he could eat the bulbs hanging from the ceiling, these electric fruit. He could drink the language of men, and be sustained by the mere scent of chicken skin and buttery greens.

He blinked.

Now a pair of young women were standing before him, wearing hats. Their teeth were unbelievably white, as if store-bought, their breasts sharp as weapons beneath their blouses. Their nails were painted the pale pink of kitten paws. Rory backed up a step.

"Your name is Rory Docherty, right?"

Their accent was clipped and clean, as if they were from Charlotte or Richmond. Rory nodded, distrusting his tongue. He took another step backward, unable to help himself. There was little room; the wall nudged his shoulder blades.

"Janette and I, we're in school at the teachers' college?" The girl looked left, right. "We heard, if we want whiskey, we should talk to you."

Now the other one touched his arm.

"We're hosting a little mixer next weekend. Saturday?"

Rory could see the stream of normal thoughts he should be having, and slightly apart from these he stood, bewildered. He was not sure if they were asking him to come to the party or did they want to buy whiskey now. He waited for this point to be clarified, but both of them simply stood smiling before him, their heads slightly cocked, waiting.

The one with her hand on his arm squeezed slightly, as if testing him for quality, but he hardly noticed. He was looking at the flowers in the other girl's hatband, bright-wheeling blossoms that made him think of Christine's cloche hat.

"Well?" she said. "Can you get us some?"

Rory eyed a pink rose in particular.

"Some what?" he asked.

"Whiskey, of course."

Without thinking, he leaned forward, poking the flower with his finger.

"Silk." He grunted. "It ain't real."

The girl stepped back, giggling behind a cupped palm, as if he'd touched a funny button on her. The other girl's face darkened.

"Of course it isn't real. It would rot."

They were wearing perfume, not the oils like Granny used. Something factory-made for fancy parlors, hovering all about them in invisible clouds. The two of them closed in again, all smiles and smells, and he thought of Christine. He was struck by the terrible notion that if the sharp points of their breasts so much as grazed him, hers never would.

"You got the wrong man." He slid edgewise against the wall. "I'm a clean-liver, pure as the driven. Wouldn't touch the stuff with a mile-long yardstick." He was nearly to the door. He flattened his back against it. All he had to do was lean back.

"That's not what we heard."

"Tell you what. If you two are hell-bent for whiskey, I advise you to go see Eli Uptree at Howl Motors, just up the mountain. He can square you away."

Before they could reply, he was through the door. He found himself in the sanctuary. The pews sat in rigid formation, burnished by decades of satin-clad rumps. An aisle ran crimson from the back of the church like an open vein. The ceiling arched high, ribbed and timbered like the belly of an upturned ship, as if the whole place could be upended and set sail. Past the altar stood the organ, the ranks of silver pipes thrust upward from the wind-chest.

He could feel the sudden soundlessness of the place pulsing against his eardrums, the weight of old voices and hymns. The shudder of silence. He felt tuned to the underside of the world, the things laid aground. His wooden foot had begun tingling at the end of his leg, as if newly fleshed. He could feel blood popping and whistling, as if through the grains of wood, a capillary slink. As if some miracle had been performed upon him, his sawed-off shinbone sprouting a new foot like the eye of a potato in the root cellar too long. *Phantom limb.* Here was a little ghost of his own, unseen but surely felt, realer than any black-veiled lady walking the hills of a night. Despite this, he kicked a nearby pew, making sure. A wooden thud echoed through the darkened whale's-belly of the place. Right then—sure as the blow of an ax—he knew Granny had sabotaged the cake.

"Damn crazy woman."

He crossed to the far side of the sanctuary and pushed through the door, emerging into the evening. He made for the back of the place, creeping in the shadowed lee of the wall like a thief. The land sloped down from the road, revealing a basement floor, and a line of golden windows hovered a story over the rear lawn, looking onto the fellowship hall. He found an old ladder in the maintenance shed and leaned it against the wall, the stringers trembling and twisting as he scaled the rungs. He climbed just high enough to peep over the window ledge, eyeing the people at Sunday dinner.

"Jesus God."

They were fat-cheeked and slit-eyed, their faces beaming like spotlamps, as if Granny had conjured them into a congregation of round-faced idols, newly enlightened. Some sat bemused in their seats, smiling at the walls, and others had taken to examining patterns in the tablecloth. Many were still eating, bent low over their food, their jaw muscles pulsing over pouched cheeks, their utensils stuck like communication antennas from resting fists. They'd laid waste to the serving table, the surface littered with scraped-clean dishes and plates and trays. No rubble of stackcake remained. The plate gleamed as if tongue-polished, and maybe so.

He saw two men bent double, guffawing over their shoes, their bellies held in place with both hands. When they looked up, their faces were red and wet as sink-washed beets. He saw prim little housewives who must survive on leafy greens and boiled eggs during the week, and they were ravaging drumsticks with their teeth, their lips puckered over clean-sucked thighbones. The pastor, an aging white crane of a man, sat at the head of one table, his flat belly fronted by a flotilla of deviled eggs. He was palsied, each egg riding waves into the red pit of his mouth. A blue-haired woman at the far end of his table belched, clapping an age-spotted hand to her mouth, her eyes wide, and the rest of the table roared. One of the women laughed so hard a white mustache of cookie-milk sped from her nostrils. The table roared yet louder, the old-timers heaving, gripping the table edges to keep themselves from flying away. One or two might die soon, thought Rory, stroking slack-faced onto the floor. He decided to make his escape.

He was nearly to the street when Big Carling stepped out from a side door, adjusting his belt. His bulk blocked the sidewalk. He turned and saw Rory, clapping a hand onto his shoulder.

"Jesus wept," he said.

"Sir?"

"Jesus wept. John eleven: thirty-five. Shortest verse in the Book. He wept before the sisters of Lazarus." No moon tonight, but the big man's face shone, his eyes red-edged, as if he himself had been weeping. "You know what come him to weep?"

Rory shifted his weight.

"I ain't put much thought toward it—"

"I'll tell you," said Carling. He scrunched up his face and looked to the distance. "He knowed what he had coming. Seen it." He nodded. "It's a blessing, son. Most of us we couldn't but weep, seeing such-like for our own selves."

"That's mighty pessimistic of you, Sheriff."

Carling shook his head.

"It's a blessing, got-damnit. I knowed what was on the ground waiting for me, I never would of rolled that tank off the boat." He looked at Rory. "You, you might not of rode that ship to Korea."

"You don't know what I would of done."

"We can take what comes, it comes out the dark. It's the blindness that bears us along."

"I better get along myself, sir."

"There's something coming, son. I've felt it. The world is speeding up, whirling like those winds high on the mountain. You aren't careful, it'll blow you right off."

"I'll keep that in mind, sir."

His fingers dug hard into Rory's shoulder.

"See that you do."

Granny was on the porch, her eyes bright with expectation. Rory bent and kissed her cheek.

"How they like that cake?" she asked.

"You might of earned yourself some new customers, they don't burn you at the stake."

"I'd like to see them try it."

That night Rory lay in bed thinking of Christine. He thought of the wide slash of her mouth and bold green eyes, her milk-white skin. He thought of the dark hollow at the base of her throat, an invitation as if for his thumb. Her breasts, naked and ripe, floating silver-bright above him, the nipples like hard little stems beneath his tongue. He thought of the pink furrow, dark-furred and glistening, he wanted so bad to taste. He slid his hand under the covers, between his legs, and closed his eyes to see it all, clearly.

V. SICKLE MOON, WAXING

Bonni knew the old hollowed-out sycamore by the rope-swing nearby. Here, when she was a girl, her mama and the other working girls would come on Sundays while everyone was at church. They would strip down to their skinnies and swing hooting over the green water. They would drink beer and eat fried chicken and smoke thin cigars, their white breasts bobbing in the river like buoys. They would wring the water from their hair, and Bonni would marvel at the mottled bodies of these giantesses, at their bruised and curdled thighs, the furry pockets between their legs. The girls would speak of men's organs like garden-grown mushrooms, discussing attributes of length and girth and straighthood, coloration and flavor and scent. Bonni would envision them squatting on their beds each night, inspecting these strange growths that sprang newly from each man's trousers.

They found no parakeets in the tree hollow, but Connor wasn't discouraged.

Let's wait awhile, he said. Maybe they'll come back.

Bonni went to the horse, brought down his violin case.

Play for me, she said. I want to dance.

The instrument wailed under the flick of his bow. She kicked off her shoes and let down her hair, wheeling and bobbing on the riverbank. Her face shone; sweat gathered in the shallow valley between her breasts. She slid the loops of her dress from her shoulders, her nipples berry-firm under the sun. She drew him toward her, her hands on his wrists. She unbuttoned his shirt. When it fell, she saw the purple storms of bruise over his ribs and kidneys.

She drew him into the green river, as if into healing waters.

CHAPTER 20

You think she'll put out?"

"I ain't really considered it."

Granny just looked at him, her mouth flat.

"They cut off your leg, son, not your pecker."

"Jesus God," said Rory. "I know good-and-well what they did and didn't."

"Well, you ain't been laid since coming home."

"How in the hell would you know?"

"You wouldn't be so ornery you had."

"I ain't ornery."

Granny sucked her teeth, squinting at his red-riled face. It was Thursday, dusk, and the bullbats were out, lone silhouettes over the purple meadow that surrounded the house.

"The hell you ain't."

"Only because you're riling me."

"Let me tell you something: one that don't put out ain't only a waste of time, it's a unnatural phenomenon."

"Jesus God."

"There you have it. Them Christers like to lock they little pussies up tight, keep your pecker a-hunt like a witching rod. Want you to marry them first. Hell, would you buy a car you ain't test-drove it yet?"

Rory bolted upright from his rocker, clapped his hands over his ears.

"I can't hear you. Really I can't."

"Oh, you heard me, all right."

Rory stared up at the haint-blue ceiling of the porch.

"I got to go."

"Go where?"

"I don't know. Somewhere."

"Well, go on, then, wherever you got to go. Ain't no skin off my nose."

"I will."

He tromped off the porch, heading for the car. She called after him.

"Don't wed 'em till they spread 'em, son. There's words to live by. Any girl wants Jesus in her more than you, something ain't right."

"Jesus God," she could hear him muttering. "Jesus God."

He got in the Ford and fired the engine and swung in a circle back down the drive. Granny watched him go, smiling to herself. She didn't know this girl, no. But she knew her boy. Sometimes he needed a little prompting.

Rory idled past the Adderholt house—a foreman's bungalow, white and tidy in the mill-workers' section of town. He parked down the block, then walked back toward the house, hands in his pockets, as if he were just another worker from the mill ho-humming his way home. But his hands were fists in his pockets, his breath short. His heart thundered like a bloody stormcloud against the wall of his sternum, lightning searing through his veins. There did not seem to be enough air in the world. He wondered if he were going crazy. If he had been dosed or cursed or cast beneath a spell. If he were sick in his blood. He was shivering with desire.

The moon was the thinnest sickle now, carving itself from shadow. He stopped and leaned breathing against a telephone pole, casing the place. The house had a low-pitch roof, gabled, and a front porch that sat beneath a shingled overhang. Above the porch were two small, square-shaped windows set side-by-side. They gave onto an attic space, the glass panes glowing in the night.

Her room.

A pebble rolled between his fingers. That age-old suitor's device. He was halfway across the yard when a dog came tearing around the corner of the house at speed, a mongrel beast with a black mask and purple tongue, a cage of white teeth. Rory juked one way, then lurched another. The beast bellied itself in the yard, legs spread, watching this absurd dance with a ragged smile. When it pounced, Rory gave it the calf of his wooden leg.

The dog drove its teeth into the limb. Rory dragged the beast stiff-legged and growling across the yard, making for the one-car garage at the house's flank, praying the door was unlocked. If it wasn't, he was going to cave it beneath his shoulder, to hell with the noise. Anything was better than the dog turning up tail-thumping on the girl's porch with his leg for a trophy, or else burying it somewhere on the grounds like a bone.

He twisted the knob and the door gave and he tumbled into the darkness, kicking back the dog with his good foot while he slammed home the door. The beast whined and scratched. Rory sat spraddle-legged on the floor, breathing hard. He pulled up his pantleg. The maple calf was scored and furrowed in a dozen places, ravaged. He shied to think of the gashes those teeth would have made in true meat.

Small blessings.

The darkness was absolute, the windows papered, and he stood slowly into the cavelike space. He spread his arms out to either side and twisted a slow circle to find his bearings. The dog sniffed back and forth along the bottom of the door, hearing him move.

Rory's fingers found something smooth and round, the size of a skull. Now others. Wooden heads, faceless, each adorned with a hat. His hands found the fabric orchids of cloches, the feathers of fascinators, the veils of pillboxes. Now something else. A hard corner, covered in a sheet. He stepped toward it, spreading his arms to the question. He hand-shaped the machine from the darkness, a steel ghost rising beneath the sheet. A car of another era. Stubby hood and upright cab, shaped like a man's top hat. The wheel hubs were octagonal, with letters cast on their faces. He knelt down, remembering his lighter, and thumbed a flame. A bouncing orb of orange light. The initials *DB* on the wheel hub. Dodge Brothers. A Prohibition-era coupe with a 35-horse motor, nearly twice that of a Ford of the same era. He wondered if it was stock under the hood.

He bet not.

The flame turned blue and waned, winked out. The darkness came back in a rush. He ground the thumbwheel again, again. Only sparks. He stood upright into the returned dark, too quickly, and felt dizzied. The blood swam from his eyes in silver threads and the ground tilted beneath him, out of plumb; he cast out a hand for balance. His palm pushed a can from the shelf, and he heard it crash on the floor as he landed alongside it.

The sound that followed, he would never forget it. A serpent's rattle, that perfect frequency of threat, eons in the making, came echoing from inside a tin lard can. The sound amplified to something modern, machinelike, a new and terrible weapon, like the machine gun of some war yet to come. Now others joined in, who knew how many. The little garage alive with their anger, a thousand maddened marbles. Each serpent speaking the same message to him, the only one they knew: *I am death I am death I am death.*

A ripple in the dark. He scrambled to the door, flattening his back against the wood. He could feel the beast through the thin pine, the barreled ribs quivering with lust. He tried to find a quiet place inside himself, an attic of calm. He closed his eyes. The temple of stone.

The door fell open behind him; he fell flat on his back in the yard. He held out his palm, as if that would calm the red fury of the dog, stop the coming teeth. Instead he found himself looking up a woman's shift, a pale gleam of panties cradled between her thighs.

Christine.

She stepped back. The dog sat beside her, whining through an open mouth, waiting for permission to dismember him.

"*House.*"

The dog dropped its head and slunk toward the porch. Christine's arms were crossed under her breasts, her hip kicked out. Her eyes had that catlike glow.

"How'd you find me?" he asked.

"How couldn't I? You got Ornias all worked up."

"Orn-yus? The dog?"

"The snake."

She stepped over him into the garage, silent on her bare feet, and pulled the chain of an overhead bulb. A weak yellow light splashed across the garage. There were hats everywhere, sitting on mounts and hanging along the walls. A wide, sawhorse table piled with scrolls of fabric and felt. Cut dresses and neckties. Paisleys and flowers and stripes. Shears of various sizes hung from hooks behind the table, and rolls of framing wire.

"I could hear him from the house," she said. "Rattling."

In the middle of the floor lay the lard can, quiet now. It had a piece of tape on it. ORNIAS, it read. She picked it up, arms outstretched, as if she were handling a live depth charge.

"What kind is he?"

"Eastern diamondback. He's Daddy's favorite."

" 'Favorite'? There's a word I never heard applied to a rattlesnake.'"

She raised up on her toes to place the can back on the shelf. There was a row of them, lined up like munitions in the belly of a ship. The back of her shift displayed a dagger of bare skin, her spine studding through a valley of flesh. He watched the muscles of her upper back ball and slide as if of a mind themselves.

"You work in here, with them?"

She threw her chin over her shoulder, her eyes alight.

"They ain't such bad company, long as nobody knocks them off the shelf."

"It wasn't my first choice for an entrance."

She turned around, flanked by the perforated lard cans in their rows.

"Want to see what I been working on?"

"All right."

She strode past him. His sleeves were rolled up; he felt the colorless fuzz of her arm tickle his skin as she passed. Her shoulders hovered motionless as she walked, her lean hips swiveling beneath them. She was slightly splay-footed, her toenails unpainted. He followed her to the worktable, where a brimless pink hat was perched rakishly on a wooden head.

"Pillbox hat," she said. "You know who was first to wear them?" She didn't wait for him to say. "Roman soldiers. Called it the Pannonian cap. Can you imagine all those scar-faced legionaries wearing hats like this?"

Rory shook his head. He was hooked on how far her words could range, carrying him far beyond the mountains, into other centuries and countries. They told him how little he knew, how much he still wanted to know.

"The special thing is the color," she said.

Rory leaned closer, looking over her shoulder at the hat. It was a fleshy pink, like a dog's tongue or wad of Bazooka gum.

"They say Eisenhower is going to be elected next month," she said. "And Mamie's favorite color is pink."

"Mamie?"

Christine rubbed her fingers lightly over the flat crown of the hat.

"Ike's wife. They say she got married in pink, drives a pink car, even dyed her pets pink once. Pretty soon women are gonna be lining up for hats this color, you watch. It's going to be *the* thing, and I'll be ready."

A vein pulsed in her neck, small as a worm. Rory wanted to rub his chin against it, to find it with his tongue and teeth.

"That's smart of you."

"It's my ticket out of the mill. I don't aim to be a toe-sewer the rest of my life."

He placed his hands on her waist, lightly. She rotated in place, facing him, pulling her hair across her mouth like a mask.

"When I heard Ornias, I knew it was you."

"Yeah?"

She pulled her hair away from her mouth. He was breathing her breath.

"Daddy's like to catch you."

She was tiny beneath the thin cotton shift. Rectangular, hard. He placed his thumbs into the creases above her pelvis, feeling the muscles of her stomach constrict.

"Let him."

He kissed her. Her tongue found his, quick as a dart, and he felt himself flood, his blood surging up and up and up. He lifted her tiny from the floor, onto his hips, and she hooked her bare feet behind him, their breath torn ragged from their mouths. He yanked the sheet from the car and cranked open the door and they spilled panting and clawing across the seat, their faces twisted, their teeth bright and sharp.

The shift was bunched high at her waist. Her flat belly gleamed with sweat, with the wet slashes of his tongue. He pulled the thin cotton to her chin and dove for her breasts, the nipples hard as buttons in his mouth. Little cries from her throat. He wanted the taste of her, her mouth and her sex. His blood would leap the bounds of his skin.

"Rory," she said. "Rory."

His hand found the back of her neck, gripping it like a handle, his mouth seeking the hollows beneath her chin. He lapped them, the sting of her on his tongue.

"Stop," she said. "I can't."

She began to struggle, retreating farther up the seat, her legs and arms sprawled for traction.

"Stop!"

He did, waking as from a trance. He found himself kneeling on the seat, his chest heaving. She sat cross-legged against the far door like a cornered animal, the blood high in her cheeks.

"Daddy caught us out here in his old car, it'd be both of our asses."

"I ain't afraid of him."

"You ought to be."

"Why's that?"

"He wasn't always a preacher."

Rory raised up, looking about the machine they were sitting in.

"That's where this old hot rod come from, isn't it? That trunk used to jingle of a night."

"That was a long time ago, before I was born. He's past all that."

"Is he?"

She opened her mouth to say something, then didn't. Her legs and arms were still crossed, her body knotted against him.

"He says you're trouble. Says you work for Eustace Uptree on the mountain."

"You knew that the first time you saw me." She didn't say anything, and he leaned forward, across the seat. "Didn't you?"

"He says you don't have the Spirit in you."

Rory leaned farther across the seat, kissing distance from her face.

"Damn him. I'd boot the Holy Ghost from his ass for an hour with you."

She jutted her chin.

"Big talk from a one-legged man."

The words pierced him, blade-cold. A hot pang in his chest, like loosed blood.

She saw the damage.

"I'm sorry," she said. She reached out for his hand. "I didn't mean it like that."

He whipped his hand away. His heart was crashing.

"Remind me." He could feel the meanness slipping into his voice. "Remind me how he lost that eye?"

"Timber-cutting accident."

"Is that right? Funny thing is, seems he lost it awfully close to the time they flooded the valley."

"So?"

"So that's right about the time they killed that mill boss's son, and my mother cut out one of their eyes with a cat's paw."

"Don't you dare—"

"I already did."

She slapped him, hard. The echo of her palm stung his face.

Rory swallowed, slowly, and turned his other cheek.

"How's that for the Spirit?"

She was already out the other side of the car, gone.

Granny was on the porch when he tore up the drive. He stepped out of the car and slammed the door. The window glass rattled in its frame. After Christine left, he'd stood a long time before the rows of serpents in their round tin homes, imagining what the venom of a viper might feel like under his skin. He remembered the schoolhouse words.

Hemotoxic. Necrolytic. He imagined the shuttled cells of his arteries bursting, his blood whirling water-thin, unclotted. His flesh deep-eaten at the wound, a dark sink of rot spreading from the bite like the very spirit of evil.

He'd turned off the light, closed the door. Christine had chained the dog to a metal post in the yard. It lay watching him, whining, as if with love. He walked across the grass, toward the road. He passed alongside the house, and out of the corner of his eye he caught sight of something in the window, white as a ghost. He turned, and there it was, the bone-white visage of the little boy, Christine's brother—Clyde—watching him from inside the house. Rory waved, but the face registered no change. Just that same scowl, like something shaped in a mold.

Now he stomped up the porch steps in his shirtsleeves, the cold stinging him, and stood in front of Granny. The wind was up, the near-naked trees clamoring and swirling at the edge of the meadow. The bottles moaning, clinking in their branches. She blew smoke from her nostrils.

"What?" she asked.

"You're going to dig up that fucking eye from wherever you got it hid and give it to me."

"Say I am?"

"Damn right you are."

She hawked and spat—the gobbet hit the planks with a thud.

"Just 'cause you got a cock swinging between your legs don't mean you can order me around. I never bent to no man and I ain't about to start."

Rory picked up the rocker beside her and swung it into a porch column. The chair shattered, the skeletal fragments falling curled and broken at his feet.

"You bent plenty," he said. "Ain't you now?"

Granny stood from her rocker, slowly, unfolding herself sword-straight beneath him, her heavy breasts nearly touching the heaving planes of his chest. He could feel her breath against his neck, her voice playing like a blade against his skin. An edge he'd never heard.

"Careful what ye say," she whispered. "Lest some old woman don't cut ye pecker off some dark night."

"I'm in love with her, Grandma."

Her chest rose, fell. Her tongue worked around the inside of her mouth. She lifted a hand to touch his face and nodded, a slight wetness in her eyes. Then she walked off the porch, into the night.

CHAPTER 21

Rory was up before the cock's crow. The floorboards groaned beneath him, the eastern ridges blood-edged by the first sliver of sun. A jar sat gleaming on the porch rail, still covered here or there in chunks of dirt and turf from its moonlit excavation. He sat in one of the unbroken rockers, the jar clutched in his lap, and he was the greatest fool in the world. The king of fools. If the printers of playing cards saw fit to introduce a fool into the deck, it would be a character of his likeness, a man holding the bloody lump of his heart in his hand—an organ he'd cut out himself.

He held the jelly-jar before his face. In it floated a detached eye, ball-shaped with a red tail of nerves like a creature netted from the black depths of the sea, jarred and preserved for exhibition. For the profit of carnival showmen or museum curators. An organ not torn from the socket of the man he suspected and accused, whose daughter he loved. This eye was blue, a sealike color he didn't recognize, and he didn't know whether to be relieved or punch a hole in something.

The wind rose, rattling the curled bones of the broken rocker. The bottles and branches and leaves, the very contours of the land, heaved beneath him. He squeezed the jar in his hand, veins rising like worms from his flesh. He pictured the glass crushed in his fist, the eye bursting in his palm. A world destroyed, yolked through his fingers, lost like all those stories at the bottom of the lake. He held the jar to eye-level, staring unblinking at the bodiless orb, trying to detect any provenance in its shape or color or pattern or gleam.

"*Rory.*"

He turned, startled, to see Granny lashing a robe about her waist.

"I told you there wasn't nothing in that eye but trouble."

He looked again to the jar, the eye warped slightly behind the time-crazed glass.

"It isn't him."

"Who?"

"That pastor. Adderholt."

"Well, now you know."

He set the jar on the porch rail, turning the eye away from him, outward, like some terrible sentinel.

"I don't know shit."

It was about noon when the ranch-wagon came grumbling up the drive, bouncing over ruts and churning through slogs. Granny set aside her knitting and lit her pipe. Rory was down at Eli's—so he said—and she thought she had new customers until the men stepped out. There were two of them, bearded. They wore rumpled suits and eyeglasses with thick black frames and each carried a leather notebook. They looked up at the chestnut tree a long moment, open-mouthed, before approaching the porch.

"I ain't buying," she said.

"Ma'am?"

"Whatever it is you selling. Some new god, probably, or *Britannicas.*"

One of the men was short and round, the other tall and gangly. Neither would fit very well in a store-bought suit, which is what they wore. The short one spoke.

"We're biologists, ma'am, with the university in Chapel Hill?"

He said it like she hadn't heard of the place.

Granny blew the smoke from her nostrils.

"What is it you want?"

"This tree you have here," the man swept his arm, "it's an American chestnut."

"That's right."

"Are you aware how rare it is?"

Granny shrugged.

"Some. They's about all gone."

The man nodded.

"Yes, ma'am. We estimate three and a half billion blighted since 1900."

Granny raised her eyebrows.

"Billion?"

She remembered, after Anson's death, seeing whole hillsides blighted, the once-mighty hardwoods toppled over their rotted-out trunks, their felled branches clinging to one another as if in mourning. She remembered wondering if it was somehow related. All those dead boys in that Great War and the previous, maybe the earth was too sad to support such mightiness. Maybe something cankerous had gotten into the dirt along with all that blood, here and across the oceans.

The man smiled grimly through his beard.

"Billion," he said. "They are nearly extinct in the wild. My colleague Dr. De Groot and I have been on the road for six weeks searching for a live specimen. We've been as far north as Pennsylvania, in fact. Then we heard rumors of one up on Howl Mountain. So here we are."

"Well, you found it." Granny gestured with her pipe. "You ain't cuttin' on it, though."

"No, ma'am," he said. "We just want to take some samples is all."

"What for, you hunting for its secret?"

"Something like that."

"You got a theory?"

"A few, actually. Best one being it's contracted a virus of some kind that fights the blight fungus. If we can identify such a viral agent, we can—hopefully—inoculate others with it. It would be a great step toward saving the species."

"Have at it, then. I don't aim to stand in the way of that."

The man turned and looked at the tree.

"May I ask about the bottles?"

Granny sucked her teeth.

"You got vials in those laboratories of yours, full of things shouldn't never get out?"

"Some."

"There you go."

"And that?" The man pointed to the jar still sitting on the porch, filled with the bloated tadpole of an eye.

"Too late," she said.

She eyed them close while they made their study of the tree. A lot of evil things had been done in the name of science. Not under her watch, they wouldn't. But the men proved kind, even reverent. They fawned over the big survivor. They studied the bark, making notes, and erected a tripod, taking close-up photographs of the heavy threads of bark that twisted their way up the trunk. They measured the tree's circumference with a tape measure made of waxen cloth and stood far back in the meadow, bending to examine the tree through the scope of a surveyor's device. They donned rubber gloves and picked leaves and twigs from the soil, housing them in labeled jars, and they filled vials with soil from the base of the tree. They collected the spiny, palm-size burrs that had fallen from the branches.

Not too many, Granny made sure. Each burr held up to three nuts that she used for turkey-stuffing and open-fire roasts. Rory fed them to the hogs to sweeten their meat. What the people and hogs didn't eat, the whitetail did. They would come out of the woods at dusk, light-hoofed and slim-born, like beasts made of smoke and light. She would sit stock-still, hardly breathing, watching the black velvet of their noses, the dark gleam of their eyes. The way a buck's antlers glowed bone-white in the dusk, cradling the dying sky. This tree, whose kind once fattened the beasts of the mountains, would stand kinglike in the meadow, crowned in golden leaves, as if shielding the deer from the coming dark.

The scientists approached the porch after finishing their study.

"You get what you need?" Granny asked.

"We hope," said the short man.

"You the only ones working on this?"

The scientist shook his head.

"No, ma'am. The Department of Agriculture, they're trying to crossbreed American chestnuts with Chinese specimens like those that carried over the fungus. But it isn't going to work."

"No?"

"The hybrids might be blight-resistant, but they'll be too stunted. To compete in these mountains, you have to be strong and tall. Otherwise, you won't be able to reach the light."

Granny nodded. This little man, she might have underestimated him. He seemed to have the right idea about things. The scientist looked at his shoes a moment. They were dress loafers traumatized by weeks on the road, scuffed and seam-split, bulging at the sides.

"Ma'am, may I ask what herb you were smoking when we arrived?"

Granny narrowed one eye, as if aiming down the barrel of a gun. "What's it to you?"

The scientist crossed his hands behind his back.

"Dr. De Groot and I, we have our own, ah, side project. Not sanctioned by the university, you understand. Our interest being, well, not purely academic. Dr. De Groot here, he is a Dutchman, has traveled extensively, collected seeds from a number of locales. Thailand, Tibet,

Morocco. We're developing our own strain of cannabis. An optimal blend of the sativa and indica species."

"Optimal, huh?"

The man produced a glass vial from the inside of his coat, stoppered with cork. It contained two large buds.

"Flying Dutchman, we call it. Problem is, ma'am, we are plain out of rolling papers."

"Say you are." Granny knocked her pipe against the heel of her hand, clearing the ash. "I might could help with that."

"Teeth like butter mints, hair like spun gold. You should of seen them, boy."

"I did see them," said Rory. "I'm the one sent them to you, if you don't recall."

"We could have us a double date or something."

They were sitting in Eli's garage, the hood of the Ford propped open.

"I think those two are looking for higher-class cuts than us."

"They invited me to their party tomorrow, didn't they?"

"And who's bringing the whiskey?"

Eli leaned back on his shop stool, eyeing Rory over his cigarette.

"Got-damn sourpuss is what you are. What happened, that little heart-sabotager of yours went and sabotaged your heart like I said she would?"

"I don't want to talk about it."

"What'd you do? Tell her you suspected your mama scooped out her daddy's eye with a cat's paw back in '31?"

Rory didn't say anything.

Eli leaned forward, squinting through his own smoke.

"You did, didn't you? Jesus H., what's in that head of yours? Sand? Pea-gravel? You might be dumber'n I ever thought."

Rory folded a rag on his knee, set it on the workbench.

"I said I don't want to talk about it."

"All you need is some strange, son. Beats anything for forgetting your troubles. Beats electroshock."

"When did you get to be such the expert?"

"I had a couple stumbles in that area lately, but I turned over a new leaf. Got it all squared away."

Rory looked up.

"What kind of stumbles?"

Eli looked down, tugging on his beard.

"I don't want to talk about it."

Suppertime and the sky had that violet glow, the trees conspiring in the coming dark, melding into jagged battlements that lined the road. Rory was headed home. The Ford complained its way up the ruts, squeaking and groaning and clanking as it went. It was no easy task to cut a road out of the mountain, out of long-buried rocks and hardwood roots the size of men's thighs, and once you did it was under constant threat. No matter how smoothly graded the road started out, the mountain seemed always to turn it into a battered washboard that threatened to beat you to death.

A wagon was coming down the mountain, turning a switchback above him, and Rory pulled partway onto the shoulder, slowing for the car to pass. The driver's window was down. A tall bearded man sat behind the wheel, long-jawed over a loosened tie, while a shorter man rode shotgun. Their faces beamed in the failing light, their eyes red.

"*Hallo!*" shouted the driver as he passed. He held up a giant white hand in greeting. "*Tot ziens!*"

Rory stopped, but the wagon kept bouncing down the road, jaunty, the brake lights flaring now and again against the grade. The rear bumper had been caved, a chromium smile.

When Rory pulled under the chestnut, the tires crunched. Broken glass.

"Hellfire."

He looked up to the porch. Granny wasn't in her rocker. He got out of the car and found the old poke in the backseat and knelt, picking the shards from the grass, quickly, dropping them in the bag. It was a cobalt-colored bottle that had fallen. The best for catching spirits, Granny said. The wreckage glittered blue in the bluing dusk, like a burst planet. No mark in the chestnut's trunk, but he guessed the wagon's bumper had met the tree in reverse. He wondered what wares the salesmen had been hawking. Bibles, probably, with Christ's words stamped in red, or encyclopedias. As if either could survive the page-swelling damp of a high spring on the mountain.

"Ouch!"

A red slice in the meat of his thumb. The offending shard lay smiling, proud of itself. The cut began to bleed. Blood spattered the riblike sections of exploded glass, and Rory worked only harder, faster. He couldn't have Granny knowing what had happened, that one of the bottles had dropped. Anger crackled under his skin. She carried around such notions, such a truckload of lore and superstition he was forced to shoulder. Despite himself, he worried if bad luck was seeping invisibly from the blue wreckage of the bottle, uncoiling like a waking curse.

"Cut ye self?"

Rory looked up. There was Granny, armed with dustpan and brush. Her face shone like the salesmen's, as if smeared with oil.

"Got-damnit!" He was caught. He punched the door of the Ford, hard. He could feel the blood from his cut, squishy in his palm.

"Boy, what the hell's got into you?"

"Nothing," said Rory. He could feel the anger welling yet, his mouth shut like the safety valve on a steam boiler. He took the dustpan and brush from her. "Not a damn thing."

He finished cleaning up the glass and stood, the shards shivering in the pan.

"Let me ask you something."

"I ain't stopping you."

"How was it you let my mother grow up in a fucking whore-house?"

The light fled from Granny's cheeks, quick as a lamp put out. She looked suddenly old and gray, sad. Still, her chin was high, unfallen.

"Easy," she said. "I was a whore."

Rory wiped his mouth with the back of his hand. He couldn't stop himself, the words bubbling hot from his chest.

"You hadn't, wouldn't none of it happened to her."

"And you wouldn't never been born."

Rory stood.

"Well, ain't that convenient for you."

He turned and slung his body toward the house. The bottle shards rattled in the pan. The eye in the jelly-jar watched him come.

VI. HALF-MOON, WAXING

The cool shadows along the river became their place. They would cut out early from school, riding into the valley on crooked paths used by bootleggers and truants. They would pass the old nip-joints, many of them empty now, and smell the smoke of wood-fired stills. They would hear the crack of ax-felled timber, of rifles. Logging crews with strange accents were clearing the land, readying the valley for flood. There was talk of violence, even war. One time a string of men with painted faces crossed the path before them, quick as deer, carrying shotguns and clubs. Another time they saw men on horseback, wearing sackcloth hoods, rifles slung across their backs.

Still, they were never afraid. The valley was theirs. Their love gave them dominion. They were cloaked in power, fearless but for the throbbing heart of the other. Heedless but for the taste of mouth and tongue and sex. They were invincible, burned free of the shadows of death and men. The valley was being emptied just for them. Each day they looked for the parakeets, watching for a miracle of green fire from the hollows of a doomed tree. Bonni imagined the birds sweeping heavenward on the sound of Connor's violin, safe from the flood to come. He was writing a man in Washington about them, a museum curator, who had friends in office.

Each day they swam in the river, and Bonni kissed the purple storms of bruise on her lover's body. She ran her tongue in the grooves between his ribs, along the keel of his prick. She could not be sated. They tasted each other again and again, curled gasping in the leaves. They grappled in the green water, on the riverbank and under the trees. They were breathless, desperate, as if they knew such agonies must end.

CHAPTER 22

Granny May rose early, an hour before sunup, and began assembling the fire pit in the yard beneath the chestnut tree. First frost had come and gone, and the moon was growing fuller every night. It was up there yet, halved low in the sky. It would be full again in a week. The Hunter's Moon, when the beasts of the mountain crunched through the fallen leaves, the woods nearly naked of cover, and rifles cracked the brittle air. She had always held with killing a hog on the growing moon. It made the meat swell up when you cooked it. Kill one on the new moon, or when it was waning, and the meat would shrink in the pan, popping and spitting like a baby devil.

For the fire pit, she used the same stones she and Anson had collected in times long ago, the ones she kept stacked against the hoghouse. Rory was up before long, yawning as he came out the door, drinking the coffee she'd left him on the stove. He left his cup steaming on the porch rail and dragged the cast-iron wash pot from behind the house—a wedding gift from her mother. She had the fire crackling and smoking as the dawn light broke jagged over the hills. Rory set the pot on the fire and began sloshing it full of water hand-pumped from the well. He carried two pails with each trip, the water quivering in silver discs as he rocked his way across the yard.

Eli turned up soon, emerging from the trail at the edge of the meadow. He and Rory disappeared inside the hog-house, and she heard the pop of the pistol shot. They dragged the fatted animal across the yard, each holding a leg. They spread the hind-legs and pierced the ankle tendons on the outer hooks of a singletree, then threw a rope over a low-hanging branch and hauled the animal off the ground like they would an engine.

Granny stepped forward with her razor and sliced the big vein in the neck, just back of the jawbone. She set out a stone jug to catch the streak of blood, life-bright in the gray dawn. She would use it for making blood sausage. Once it was bled, they lowered the animal into the near-boiling water of the pot, going to work on the bristles as they heaved it steaming from the water. They dunked it again and again this way, scraping down the hide.

"Not too long," Granny told them. "Don't let them hairs set."

The sun found the bare skin glistening over the wash pot, pink-scalded and ready for the knife. Granny made the cut, a long red vent from nethers to chin, careful not to puncture the organs. She cut the entrails out, letting them fall glistening and ropy in the tub at her feet. She went to work cleaning them for use as sausage casing, and Rory and Eli disassembled the carcass with saw and hatchet. They put the fat they trimmed into a lard pot for rendering, and they got the tenderloins and fatback and middling meat, the shoulders and hams. They cut the ribs in two-inch sections on a board table they set up.

They worked over the carcass all day. They salted the meat white, their red-stained hands leaving little prints on the icelike shapes and hunks. They stuffed the casings with ground trimmings and tied them off into links to hang in the smokehouse rafters. They hung the rest of the meat on rafter hooks to cure. They talked little as they worked, and Granny didn't know if it was the nature of the work or something else.

She thought about what Rory had asked her, about his mother

growing up like she had. In a whorehouse. He had every right to ask. For years, she'd turned it over in her own mind. But it never seemed so bad back then. She'd had to keep a sharp edge on herself—anyone did around whiskey-drunk men—men with twice-broken knuckles and pinching fingers, cocks like billy clubs. But Bonni's room was high above the working rooms, hardly in earshot of the moans, the wincing of bedsprings. Only the girls even knew she lived up there.

She knew there were rumors among the men of a raven-haired beauty who stayed in one of the upper rooms, a white virgin kept from lesser eyes. But these were halfhearted, few. The men got what they needed downstairs, and cheap, and Granny and her kind taught them it wasn't a virgin they wanted. It was the talented few.

Still, she'd come over the years to wonder about the one theory she didn't want to. The one she could never say. She'd come to wonder if the townspeople were right. If her Bonni had turned to doing what her mother had done. If that's what she was doing with that mill boss's son. More than once, Granny had climbed gin-buzzed and sore up the stairs and stopped outside her daughter's door. In those late hours, the house empty of men, she'd sensed the girl was not in her room. That she'd slipped out the window, shimmied down the tree. That she was out, gone.

Never once did Granny twist the knob, check the room. She thought the girl should have a life of her own. Bonni was too quiet as it was, staying always up in her room, unaccompanied but for the birds and beasts she painted for herself, a kingdom perched shining on their white leaves of parchment. If she snuck out, then good. Granny never thought something so terrible would happen. She was dumb.

She was relieved when the baby was a boy, a quiet child like Bonni but harder to hurt, a body filled as if with grit and sand instead of softer jellies. He fell down the porch steps at two and never cried, poking at his bruises with a studious look. She was relieved because he would be better protected from the world, or so she thought. She'd forgotten how quick men could strike off in ways their own, heedless, giving no account of themselves or the things they sought.

Granny sighed and tried to think of other things, better things. She tried not to look at Eli's hands, how he went about salting that ham hock.

Eustace showed as the sun was falling, spilling red down the mountains like blood on teeth. He was not in his old flatbed. He was driving a deuce-and-a-half, a six-wheeled military cargo truck. Rory was sitting on the porch, trimming hog's blood from his fingernails with a penknife. Seeing the truck, Eli set down his flask and hopped from the porch, nearly skipping across the yard.

"What happened to the old one?"

Eustace climbed down from the cab and spat in the grass. He looked at the black scar in the fire pit, still smoldering, and the dark-dried blood that flecked the stones.

"Hog." He looked at the sky. "Moon's about right."

"Your truck," said Eli.

Eustace looked at him.

"Threw a rod last week."

"I could of rebuilt it."

"I know a man," said Eustace. "Quartermaster down at Fort Bragg. Got this one for next to nothing from him."

Eli was walking around the machine, squatting and eyeing, poking and prodding.

"Two-seventy straight-six," he was saying. "Two-speed transfer case. Rated for five thousand pounds off-road but they say she'll haul twice that."

Eustace watched him.

"Tailpipe's in back," he said, "if you're wanting to fuck it."

Eli straightened, jutting his jaw. His beard bristled like hackles.

Eustace ignored him, pulling the tarpaulin back on the night's whiskey.

"Well, boys," he said, rocking back on his heels. "Y'all best hop to it. I got business to attend to."

He hooked his thumbs in the straps of his overalls and rumbled up onto the porch, dipping to kiss Granny's cheek before stepping through the door. She got up and followed him, blowing smoke from the side of her mouth. Eli watched them, arms crossed, the wires of his forearms twitching beneath their thin forest of hair. He gripped his beard.

Rory leaned against the bumper of the truck, grinning.

"You ain't jealous, are you?"

Eli wheeled.

"Jealous? I got a date tonight. What I got to be jealous about?"

"I was meaning the truck."

Eli's hand dropped from his beard.

"Oh," he said. "Right."

Dark came fast into the valleys, a flood of shadows, daylight cut ever shorter as the season stretched on. The trees cascaded down from the mountaintops, skeletonlike, pooling rust-crowned in the valleys. The air bore an edge, an October bite that promised harder cold. Rory let it sting him as he drove, his face growing so cold he could hardly feel it, the skin stretched pale and taut as drum hide. A face that would not blush or skew, staring grimly on at the world skirling through the headlights.

He was into town early. He drove past the shothouses, the whorehouse, the filling station at End-of-the-Road. Past everything, down to where the road really did end. It led right on into the water, spearing into the shallows. Rory drove the car to the edge, the lake lapping at his front tires. He got out and sat on the hood and looked out across the flooded valley, the half-moon and attendant stars puddled on its shifting roof.

His lighter snapped. A cigarette burned from his lips.

He toyed with the little bandage at the ball of his thumb, looking at the lake. He thought of his days at Parris Island before being shipped out. He made friends with a Georgia boy, Coosa, raised in a family of turpentiners who spent their days in the lower flatwoods of that state, cat-facing pines for resin. One night Coosa took him to the Gutbucket, a long shotgun shack that squatted under the oaks of the Harbor River. Warped walls, salt-rimed sheathing, moths braining themselves against the yellow bulb over the door. The place seemed almost to throb, the pine planks given second life. He could see red fireflies of ash swirling in the darkness. Coosa went ahead of him, clad in the sharp creases of his service khakis, his overseas cap set rakish over one eye. A flat hand kept his tie in line.

They walked through a dark forest of limbs, men and women open-mouthed or grinning at the sight of Rory's skin. Their cheeks shone as if varnished. Blue reefs of smoke distorted the low-wattage bulbs. In one corner a man sat on a milk crate, playing the guitar. He was picking the strings with bulletlike fingertips. On his fret hand, a glass slide cut from a bottleneck. He slid the glass down the frets, and the instrument cried in his arms. The strings jounced and twanged, and the man rocked stiff-necked, eyes mashed shut, as if listening to a sermon. Finally he raised his face, features all twisted, and sang.

"Wish I-I, I was a catfish Lord.
Swimming down, down in the deep blue sea.
I wouldn't have nobody, nobody settin out hooks for me.
Settin out hooks for me.
Settin out a hook for me."

Rory thought of prowling the black river bottoms, his body bullet-sleek, finned for grace, and he thought of the deep of the lake. He imagined himself weightless down there, gilled and tail-flicking, hunting for the man that sired him, the girl his mother had been. He would glide over the valley as it once was, moonlight shafting down on old tin roofs and copper pots, junked cars and tractors and hillsides cavitied with the gravesites of the evacuated dead. His troubles a world away, muffled and small, heard as if from the dark of a womb.

He opened his eyes and unscrewed the lid of a jar. A sharp odor, dangerous almost, like nitro or cordite. A spirit that tasted like water lightning-struck, electrified.

He sipped.

A dream, he thought. If he ever made it to the bottom of the lake, it wouldn't be as a fish.

"Oh," said Granny. "Yes. Right there."

She was striving to put conviction in her voice. Eustace hulked red and huge above her, his fists driven into the mattress on either side of her head, his great white thighs slapping against the backs of her legs. He smelled not like a man, but something wild and old. There were beasts rumbling beneath his skin, loosed and unbroken, and great ageless stones. His sweat was oil that would crackle in a pan. His teeth wet, as if freshly honed. White gobbets hung at the corners of his mouth. He labored on, and she was wondering how her Anson would have been had he survived the war. How cold, bestial. She wondered how her Rory really was.

She looked up and saw beads of sweat quivering in the white-gray curls of Eustace's chest, a red apron flaring down from his neck. Getting close. He wasn't reaching where she needed him to—he never did—and she began to inch her hand down her belly, over the puckered flesh of her navel and down the long slope to the woolly mound between her legs.

He raised up on one arm and slapped her hand away.

"I done told you I don't like that," he said. "It ain't womanly, playing with yourself."

She bit her tongue, wishing her mouth wasn't the only place with teeth. She slid her hands up the backs of his arms and gripped the three-headed muscles there, opening herself yet wider beneath him, thrusting him home with her heels, hurrying him toward the shuddering, wheezing, spittling brink—his breath exploded from his mouth, a long roar. *Yes*, she said, *yes*. Eustace pulled out, as if still afraid of making children after all these years. Sons. His seed shot hot across her belly, his prick jerking like a hammer. Afterward he crashed onto his back, unwilling to touch the stuff come curdled and sticky from his own balls.

"Fuck," he said. His great chest heaved. His organ shrinking now, curling like a pig's tail beneath his belly. Granny rose and dipped a rag in the washbasin and began scraping him from her body. She parted herself slightly to clean between her legs.

"You don't got to be in such a hurry about it," he said.

She came back to the bed.

"Since when were you one to cuddle?"

"That ain't what I mean."

She knew it wasn't. She knew he would rather his seed dried across her flesh, glistening like the trails of slugs and snails she found on the porch of a morning. A web of dominion, possession.

"Let me ask you something." She lit a tobacco cigarette.

His nose turned up at the smoke.

"What?"

"That boy of mine, you think he's all right?"

"'All right'? The hell does that mean?"

"Means you've seen some of the same things he has. I want to know what it done to you. Whether you think he's all right."

Eustace started to rise.

"Woman, I don't got the time."

She grasped his wrist.

"Eustace. I don't ask you much."

He lay back, inhaling through his nose. His eyes reached through the ceiling.

"Please," she said.

"What it done," he said. "Time I was nineteen, I'd killed a hundred men, seen them tangled in bobwire screaming for they mamas while my Lewis gun tore them to pieces. They say a million boys went down in three days at the Somme. I don't doubt it. Tribes of monkeys in matching helmets with the worst toys their monkey-brains could think up, blowing one another to pieces. Thinking in they heads they was something special in the world, made in the image of God. A sick god, must be, or blind or cock-hard for the spilt guts of boys screaming his name. I seen them out beyond the wire in they gas masks and coal-scuttle helmets, scurrying here or there, and pretty soon they was just ants to me. I seen them as God might, from high up, hordes of them nameless, cut down at the end of my gun, pink-popped like under a magnifying glass. Pretty soon it wasn't nothing. I'd of killed them all if I could. They wasn't no god but my Lewis gun."

He rose from the bed and Granny grasped his arm.

"You didn't answer my question. About Rory."

Eustace's teeth ground sideways in his mouth.

"I just did."

He pulled on his shirt and overalls and boots and walked out, the house trembling as he went. She heard his boots clomp down the porch steps, his truck coughing to life in the yard. He gunned the engine once, twice, warming it up, and then she heard the churn of the tires in the dirt. She lay back, her cigarette half gone, and leaned to flick the ash through a knothole in the floorboard. She had another long night ahead of her, alone, and when she rose she would have to take down the shotgun. Who knew what evil might come to call. She could have asked Eustace to stay, but she'd asked a favor of him once tonight and didn't like what she got. She was not afraid, really. She was tired, heartsore, and she could not quit thinking of that blue bottle burst twinkling in the yard. She closed her eyes and inhaled, letting the smoke curl into the deepest branches of her lungs. Exhaling, she imagined the little black nests of doubt and fear being blown right out.

CHAPTER 23

Rory woke with a start. He was lying naked on a frozen plain, white under a white sky, and he'd never been this cold but once. Black stars hung above him, tattooed into the white vault of the heavens. No, not stars, for they were moving now, soaring, circling into a slow-turning cyclone of something: carrion birds. Ravens, black-winged, silent as what they sought.

He tried to sit up but couldn't. Couldn't will his body to move. Just his head obeyed, and he saw, on either side of him, men in uniform. Dead men, slack-jawed in some ultimate awe, staring blindly at this last unkindness. They were laid out on both sides of him, as far as he could see, a highway of the gutshot and disemboweled, the stabbed and bludgeoned and brained. He blinked and they were not men now but stone Buddhas in soldier's uniform, a thousand faces of serenity shattered and split and crumbled, as by chisel and sledge.

Sato was one of them, and Connor Gaston, and the Chinese infantryman he killed.

Rory cocked his head back and saw her coming. Christine. It was her and it wasn't. Because her hair was alive, writhing, a great mane of satin-black serpents that floated all around her face, like the halo of something evil. They had forked tongues, pink, and eyes like volcanic glass, and she wore nothing at all but them. He tried to rise again but couldn't. He was dead, frozen, like all the god-men laid out shoulder-to-shoulder. His brothers.

She stood over him, looking down, her sex flushed red like a wound, and he felt himself unfurling, hardening despite the cold. She lowered herself onto him, slowly, and buried her face into his neck. She began to move on him, skin to skin, and the serpents did, too. She slid high enough to unsheathe him, or nearly, then down. Again, again. The serpents all around him now, stroking him like the arms of lovers, an orgy he couldn't track. It felt so good, all of it, that he didn't care when the first one sank its fangs into his arm, the second his shoulder, the third his neck. Then all of them, loosing themselves into him. Their venom. He didn't care until the pain came and his blood was two hundred degrees, boiling, and he was only afraid she'd stop.

Rory woke with a jolt, something wet in his lap. His jar of shine lay overturned between his thighs, his trousers darkened like he'd pissed himself. He righted the jar and rubbed his eyes, but he still had whiskey on his hands. He got out of the car and leaned on the hood, trying to blink the fire from his eyes. Cars were parked all around his, humped under the moon, and he could hear the guitar thrumming from the filling station, see the shadows bounding against the blinded windows. The green dinosaurs on the pumps seemed to quiver, as if they knew what was coming. Rory gave his eyes one last swipe with the back of his arm and started inside, whiskey running in ant-crawls down his legs.

The preaching was over, the music begun. The believers were testifying in this tongue or that, man's or God's. Combinations thereof leapt from their throats. Some of them were pogo-ing in place, hands raised as if to snatch some spirit from the air, while others twirled and twirled, arms out, tornados of flesh that bounced among chairs and walls and shoulders. A few of the women had simply crumpled on the ground amid their skirts, bawling faceup into the light.

Rory stood in the back this time. He knew he smelled of whiskey but it wasn't that. He felt no part of them, a stranger, soot-blacked and lifeless as one of the stones that edged the slaughter-fire that morning. His eyes cut through the crowd, looking for Christine. He found her at the front, keening like something not quite human. Her eyes were mashed closed, her brow furrowed, her cheeks flushed with blood. Her mouth agape, like she was being tortured. Like the thing she most wanted in the world was slowly being given to her or taken inch-by-inch away. Rory watched, and he was jealous. A green-black burn, like venom beneath his skin. He wanted to be the thing alive inside her, searching her furthest places, not hurting her but almost. He wanted to be the deepest thing. The only.

He stepped back. He was alien to this place, a dark spirit in a house of light. He was the black thing that foo dogs guarded against, the slinking wickedness caught in Granny's bottles.

Pastor Adderholt, slick-haired in his shirt and tie, skipped sideways across the floor, his heels clicking the boards in a frantic, bowlegged jig.

"Ho Jesus!" he said. "Praise him!"

Rory walked out.

It was a cold night, and dark, and he thought he just wanted to go home but found himself sitting against the side of the building instead, sipping from what remained in the jar. He spread his back wide and flat against the wall, and he could feel the place throbbing like an engine against him. He swelled his lungs with air, and it echoed in the hollows of him, that power, in those empty places that never did fill up.

He left when the music died, before anyone could see him. He pulled out of the lot and into the road, gunning the motor. He glanced once in the rearview mirror, and he thought he saw a girl-like figure standing in the road behind him, watching him go.

Probably just a trick of the light.

———

The Sheriff's white coupe sat idling at the top of the road, plumes of exhaust smoke throbbing from the tailpipes. The spilled whiskey fumes still burned in Rory's nostrils, heady as nitro, and he gigged the motor as he passed, a machine growl, like one dog threatening another. Rory took a detour through town, passing down a street of long-fallen glory, the once-smooth pavement ribbed and potholed, the old Victorians clutched in thick jungles of weeds and mosses and creeper vines. Their windows were dark, their fish-scale shingles rotten and stained and missing in swaths, as if scraped by the hand of a careless fishmonger.

He stopped before the blackened ruin of the one at the end, the old bawdyhouse where Granny had lived in Prohibition times, his mother hidden in one of the upper rooms. He pictured her in the corner tower, in the tall window beneath the witch-hat turret, her shadow swelling spiritlike against the pulled blinds. That tower was nothing now but a black-charred spear, snared in a maze of low-hanging limbs, the house itself an obscene negative of what it once was. A white house scorched black. A miracle it even stood. It burned in the early thirties, not long after the valley was flooded and the sin-houses popped up at the end of the road. The story was, a drunk passed out with a cigar burning in his teeth, a whore working in his lap. The cigar fell on the bedspread, catching fire, and the girl didn't notice until she smelled the smoke. She said his thing never flagged an inch.

When Rory got his draft notice, he thought of climbing up into that tower. He did not know if he would come home again, and he thought he might find some part of his mother still up there. He might hear the echo of her voice. He did not even make it onto the porch. His foot stove right through the first step, the handrail collapsing beneath his hand.

The whole place seemed pasted together by memory, as fragile as that, the thinnest conspiracy of soot and ash that would collapse one day under the alighted feet of a sparrow or crow, implode on a band of trouble-seeking boys. All the past seemed like that, constructed of the most tenuous of blueprints, waiting for the wrong wind to blow. A history you could bring crashing down with a single kick to the right beam or post, a structure risen up in ash and smoke. He had the sudden urge to find that linchpin, that column or stanchion or joist, for if he collapsed the place it might swallow up the ghosts that haunted him, the shadows that roamed in his skull. All forgotten in a tangle of timber-bones.

Instead he pulled the car into gear and slipped away, easy on the throttle, as if even the throat of the engine could splinter the foundation stones.

The town square was empty, the grass browning at the courthouse steps, the darkened windowpanes of shop after shop rattling as he passed. He crossed the dam, the lights of lakefront houses scampering in and out of the trees. In the rearview mirror a panorama of the town in miniature, diminishing, the yellow-starred constellation of clapboards and shacks and mills powered by a hundred thousand acre-feet of river pent against the Gumtree Dam.

He was a mile out from town when the headlights appeared on his tail, growing fast, and he knew they were the same ones from the week before. The car rode right up on him, blasting high-beams into his mirrors like an insult.

Rory downshifted and stomped the gas.

The motor bawled, shoving him into his seat, the speedometer spinning wildly clockwise. The roadside trees shuddered, liquefying with speed, blurred to torrents of a parted sea. The machine was vibrating on every side of him, galled to fury, and he was not slow now, not crippled. The world was unspooling before him, delivered at the beckon of his foot. The trees fell away, the night rushing in over the fields, and he knew that old tobacco road was coming up.

He rounded a wide bend and began braking, downshifting, blipping the throttle with his heel to keep the rear wheels from locking up. He swung the wheel hard onto the red road and laid into the gas, shooting a rooster-tail of dust. His eyes flicked to the mirrors. The twin lights of his pursuer burst through the rolling cloud of his wake, undaunted. The road straightened, the tires kicking sideways over softer patches in the clay, Rory fighting the wheel to keep the car out of the ditches. The T-junction with the logging road was a half mile ahead, mere seconds. He sang between a pair of curing barns, tin walls flashing, and then he was out of the fields and into the hardwoods, trees thrust in phalanxes on every side. He spun the car onto the gravel of the logging road, balancing the machine on the very edge of itself, sliding, and came out of the junction hard on the throttle to find a roadblock waiting for him. Two cars parked nose-to-nose between the trees, flanked by government men with hats and ties and guns.

He flicked the wheel one way, then hard the other, stomping the hand brake to cut loose the rear end. The tail swung violently against the weight of the engine, the car reversing itself in a spray of thrown dust and gravel, and he hit the gas going back the way he'd come, peppering the roadblock with pebbles and grit. He broke from the swirl of dust and saw his pursuer turned broadside in the road, penning him like a bull in a stockade. It was Cooley Muldoon in his big green Hudson, smiling.

Rory started to let off the gas, beaten, then didn't. He drove the throttle to the floor. The smile drained from Cooley's face. He realized his mistake. He'd turned his driver's door to the front. He looked down at his gearshift, his arm working frantically, but there was nowhere to go. There were trees to both sides, crowding the road. The Hudson jerked, the brake lights flared—he'd stalled.

Rory was almost upon him, straight-legging the accelerator, when he mashed the brakes with both feet. The coupe hove hard onto its nose and plowed down the road, shuddering and rattling, squabbling for traction in the gravel. Slowing, slowing. The Hudson reared large in the headlights. The Ford bumped the driver's door with a jolt. A hard sock in the shoulder, like it had only been a joke.

It hadn't.

Cooley spilled out of the shotgun door and bolted upright, pointing over the roof, his face skewed monstrously under the moon.

"You're dead, Docherty! You hear me? Bring it on the track and I'll kill you legal. They'll be sucking you out that shit-can with a vacuum hose."

Rory leaned out the window, one hand palming the wheel.

"Wait till I tell everybody old Cooley Muldoon's a federal bootlicker."

Cooley started around the car, his hand on his knife.

"You won't be telling shit, Docherty."

The tax agents arrived first, crowding the windows on every side, all barrels and shouts. Rory placed his hands behind his head, winking at Cooley.

"See I won't."

The agents reached in and yanked him from the car. There were four of them. They pushed him up against the door and kicked his legs out wide and one of them went right for the pistol housed in his wooden leg. That surprised him. The agent dropped the magazine and worked the slide, jacking the chambered round into his palm. Rory watched him over his shoulder. The man was not large, but he had the close, balled shoulders of a footballer and a handlebar mustache. His hair was regulation cut, slicked from a part that gleamed like a scar on his head, like someone once tried to cleave him and failed.

Rory sniffed.

"Kingman."

The man looked up. His tie was wide and flat, his tweed trousers worn high-waisted and trim, their bottoms tucked into a pair of polished jump boots.

"You know my name. That's good."

"I knew they were sending some new revenue man down. I didn't figure him for the spitting image of the Archduke of Prussia."

"Ah, you know your European history."

"I know it didn't end so good for Franz."

"Yes, his assassination set off the powder keg of Europe, a war the likes of which the world had never seen."

"Well, somebody went to school."

"Yale."

"They teach you to use turncoats to run interceptor?"

Kingman flicked the extra shell into the trees.

"Perks to working for Uncle Sam, you might be surprised."

"Oh, I'm familiar. Got me this fancy leg, for instance." He knocked his wooden leg against the fender.

"Let up on him. We know he can't run off."

The agent retracted his forearm from the back of Rory's neck. Rory stood and shook himself off.

"You must of pissed somebody off, they sent you down here."

Kingman smiled.

"I wouldn't say that."

"No?"

"I have my uses. You see, there's been some mythmaking going on in the papers of late. Saying there's some kind of a camaraderie between you boys and us. Some kind of code. But we both know that's a lot of bull, don't we? We know one of your kind would kill one of mine just as quick as he'd take a piss, and has. So they decided it was time to quit pretending. That's why they brought me in. I'm not the pretending type."

"Some speech," said Rory. "You practice that with your prick in hand?"

Kingman smiled, planting his knuckles high on his waist. Rory saw he had a commando knife sheathed on the right side of his shoulder rig. A stiletto blade, double-edged, designed to kill. Members of the Office of Strategic Services had carried them—the OSS—Ivy League operatives who parachuted alone into France, organizing resistance groups and blowing bridges, assassinating enemy officers and collaborators.

Kingman looked out at the long ranks of hickory trees, each straight-spined as an infantryman.

"To become tables and chairs," he said. "What a shame."

"What?"

Kingman turned.

"A lamentation, Docherty. Now, let us see what you have in the trunk."

He held out his hand. Another agent stepped forward and handed him the keys.

"You do know I was *leaving* town?"

Kingman sighed and stuck the key in the lock.

"Mr. Docherty, I know all sorts of things." He opened the trunk. "I know, for instance, that you are easier to catch on your way out of town, when you assume the law won't be pursuing you. When you won't resort to oil slicks or caltrops or some other improvised device."

Rory didn't say anything.

The man patted the big tank in the trunk, a hollow thud.

"I know this tank is empty. I knew it would be. I could, of course, impound the vehicle and cut it open, check for residue."

"Whatever tickles your tackle."

Kingman smiled. It was a tired smile, as if he found all of this taxing. As if it pained him to be cruel.

"The thing is, Mr. Docherty, I know even more useful things. I know, for instance, a number of people in the state department of corrections. In Raleigh? They tell me the washouts, the ones let go for mistreating prisoners and such—several have ended up as orderlies in the state psychiatric hospital. Dix Hill?"

Rory stiffened.

"One of them oversees an inmate there. Bonni Docherty? You might know her. I tell you, those washouts from corrections, they're downright mean, some of them. Spend too much time in lockup alongside killers and pederasts. Rubs off on them, I guess. A contagion. They'll throw somebody in a straitjacket just for nothing. Beat them silly first, of course. Get them so bruised they have no way to lie on the floor that doesn't hurt." He sighed through his teeth, shook his head. "And what they've been known to do to female prisoners? With their batons and all? I tell you, it's medieval, son. Attila the Hun would turn his head."

Rory licked his lips.

"What is it you want?"

Kingman set his knuckles on his hips again, two a side. He leaned close to Rory's face.

"The big prize, boy. Eustace Uptree. And I want him tonight."

Rory rode handcuffed in the back of his own car, shivering, while Kingman sat shotgun. One of his agents drove. A crimson Hudson trailed them, the Muldoon machine impounded the week before—the one with a tommy gun found on the floorboard. A party of still-raiders couldn't drive a string of their own vehicles up the mountain, not if they meant to surprise anyone. Eustace had spotters posted along the roads, old women on porches who knew a government car when they saw one, who could discern the factory purr of a federal unit from the loping throb of a whiskey car. Some had shortwave radios, the dials already set.

Kingman looked back at him.

"Comfy, sweetheart? You want a blanket?"

They'd pressed him against the side of the car and stripped him of his shirt and jacket, then poured a canteen of water down his spine, over the swell of his chest. A cold cloak of pain, the icy fingers slipping beneath his waistband, sucking short his breath. Now they drove with the windows down, their elbows perched on the sills. Casual-like. The wind lashed and tore at his flesh, a frenzy of white teeth ripping him down to the bone. He could close his eyes and see wolves, ice-white, like ghosts of their kind. A whirlwind around him. A white death. He tucked his hands trembling between his knees, heaving, trying to flush blood into the dead pale of his flesh, to will some fire of rage or spirit into the upper branches of himself. Whatever might warm him. His jaw chattered uncontrollably; he could no longer feel his heart. It was buried deep in his breast, blue as a stone.

He thrust his chin at the men.

"I been cold," he said. "This ain't it."

Kingman just smiled. He seemed to know what he was doing. He would wring out the prisoner's energy, suck him dry of will. Leave nothing for deception. Hunger was good. Cold was better. He took his revolver from the holster beneath his arm and swung out the cylinder. One of the chambers was empty, where the hammer rested during daily carry. Kingman took an extra shell from his pocket and slid it home. A ring of brass rounds, glinting like small gold coins. He pushed the cylinder back into place and slid the pistol beneath his armpit, then looked over his shoulder at Rory.

"Never can be too careful up amongst the savages."

Rory tucked his lips inside his mouth. They were bloodless, he knew. Bluing.

"You really are a bastard, aren't you?"

"You just keep giving the directions, sweetheart, and try not to freeze to death."

Rory sat back and stared through the windshield. They were in the foothills now, the road rolling and twisting through vast forests of hardwood. Before them the mountains shouldered into the sky, the swells of a great black sea that might just swallow them up. A cold sea. Rory tried to find a lighted place inside him, a warm place, but couldn't. No temple. No chambers of stone. The warm rivers that ran him were going cold, darkening. He leaned forward, the words coming strange from his wind-numbed lips.

"You have to strong-arm Cooley into turncoating, or was he just itching to make a run at me?"

Kingman pulled Rory's little automatic from his back pocket. An ugly look on his face, like he'd sat on a wad of gum.

"Little of both, I suppose."

Rory watched him.

"What about that pistol? Cooley wouldn't have known about that. The Sheriff, maybe. He tell you? He the one set me up for this?"

Kingman sighed and put the pistol in the glove box.

"Sometimes a man's whole life is a setup, Mr. Docherty, and he doesn't even know it. It's a fate that always surprises. I've seen it time and again."

"And what, you think that's what I got coming down the pike?"

Kingman shrugged.

"I can't say yet, but I'm a curious man."

"You do know what they say about curiosity, don't you?"

Kingman cleared his throat.

"'Helter-skelter, hang sorrow, care will kill a cat, up-tails all, and a pox on the hangman.'" His eyes flashed over his shoulder, his mustache arched like wings. "The playwright Ben Jonson. *Every Man in His Humour*, fifteen hundred and ninety-eight."

Rory narrowed his eyes at him.

"You are by far the queerest revenuer they ever shat out of Washington."

"It's possible you have a narrow view of the world, Mr. Docherty."

Rory raised his cuffed wrists, cupping his palms.

"Here now, I thought I had it all just sitting in my hands."

Just then a white light flared through the cabin, and the green whale of Cooley's Hudson roared past them in the other lane. Rory could have sworn he heard, in the wake of the machine, the scream of a panther-cat.

CHAPTER 24

It was nearing midnight. The sky looked ice-glittered, a black veil cast over the sleeping ridges. Granny locked her jaws against a yawn, the cold sucked whistling through her teeth. Slowly she stood, her joints rusty and night-seized, popping and smarting as she rose. Her hips ground in their sockets like seeds in a mortar bowl. Her thighbones were a pair of heavy pestles. Her back an old king post, worm-eaten and warping under the raftered weight of her collarbones. Used to be, she could stay awake all night if she wished, neither man nor coffee needed to race her blood. Now she could use a little of each.

She set the shotgun against the wall and stepped through the door, feeling the aural heat of the woodstove. A tiny hell seen flickering through the slit windows of the iron door. A pot of coffee sat warming on top. She drained the dregs of her previous cup, then tilted the blue well of the mug to the firelight. She would see what signs the grounds had left, what emblem of the world to come. The firelight licked down into the enameled hollow, glazing a coil of remnant grounds, and the sign rose to the red dart of her tongue: *snake*. An omen of both deception and wisdom in the annals of sign lore.

She tilted the mug this way and that, the serpent alive and glistening in its well, and she saw that it had struck itself. She saw jaws unhinging over a ribbed tail, and she did not know which omen would be swallowed rattling into its throat. Wisdom or deceit. Surely one would destroy the other. She splashed a little extra coffee into the mug and swirled the grounds, erasing the sign, crushing the snake yet finer between her teeth.

The language of sign, like so much the old widow had taught her those winters back, seemed but a skeleton-work of knowledge, the final weights and portents waiting to be fleshed and filled. Granny knew the remedies she prescribed—the herbs and roots and tinctures—were in part but talismans, the faith that imbued them more powerful than any sum of their ingredients. A faith of which she must stand as her own deep well, ladling its remedy among they who came to her porch in supplication. Sometimes it was a heavy weight to carry, and little wonder the old widow had made her to sit three days alone under a falling snow. Somehow, the burden felt heavy tonight. Her body old.

She was refilling the cup when the planks trembled beneath her feet, bespeaking intrusion, a foot on the porch, and she was out the door in an instant, mug in hand, ready to cast a wing of scorching coffee into the face of the intruder. No one. The world was still. Then Eli appeared from the trees, as if tardy to the sound of his own steps on the porch. He was plodding, head down, and she knew right then that the holy-oiled ginseng had not worked as hoped. He stopped at the edge of the porch and raised his head, his face purpled and swollen like a battered, bottom-barrel fruit.

"Jesus, son. What did you run into?"

"About twenty knuckles and a steel-toed boot."

"Sit." She pointed to the rocker beside her. "Talk."

He climbed the porch steps and sat with his elbows on his knees, tugging two-handed on his beard. She watched him.

"I ain't got all night, son. Come now, spit it out."

He turned an eye up at her through the bruised flesh of his brow.
"You think it's easy to talk about?"

Granny sniffed.

"If you come all this way to waste a old lady's time—"

"Okay, okay. Jesus. Here goes." He cracked his knuckles. "I figured
it all started at the church supper last week. Rory, he met these couple
girls from the teaching college, were asking him about getting them
some whiskey. Said they had a party coming up. Well, him being all
knotted up on that Gumtree girl, he told them to come see me if it was
whiskey they were after. Which they done. And let me tell you, they
were a right fair couple of gals when they shown up, bright teeth, skin
like—"

Granny spat on the porch planks, a hard smack like a period. Eli
cleared his throat.

"Anyhow, I show up about nine o'clock tonight at this boardinghouse of theirs with a half gallon of high-proof, as agreed. I figure I'll
be the spark of the party, you know, bringing that stuff. But they
don't crack the door but a inch and slide the money through edgewise, tell me to leave the whiskey there in the hall by the door. I can
hear the party going on in there, glasses tinkling, people laughing,
and they send me packing with a two-dollar tip."

He shook his head, pulled on his beard.

"I was feeling pretty sorry at that point, so I had a quarter jar and
went on down to the roadhouse. Thought I'd see Edna-Lynn. I turn
up, there's not one but two old boys coming out her door—together—
the both of them tucking in their shirts. Big timber-cuttin' sons of
bitches, drunk as Cooter Brown. I been using the root like you told
me—anointin' myself—and I was pretty good down there, like old
times. Then she pulled me in the door and we start fooling around—
and just like that, it starts to wilting on me, sliding home like a worm
in the dirt. She goes to work on it and it's nothing doing, like last

time, but this time she doesn't have the patience. Says, 'I always did know you was a queer.' Kicks me out the door before I even got my trousers up.

"I come downstairs and there's them two timber-cutters bellied up at the bar, drinking whiskey, and one of them says with this big shit-licking grin: 'Some matter, bud? She ain't like that rope you was pushing?' I'd like to think I loosened a couple of his teeth with that first punch, but that was the only one I got in. I made their night for them, I reckon. They got laid and drunk and whupped a man's ass—it don't get much better on a Saturday night for a couple sons of bitches like that."

He shook his head, his breath shuddering from his lungs.

Granny patted his knee.

"Let me get you something for them shiners."

She started to rise but he caught her wrist, the shock of his rough hand dizzying her slightly.

"It wasn't the shiners I come about. It was . . . the other thing."

Granny looked down at him. Her blood drummed in her ears.

"I know, son. And don't you worry. I got just the thing."

She went inside and got down a jar of high wine she kept hidden on the topmost shelf, triple-distilled corn liquor north of 190-proof. She funneled a double-dram into a brown glass vial of ground ginseng and shook it for a full minute, then poured the tincture over a sugar cube set into a teacup. She opened a trifle-box and got out Anson's windproof lighter, the one made from a brass bullet casing—sent home with his body—and walked back outside. The wind had picked up, the black branches clutching one another, the bottles moaning. She held the teacup before Eli's lumped and broken face.

"Hold it steady," she said.

He took the cup in both hands.

"What is it?"

"Hush."

She snapped the thumbwheel of the lighter. There sparked an orange leaf of flame that quivered in the night. She set the potion alight, a cold blue cone of flame held hissing between them. Now she bent forward, close to his face, and blew it out. A curl of whiskey smoke.

"Drink."

He turned the cup to his mouth, both-handed, his long throat working down the scorched potion. His head whipped back and forth in the wake of the dose.

"Got-damn," he whispered.

She took the cup from him.

"Is that it?" he asked.

"No," she said. "One more thing."

She went back into the house and slipped off her boots and set the woodstove to roaring. An iron hiss traveled up the stovepipe. She slipped off the shawl she wore and the sweater, too, and she knew he could hear the pad of her bare feet along the cold-groaning floors, the squeak of the stove-door. When she stepped again onto the porch, she was wearing nothing save her old faded dress, the thin calico no help against the night. Cold, black fingers slid under her arms and along her ribs, around her neck and up the backs of her legs. Seeking her heat. She stood over him, and she could feel herself whelming with the power of old, his blood rising beneath her. His breath gone ragged in his throat. She watched his eyes widen as she unlaced the bodice of the dress. The flaps swung open like a set of saloon doors, her breasts uncaged. They hung shapely and blue-veined against her ribs, the nipples pert despite their age, buttonlike in the cold. His mouth was open, his eyes fixed, his face stunned as if with religion.

"See something you like?"

He nodded, not daring to blink.

"Yes, ma'am."

Her eyes roved him. Settled somewhere.

"Sporting a sapling down there, are ye?"

He breathed in, licking his lips.

"Oak," he said.

She knelt before him.

"Sounds serious," she said. "I might should take a look."

The men crowded the trunk of the crimson Hudson, divvying up their raiding tools: shotguns and axes, black-taped bouquets of dynamite. Rory stood shivering next to the warm hood of Maybelline, his shoulders rolled forward, his cuffed hands clenched at his belt. Between his palms, clutched like a talisman, was the key to the Ford, stolen while the men tightened their boot laces and filled their pockets with shot shells. He tried to control his body but couldn't. Shivers wracked him, again and again. The sound of clicking jaws filled his skull.

Here came Kingman, his tie tucked between the buttons of his shirt, a shotgun cradled in the crook of his arm. A man out hunting pheasant or grouse. He smiled.

"Douse him again," he said.

The water, so cold, hit him like a sledge. He fell to his knees, his hands thrust between his thighs. His lungs burned, fighting for air. He could see his spirit escaping from his mouth, ghost-white. He blinked, looking up at Kingman.

"I shouldn't warn you, but I will. He already knows you're here. He's ready. He's been ready for you his whole life."

Kingman fingered his mustache.

"Get up, boy, and start walking. Stop once, I'll shoot you in the back."

Rory rose, swaying on his wooden leg, and led them past Eustace's army truck, which was covered in a camouflaged net, and on into the trees. The same trail that he and Eli had taken. The half-moon was out, spilling ragged and broken onto the narrow path. The agents filed behind him like commandos on patrol. Rory could hear them breathing. He looked over his shoulder. Men in hats and ties and boots, their mouths smoking like barrel-fires in the cold. Their fingers were curled over the triggers of their pump guns. All but Kingman, who strode square-faced and hatless at their rear, his shotgun cradled against his chest. He winked again. Rory shook his head, looked away. The man no longer bothered him. None of them did. He was out of their domain, at the edge of their laws. Up here, it wasn't them he feared.

The trees made an archway before them, breaking onto the moon-lit bald. The rushing darkness of the creek gleamed silver-skinned under the moon, cutting through the purple meadow grass in a whisper. A cruel wind came lashing down the mountain, moaning like a ghost, burning the shivers from his skin. He could feel his blood slowed, darkened, the cold creeping into his hollows like a spell. Like it had in those other mountains, a world away, when you could only care so long. When you wanted only to sleep.

Above them stood the cloud forest of the summit, a black castle of spruce and fir. He started the raiders across the meadow, climbing toward the high trees. The meadow grass bent and whirled, catching long whips of wind, and Rory struggled, his boots slipping in the dirt. His hands were numb, his face. He felt strange to himself, bloodless, his flesh the flesh of a stranger. The stars watched him, high and bright, uncaring. The moon hung broken among them, like a hunk of hammer-split stone. They were halfway up the slope, following the creek that zagged through the grass, when Rory stopped. He stood flat-footed, closing his eyes.

Keep walking, boy, or you never will.

The rack of a shotgun behind his back, loud across the meadow, and he opened his eyes. He looked at the black forest above them, waiting. He knew what would come.

A flash from the trees, fire-colored, and the night shuddered and cracked, rent by a long streak of light. Now more of them, a staccato burst of flame from the trees, and the night was slashed with machine-gun fire, bright fates searing down from the summit like a judgment.

The earth rose up at their feet, black-sprung, and there was no cover. Rory turned, and the revenue men were already in flight, their shotguns useless at such range. They were running headlong for the lower tree line, tracers chasing after them like lightning unbent, chewing at their heels.

Rory tried to follow in their wake, hurling his wooden foot down the slope in his stunted dash, hearing the hot zip of rounds, the smack of lead in soil. His wooden leg buckled underneath him and he fell crashing and tumbling down the slope, end over end, limbs askew, seeing grass and dirt and stars. The creek wheeled overhead and he crashed into the glitter. Cold struck his temple like a hammer. He raised his head dripping from the creek, coughing water onto his chest. He was upended, his legs splayed on the bank above him. His foot gone, torn loose in the fall. A flat twist of trouser leg. The stars leered over him, swirling like glow flies, and he was so tired. He wanted only to sleep. He was numb. He was struggling, dizzied, fighting to right himself, when a new mountain rose against the sky.

Eustace.

The old man stood at the edge of the bank, an ancient machine gun shelved across his belly. The bipod was spread, the muzzle smoking. He swung the long boom of the liquid-cooled barrel toward Rory's face.

"Ought to do you here like a lame animal. Put you out your misery."

Rory looked down the black tunnel of the gun. He imagined himself blown mindless into the creek, his red selfhood sliding in bright threads down the mountain, into the valleys and lowlands. He didn't want it that way, but all his wanting had retreated down into the deep of him, so cold he could hardly feel it.

"It'd be a neat place to do it," he said. "Little cleanup."

Eustace crouched before him, a smile belying what was in his eyes. What malevolent light. His forked spoon peeked from the bib pocket of his overalls, shining, too, a mean little face catching the moon.

"You think you'll live from crossing me?"

"I didn't count on it."

"That's smart."

"They were threatening her."

"Granny?"

"Mama. That new agent, Kingman, said he'd have her straitjacketed. Beaten. Said they'd do . . . bad things." He took in a breath, held it, looked the old man square in the eyes, steady as he could. His only shot. "I done what they told me to, Eustace, and I would again. What would you do, it was your mother?"

Eustace looked at him a long time, his head slightly cocked. Rory could see thoughts silvering behind the man's eyes.

"The same," said Eustace. "I would of done the same."

Now the old man rose, swinging the barrel away from Rory's face. He looked down the slope, sure as a lord.

"How was it they caught you?"

Rory sat up. A cold ball of pain in his skull, heavy as stone. He tried to blink it away.

"They had another tripper in a pursuit car. That Cooley Muldoon."

"And they were waiting for you?"

"Yes, sir. I think they tried it last week, but I didn't bite."

"You seen the Sheriff tonight?"

Rory nodded.

Eustace swelled with breath. He lifted his head and squinted at the stars, as if reading them for signs.

"There's something I got to tell you, son." He paused, licked his lips. "Something I been keeping from you. About Sheriff Adderholt."

"Keeping?"

Eustace rubbed the top of the rifle with one hand, nodded.

"He's got to give them revenuers somebody every once in a while, just to keep his place. This new one, surely. Kingman. But that ain't what I'm talking about." Eustace looked out across the meadow, pinched his beard. "Goes back a long time," he said. "Having to do with that mill boss's son. And your mama."

"What about them?"

Eustace had a faraway look in his eyes.

"Winston Adderholt, see, he was the one done them all that."

"Say what now?"

"It was him," said Eustace. "That done it."

"That beat Gaston to death?"

"And struck your mama dumb."

Rory's eyes burned.

"No."

Eustace nodded again.

"Them Adderholt brothers was kings of the valley before they flooded it. Asa trucking the whiskey and Win—just a deputy then— running protection. Thought they was kings of the world. Win, he was sweet on Bonni, see, and she was the one thing he couldn't have. That only that mill boss's son could. So Winston, he went and showed them what was what."

"No," said Rory.

Eustace tugged on his beard and nodded.

"I'm sorry, son."

"How you know it was him?"

"I had ears in that valley, son. I know. There ain't much I don't."

"And you never did nothing?"

Eustace bit his bottom lip.

"The valley wasn't mine to law." He paused. "And it wasn't blood."

Rory turned his head and spat.

"You ever tell Granny this?"

Eustace shook his head.

"Never. She would of got herself kilt."

"And you weren't gonna tell me, neither?"

"I was waiting, son. Till you was old enough." Eustace twisted his pinch of beard into a knot. "Till I knowed you could do it."

"Do what?"

Eustace's breath fogged the air, clouding against the fir-darkness of the mountain. This great black temple of stone and tree and root. The cruel moons of his eyes glowed.

"What has to be done."

Granny woke, eyes wide, sensing a shudder in the night, a rapid-struck thunder from high on the mountain. An echo of her dreamworld or the one without. She looked to her bedroom window. Light flared, but it was early yet for dawn, and the word rose panicked against her throat: *fire.*

She threw off the quilt and scrambled from bed, Eli groaning as she crawled over him, his mind still thick with sleep. Her bare feet hit the floorboards and she raced across the cabin, taking up the shotgun and unbarring the door. She pounded down the front steps and around the back of the place, where she froze flat-footed as if before a wall. The stilted little house of the chicken coop was aflame, a hellish crown of licking tongues racing high into the darkness. The square door was latched closed, the ladder kicked away, the gray-weathered walls scorched in evil black teeth. They were climbing toward the sloped roof.

Eli came scurrying up beside her, still trying to buckle his trousers. Before he could grasp her arm, she was dashing toward the fire, unheeding of his cries, one arm shielding her face from the blaze. She turned the shotgun butt-first and drove the stock through the leaping flames once, twice, busting the crude wooden latch on the door. It swung open and out burst a long slug of smoke, a stricken hen squawking and flapping into the cold night that wouldn't save it. It tumbled to the earth, and then others poured out, a whole shot-blast of them arcing in smoking trajectories across the yard, crashing in spats of feathers.

Granny was already running again, her bare feet crunching in the frosted grass, Eli hollering behind her. She burst through the tree line, ripping through tangles of branches and brambles, the moon shorn ragged upon the forest floor. She could feel her flesh burning in tiger stripes of blood, the very trees and shrubs and briars trying to hold her back, a thousand outstretched arms. She tore through them, her night-gown falling away in white rags, a flock of tiny ghosts left fluttering in her wake, hanging on branches and thorns, and she splashed knee-deep through the icy sluice of the creek and knew she was close. She saw white lights dancing through the trees, bodiless as the spook-lights of lore, and then the hulking machine that bore them emerged from the darkness, growling in the road. A specter in a flannel shirt rose from where it squatted before a blown tire. It leapt across the hood and around the open door, one hand yanking the column shifter into reverse even as she burst from the trees and leveled the shotgun. The machine roared, retreating in a storm of dust, and the gun bucked against her shoulder. A fist-size crater opened in the center of the windshield, the glass spidering in long crooked legs, but the big machine kept backpedaling down the road, undaunted.

Her heart was crashing in her breast, her face burning like a skillet. She fell to her knees at the edge of the iron-spiked road, cursing her aim. Later: strong hands beneath her arms, lifting her upon jellied legs, and then the long ride through the night-forest, her limbs dangling from Eli's arms, her head against his shoulder, the white shreds of her nightgown sighting the way home.

CHAPTER 25

Rory stood behind the house, a quilt covering his shoulders. The black rubble of the chicken coop whispered smoke. The world lay undawned, cauled yet in hoarfrost, the chickens arranged in crazed attitudes about the yard. Charred lumps of beaks and feet, empty sockets of heat-burst eyes. He waited for anger to flame up inside him, or hate. None did. His blood ran cool despite the quilt, through lands strange and cold and mute.

Eli came up beside him, swollen-eyed, a steaming mug held out.

"Granny says for you to drink this here tea."

"I don't need it."

"The hell you don't. You look like something drug from the bottom of the lake."

"Just pour it out and tell her I drunk it."

"I ain't lying for you."

Rory took it. The mug tingled in his bloodless hands.

"What's in it?"

"Hell, I don't know. I seen her boiling something looked like root bark."

Rory sniffed the tea. Sassafras.

"She ought to be the one drinking the stuff."

"She is. I seen to that."

Rory lifted the mug to his lips but didn't drink. Instead he looked at Eli over the rim, the purple-blue lumps of his friend's face.

"Them timber-cutters did you a number."

"Least one of them will be shitting out a tooth or two this morning."

"What was it about?"

"Nothing. Just some drunks shooting off at the mouth."

"Well, I reckon we ought to be thanking them. They hadn't busted your face, you wouldn't been up here getting looked after. Who knows what might of happened to her."

Eli examined his boots.

"Yeah," he said. "I reckon so."

Rory leaned on his wooden leg. He'd climbed from the creek last night to find it standing where Eustace had been, a gun-shaped hollow in the calf.

"Listen, I need to borrow a car today."

"You want the shop truck?"

"Will it make it to Raleigh and back?"

"Raleigh? Hellfire, you ought to be in bed, not driving halfway across the state. I'm sure your mama would understand."

Rory looked down into the mug, the steam condensing like fever-sweat on his nose and cheeks. When he looked up, his face felt cold, hard.

"I'm not asking for advice just now, only if I can borrow a car."

Eli looked a long moment at him, then spat.

"You can borrow that Merc I been working on. Owner ain't paid his bill." He looked back toward the house. "Poor Maybelline."

The car was sitting in the front yard on shot-out tires. The windows were riddled, the glass blown pebbled across the seats and floor, the front grille punctured with a blast of buckshot. The work of vengeful revenue men. The machine had limped home, the flats skidding in the dirt, the engine running hot. Rory fighting the wheel, drunk with cold.

He scratched his neck.

"We best get to work on her directly. I need her ready come Friday."

"Friday?"

"For the speedway."

Eli straightened, his eyes widening under the bruised ledge of his brow.

"Change of heart?"

"I reckon."

"What about the cost?"

"I'll handle it."

Eli's eyes narrowed in their purple pouches.

"What about Cooley Muldoon?"

"Him, too."

"You get on that track, he's liable to kill you."

Rory sipped once from the mug, a hot root reaching down into his belly. Warming, grounding.

"He's liable to kill me if I don't."

He poured out the rest of the tea undrunk, a steaming patter in the grass.

He thought of his mother as he drove. She'd sat three days in that old cabin by the river, staring at the boy they killed. They had to peel her from the floor, the blood glued to her like a shroud. She said nothing, her voice fled from her throat. Her head swollen. Her eyes vacant, as if her spirit had been loosed with the dead man's, her body shuffling on by rote. At first, the doctors said it was only the shock. That she would snap out of it, the dam broken, her voice returning in a bright gush that never came.

Rory was wild with worry, imagining how they might have hurt her. Kingman calling in favors among the orderlies, a burly ex-screw in yellowing smock who'd more than once stepped into a cell and keyed the lock, dropping a thick wad of spit like a gift onto the end of his baton. He thought of what he would do to such a man. How he would paint the walls with his blood. He knew Kingman was likely bluffing, but his heart wouldn't listen. It was going like a siren, wailing in his chest. He could see stars at the edges of his vision before he realized he was holding his breath.

He breathed in, out. He tried to remember that temple in Korea. The safety, the calm. He could not seem to find the place in his mind. He stepped only deeper into the accelerator, the oaks of Raleigh lashing past the windows. He was constantly yanking through the gears, roaring past slow-going church traffic. Twice he went up over the curb; stop signs were but suggestions. The Colt, which Kingman had left in the glove box, rode shotgun. In the parking lot of the asylum, Rory hiked up his pantleg and fitted the gun back into the cutout of his leg.

She was the same as always when they brought her out. Unhurt, if you could call it that. A shy, gentle creature still unaccustomed to the scraping chairs and chatter of the visiting room. Her eyes bright, unguarded, as if someone had broken the shield she carried against the world. As if the light inside her could be seen naked, leaking out.

She put her hands on his and smiled.

"Hey, Mama," he said. "You been doing good?"

She nodded, her black hair falling forward to frame her face.

"Nobody's been mistreating you, have they?"

She shook her head.

He kneaded the knuckles of her hands under his thumbs. Bony ranges underneath the skin, a whole mountainous country he hardly knew.

"I come to tell you something, Mama." He looked down at their clasped hands, then up. Her eyes shone, waiting. "I know who it was that done it."

She cocked her head slightly, still smiling.

"Who murdered him." He paused. "The Gaston boy."

Her chin began to slide sideways, as if in deflection.

Rory leaned closer, lowering his voice.

"I'm going to kill him."

Her cheek was fully turned to him now, her eyes wide, like a shooed-at horse. Her mouth opened but nothing came out. She began to shake her head, her hair rising in dark wings to either side. Her grip on his hands tightened. She was so strong it frightened him. An otherworldly strength. A clinging desperation, as if she were being ripped away from him.

Then she was.

The orderlies had seen what was happening, that she was having some kind of fit. Two of them came white-smocked to pull her from the table, but she wouldn't let go. She had Rory's hands, tight-clasped, and he hers. The tabletop was rocking beneath them, the chairs knocked skittering across the floor. Then the duty nurse came hurrying from her station, needle in hand, and Rory looked into his mother's face. Such fear in her eyes, the orderlies might have been monsters coming to drag her into a well. The nurse pulled the hood off of the needle, flicking the vial, and Rory let go, his limp fingers sliding through her hands, and the orderlies had her now, each wrangling an arm. They dragged her kicking and writhing from the room, her shoes squeaking on the floor. Just before they reached the door she looked right at him, and it was like he was the thing she was afraid of. The monster. The tendons of her neck flexed, a sudden deepening of vents and hollows, as if she might speak some words wedged hard against her throat. Then she was through the swinging doors, gone.

Rory stood, his mouth dry, his heart thumping. There did not seem to be enough air in the room. He found the head orderly, Alvin, in the hallway that led to the waiting room.

"What happened in there?"

Rory sniffed and held out an envelope.

"Don't worry about it."

Alvin looked up the hall, down. Pebbled-glass doors, a drinking fountain, activity sheets curling on the walls.

"You already paid this month."

"This is something extra. You got any ex–prison guards on staff?"

Alvin slid the envelope into the pocket of his smock.

"One or two."

"They work in Mama's ward?"

"No."

"I want you to keep an extra-special watch on them for me. Make sure they don't try and get near her. Can you do that?"

Alvin tapped his pocket.

"For this I can."

Rory nodded.

"You ever wonder where that money comes from?"

"I'm not the curious type."

"That's good. But there's one thing I want to make clear. You let something happen to her in here, you better start watching for me. I'll be the one shows up with a machine gun. You ain't seen crazy till then."

Alvin raised his hands.

"Hey now, there's no need for any of that."

"You better hope not."

That night he lay a long time in bed thinking of the Sheriff. He considered the man's every feature from memory, like he would a girl's. The sharpness of his face, carved as if with a knife. The veins that reached into his collar like roots, bulged like they might burst, the smile lines so neatly creased. This king of the valley. This killer. Rory could see himself reflected in the twin mirrors of the man's glasses. He wondered if the man saw Connor Gaston in his face, risen again. The mystery of blood, carried through the long dark of the womb. He wondered would the man be surprised when his fate revealed itself, like that Chinese infantryman under Rory's shovel. Or would he seem only to expect it, as if he'd seen it coming long ago, a seed sprung into man?

Granny watched him with one eye, tapping her pipe against the heel of her hand. A storm hung throbbing over the valleys to the east, silent from this distance. Rory sat in the rocker beside her, watching, a jar held nearly untasted between his black-stained hands. His eyes were faraway, coal-dark save reflected veins of lightning. He seemed colder since his night on the mountain, more remote, as if he'd never really come down.

She cleared her throat.

"How's the car coming?"

"Fine," he said.

"How about that town girl, what's-her-name?"

"Christine," he said. "Haven't seen her."

"Them young ones, you got to keep 'em keen. She don't see you for too long, she's likely to find another buck."

"Yeah."

Granny looked down at the thin cuts that seamed her arms. They were scabbing now, the flesh already forgetting her dash through the woods even if the rest of her hadn't. She felt tangled yet in brambles, her world turned turvy, her bones heavy.

"You wouldn't believe who come by the house today while you were down at Eli's. Couple of them housewives from the church, wondering could they buy some that butter I put in the cake. Might come a day it ain't just whiskey you're hauling to them town-people."

"Might."

She could feel him slipping out of her grasp. Like Bonni had. She looked down at her hands. They were so old now, the gnarling hands of a crone. She began to reach for her pipe.

"You ever wonder who done it?"

Granny stopped, pipe in hand, and looked at him.

"Every day."

Rory sipped from the jar, keeping his gaze leveled on the far-off ridges, the blue wires of lightning racing above them.

"Somebody like that, seems they must have something in them, some evil none of the rest of us got."

Granny looked at him, then out at the darkened mountains, the leaves all browned or fallen. The bottles jingled in the spirit tree, storm-livened, as if to tell her something.

"More the opposite, I think. It's that they're missing something. They was born without it and won't never have it. They don't even know to look."

Rory squinted as if he'd caught sight of something in the distance, a lone bird hanging tiny and dark against the storm.

"Sure," he said. "That could be it." He took another sip from the jar, swallowed with his mouth open. "Could be I got some of that in me. Some hollow. Like those bottles up there, just waiting for whatever evilness happens past."

"You don't."

She flashed her eyes at him, to light her words, but he was looking at the glass jar in his hand. She saw the veins standing from his arm, risen like tiny worms or snakes.

"Could be I was filled up once, but it evaporated. Got poured out, maybe." He looked out at the mountains, so sharp and black. His hand was shaking, like he might crush the jar in his hand. "Or froze."

"Rory," she said. "*Rory.*" He looked at her, but slowly. She pointed her pipe at him. "It didn't, son. It had, you wouldn't be asking. That there's proof enough."

He looked away, back to the coming storm, his jaw locked shut.

Rory sat behind the wheel of his car, the rain hammering the roof, a barrage of tiny lead mallets. He was watching her house. In the wet night, the bungalow glowed like a lantern, a refuge of warmth and light. The mongrel dog lay beneath the porch steps, his chin on his paws, watching the sky come down. On Rory's knee sat a store-bought steak still wrapped in butcher paper. In his mind a dim plan to feed the dog, then shimmy the drainpipe and knock on her window. He would apologize. In this vision of the future she would let him into her room. She would be waiting for him, knowing he would come. She would pull him through the window, shaking, and sit him on her bed, peeling away the wet clothes that kept him so cold. She would see his leg. She would unbuckle the straps, and she would see the place that shamed him, the giant elbow where the rest of his leg should be. This appendage he kept hidden like a vestigial tail or pair of webbed feet. The flesh of it uneven, the skin scarred, as if shaped by the hands of an amateur potter.

She would touch him there.

I'll sew you a sock, she would say. *So it won't chafe.*

The stone of his heart would burst into flame. They would be a knot of flesh on her bed, trying every which way to bind themselves tighter, harder, their mouths bit shut so the house wouldn't hear.

Now a shape rose against the yellow light of her window. He blinked, watching. He wondered whether a younger Sheriff had watched his mother from such a vantage, devising his own plan of possession. Revenge. Cutting eyeholes in a sackcloth hood, loading a set of ax-handles in his trunk. Rory tried to think of what he would say to Christine, but the words would not come. They were shapeless stones in his mouth, indecipherable syllables like the language of tongues. Some things were too big to be spoken. Too terrible or sweet. No words could hold them. Only silence seemed honest.

Slowly he unwrapped the butcher paper, the hunk of meat sitting bright and bloody in his hand. It seemed almost too red, like store-bought beef always did, like some iron-rich ore from the earth's crust. He rolled down the window and tossed it, high and arcing.

The mongrel came tearing from under the porch, arriving just after the steak splashed into the yard. He stood slunk-shouldered in the rain, knifing through the offering. Rory turned and slid behind the wheel. He fired the engine and throttled gently away.

CHAPTER 26

The infield of Gumtree Speedway shone beneath the floodlights, a city of steel and chrome and glass that rattled and quaked. Grease-faced men bent beneath raised hoods, tuning and feeding the iron hearts bolted in their keeps. The motors idled and raced by turn, alive with power, speaking in their own cruel tongue. The air fairly growled above them, the streamers snapping in the wind, the track red as a wound in the earth.

Rory pulled them into an open slot and cut the engine, stepping out. The air stung his nostrils, that heady mix of burnt rubber and gasoline that smelled like speed or war. They'd been working since sunup on the car. It wore bigger rubber in the rear now, tires so meaty and new you could almost eat them, and a triangular screen of chicken wire covered the nose, protecting the radiator from flying debris. The window glass was gone, along with the liquor tank and bulletproof plates, and the headlights each wore a black X of tape to keep them from shattering. Rory had bought a surplus flight helmet and pair of tank commander's goggles from the Army-Navy store in Boone. He wondered if they might have been Big Carling's once.

They knelt beside the car with a roll of white tape, affixing their race number to each of the doors. Other drivers cruised past in their race machines, spitting or nodding as they went. Rory worked to line up his numbers with the doorjambs and body lines, cataloging the most offensive of the squinters as they passed, the ones most likely to give him trouble on the track. Anything to distract him from the plot humming darkly in his mind. The thought of what he was going to do tomorrow night. What had to be done.

Soon he heard footsteps come thumping along the ground. He looked up to see Cooley Muldoon with a kinsman on either side of him, their cheeks pouched with chaw. The boy spat in the grass.

"Maybe you ain't as yellow as I thought, Docherty. Or should I say *chicken*."

Rory rose, wiping his hands on the front of his trousers.

"How's your windshield?"

"Oh, had to get me a new one this week. Somebody threw a rock at it."

Rory nodded.

"You don't say? Some arm. Too bad they didn't aim a little to the right."

Cooley shrugged.

"Bad for you, maybe."

Rory stepped closer to the three men. Eli watched him from across the car, eyes white in his purpled face.

"I come to give you a shot in return. That's what you want, ain't it?"

"Christmas come early, far as I'm concerned."

"I want this to be the end of it then. Whatever happens out there, it's peace between the two of us after."

"If there is two of us after."

Rory nodded. "If. And if there isn't, you let alone my kin." He extended his hand.

Cooley shook hands with a lopsided grin.

"It's warm where you're going, Docherty."

"You're wrong there, brother." Rory shook his head. "It's cold."

Cooley cocked his head, confused, but Rory was already turning back to the car.

They had just finished taping the numbers onto the doors when a race official showed up. He had a seed cap perched high atop his head, a clipboard in his hand.

"Qualifying," he said. "Ten minutes."

Eli began double-checking tire pressures and lug nuts and hose clamps, whatever he could get his hands on. He fiddled under the hood, holding his breath, letting it out in stressed little chuffs like a steam engine. Things rattled and clanked under there, accompanied by grumble and cuss. He stood finally, gripping the squirrel's tail of his beard in one fist.

"Ready."

Rory nodded, donning his flight helmet and goggles. He fired the big motor and rumbled out of their spot, between the parked cars, and onto the pit lane. An official waved him on, and he throttled the car out onto the straight. It was three times the width of the country lanes that kept him fed, banked like a bowl to keep the cars from flying out. A road looped endlessly back on itself. In the flag stand stood three old men with stopwatches, their faces squinted and pouched beneath ratty newsboy caps. The wheezing gods of horse and dog and automobile tracks, meting out judgment with yellow thumbs. Rory stepped hard into the machine, the ambulance motor throating its power, the tires chewing for traction. He tore around the track in big billowing circles, casting the car sidelong through the turns, ripping a red tornado of dust from the track like some kind of clock-crazed fool.

He qualified seventh out of twenty-seven racers, impressive for a street-legal liquor car. When he rolled back to their parking spot, the motor thumping, the looks of the other drivers said as much. Eli was beside himself. He thrust his arms over his head and whooped like a savage, raining whiskey on himself. He licked it off his face and pushed himself through the open window and kissed Rory on the cheek.

"Hot damn!"

Rory cut the motor.

"It will be a whole other thing with other cars on the track."

Eli wasn't listening. He was caressing Maybelline's swelled fender, a look of awe on his face.

The moon rose against a black sky, imperfectly round, not full but nearly. It looked chunked from ice; the stars, too. The stands were full despite the cold, the spectators sitting with blankets over their knees and mittens on their hands, drinking whiskey and honey steaming from metal thermoses. Rory fit his helmet. It was cue-ball white, like those the jet pilots wore in their fighters over Korea. He fastened the chinstrap and left the goggles hanging at his throat to prevent them from fogging.

The infield was alive with open-class racers making their way to the grid. Modifieds. They seemed clumsy at such speed, each throbbing and jerking like something on a leash, not built for going slow. Their idles unsteady, irregular, on the edge of stalling—the sound of hot motors that lived at speed. Rory got in and cranked the engine. It turned over twice and caught, roaring, the big pistons chugging in the block. He rapped the throttle and the car shivered on its springs, torqued clockwise, the supercharger whining under the hood. He slid the gearshift into first. Eli put one hand on the roof and looked in, a jar of whiskey curled against his chest, his breath near flammable.

"You break any more than a leg out there, I'll shoot myself and whup your ass in hell."

They clasped hands. Rory tried to pull his away but Eli wouldn't let go, not yet, staring home his words.

"I'm serious," he said.

"I know," said Rory.

He let out the clutch, easing the car forward, their arms tautening until they snapped apart. He rolled out of their spot, between rows of jacked-up machines, making toward the starting line. The car grumbled as it went, such violence waiting to be loosed.

The cars quaked and fumed on the grid, junkyard resurrections professing allegiance to car lots or wrecking yards or speed shops, missing hoods or doors or fenders, their bodies crinkled and soldered. The drivers sat masked and inhuman as their cars beat ugly and loud beneath them, throbbing in place. A green Hudson coupe sat on pole.

Cooley.

Rory pulled the goggles over his eyes, drew the bandanna over his mouth. He watched the flag stand, keeping his grip light on the wheel. The world trembled.

Green.

He jumped off the line, roaring blind through sudden dust, and he thought he should let off the throttle but didn't. He planted it, sliding wildly in that red-gone world, braced to wreck, and then he was out of it under the bright lights, booming toward the first turn, the machines stretching into a long steely chain behind him. The cars ahead of him broke into the turn, one after another, wheeling like pinballs into a slot, and then he was flying tail-out through the corner himself, steered opposite the turn, the infield rotating before him as by merry-go-round. The tires grabbed coming out of the corner and he yanked the shifter into third, flat-footing the accelerator. The car surged down the back straight, barreling past a slower coupe as the gauges raged, needles quivering, and then he was hurling the car broadside into the next turn, fighting the wheel, the tail whipping and thrashing for traction beneath the mighty power of his foot.

Six cars ahead of him.

He ripped through the turns and sang down the straights, merciless, hoping the car would hold. In front of him a wheel sheared free of an axle, the crippled machine plunging in a blast of dust, flashing its undercarriage, the orphaned wheel bounding up off the track like a jackrabbit.

Five cars ahead of him.

The Ford rattled with speed, enraged, slashing past slower machines. The drivers tried to bump him as he passed, to cut and roll him, their silver-toothed grilles flashing just shy of his bumper. Down the long straights the motor charged on and on, an endless well of power. An engine blew two cars head, a cloud of bluish smoke unraveling from the hood, as from a stricken aircraft.

Two cars.

Ahead of him thundered a hoodless coupe, the header pipes slashed upward like gleaming tusks. The driver's face shone in his car's tiny round mirrors, blocking Rory whenever he tried to pass. Rory watched the great squared-off tires bouncing before him. They were unfendered. Coming down the back straight he pushed right in on the car's bumper, sucked to greater speed, then cut hard to the inside, his bumper grazing one of the rear tires, the coupe sent slithering in the dirt.

Second place.

They were more than halfway in now, fifteen laps to go, and the green rump of the Hudson floated just in front of him, bucking and sawing over the red-churned surface like a big animal in flight. They ran together in turn two, clanging and bullying, Rory unable to get by. He wanted to pass Cooley clean, by motor and skill, so the boy couldn't run his mouth. He drove right up on him coming down the front straight, bumpers kissing, then dove low in the turn, sliding in the rutted clay. The Ford was tail-happy, fishtailing dangerously as he came abreast of the Hudson, but he kept the power on, feathering the throttle to keep from spinning, then floored it as the track straightened, pulling ahead.

First.

He cut a look in his mirror. Too much dust to see Cooley's face, but he could imagine the boy's wicked grin hanging over the down-turned mouth of his machine. Rory looked away, but the Hudson crowded his mirrors, right on him, its brightwork glaring like a threat. The boy would drive him into the trees or pits. He would roll him, crush him to jelly in his seat. Rory drove the car harder into the turns, deeper, torturing the car to speed.

Ten laps to go.

Cooley bumped him twice, hard. Rory felt caught in a whirlwind, his machine whirling and screaming through this crazed orbit of power. He could feel cooley's desperation, the Hudson diving and missing again and again. Being driven like a weapon.

Eight laps to go.

Coming out of the last turn, the gleaming arc of a torn-away fender stood in the racing line, upended, leering like a giant metal rictus. Rory yanked the wheel hard to miss it and lost control for a long moment, the wheel spinning through his fingers like the helm of a rudderless ship, the car snaking this way and that, weightless almost, showing him first the stands and then the pits. He feared it would catch a rut sidewise and roll down hard on its roof, his world collaps-ing in a steely fist, his body crushed bloody. He fought the wheel, straightening the car, and went.

Five laps to go.

They slid all over the track, hurtling headlong toward the corners, throttles pinned, wrecking themselves through the turns. Other racers scattered before them, loose-tailed like animal prey, and they pushed past the slower ones, bumping and knocking without qualm. Cooley kept diving in on Rory in the corners, trying to use the Hudson's big nose like a ram, but he couldn't carry enough speed to upset the Ford.

Three laps.

They blasted past the grandstands, the bright and terraced faces, and Rory steered into the first turn, the hood pointed toward the infield, the tail kicked out. He looked in the mirror and saw the Hudson blow the turn, coming down on him like a missile. Cooley drove the big car straight into Maybelline's left rear wheel, never slowing. Rory's world went sudden sideways, the car wrenched out of his control, spinning, and he spun fully around in time to see the Hudson streak up the bank, unable to stop, and launch straight through the board fence, over the edge and into the trees.

The Ford came to rest tail-first at the bottom of the track. Rory jumped out and started up the bank. The cars kept barreling past, oblivious or indifferent to the wreck, a flood of churning metal that didn't stop. He kept climbing the bank, hobbled as if by ball-and-chain, holding one palm upstream. The cars parted before him, a split river of them glaring under the lights. They missed him by inches, blaring horns who had them, and he didn't stop.

Rory reached the top of the track and froze. He stood in the blasted section of board fence, looking down into the trees, and pulled the bandanna from his face. He could feel them at his back, all those spectators with cold-filled lungs, waiting for some sign of what he saw.

Slowly he took the pistol from his leg and raised the barrel. He fired three times, evenly, into the night sky.

Rory followed the splinters and boards that littered the slope, making for the wreck steaming in the trees. One of the rear wheels had been wrenched off the ground. It spun on and on, the axle gears whining in their housing. The nose was smashed against a tree, crumpled and hissing, and Cooley lay spilled across the hood, the windshield gaped about his waist, his arms outflung in final embrace of the machine that carried him here. He no longer looked like himself. He looked like some new creature entirely, something bad-birthed and bloody, with its joints in the wrong places.

The pistol dangled loosely from Rory's hand. He dropped it. The helmet, too. He found himself on his knees before the wreckage, his head pressed against the fender. One of Cooley's hands hung above him, palm out, fingers splayed, their tips bright with blood. It began to twitch and flutter, whelmed as if with holy power.

When the rescue workers arrived, they found Rory curled in the grass beside the car, a smear of blood gleaming on his forehead.

VII. HUNTER'S MOON

The leaves fell from the trees. The understory thinned, rattling brittle-boned under a cold breath of wind. The river became a river of stone they could not swim. They made fires on the riverbank, wrestling naked before the throbbing spear-point of flame, but they were uneasy. Exposed. Sounds became sharp in the falling season, unmuffled in the raw air, and you could see shadows moving far through the trees. They felt like prey, watched from afar. They had lost the army of green shields that kept them hidden, protected.

They found the cabin not far from the hollowed sycamore, hidden up a narrow path. The windows were mostly broken, the floor scattered with dead leaves that crackled like fire underfoot. There was a corn-husk mattress on the floor, a sawhorse table against a wall, a stone fireplace blacked with age. A few hand tools scattered about, ambitionless.

They made the place their own. They swept the floors and aired out the mattress. They brought quilts from home. The chimney smoked. The windows were gold-lit, like beacons in the valley dark. They whispered of the future. Connor would go to college, and Bonni would come. They would be married. They would need nothing, having each other. The museum curator had told Connor that, if he found a living Carolina parakeet, he would save him a job.

A night in October. The moon was full, skull-bright in the black sky. Bonni had snuck from the high turret of her room in the bawdyhouse, had taken the old paths into the valley to meet her lover. She'd made a fire in the hearth, laid out rolls on the sawhorse table, a chunk of butter. She held her hands to the flames, so she could run them warm under her lover's shirt, chasing the cold from his flesh. She was waiting when she heard heavy boots on the porch.

CHAPTER 27

Rory walked into the service at its peak. He did not look left or right. Did not smile. He walked straight down the aisle, a determinate figure among the shining faces, the arms that twirled and flamed. He was wearing church clothes, his hair slicked clean. A healing pink slash at his thumb. Earlier, at dusk, Eustace had brought the weekly load. The old man had seen the double-bore shotgun lying across the backseat of the Ford, the barrels sawn slightly short for close work. He nodded once to Rory, who spat in the grass.

He walked now to the front of the congregation. Pastor Adderholt was there. He was in a fury tonight. Sweat poured from his face, sprung as if from a leak in the crown of his head, and his raven hair was wild and unkempt. One foot beat the floor faster than the other, as if he were skipping in place, and he wore a banded canebrake rattler around his neck with the swagger of a new god. The tail rattled just beside his ear, and he seemed to be listening closely, translating, his eyes mashed closed in concentration.

"Praise Jesus!" he said. "For that we shall live in his living blood! For that we shall drink of his Spirit and be saved from the wretchhood of these fleshy rags!"

Yes, brother.

"For that, in his power, he shall maketh a bed for us in this world and the other, so that we shall have respite in the blackest storm."

Amen, brother.

"For that we shall breathe of his breath, for that we shall bleed of his blood, for that we shall see of his eyes, and know a vision that is not of this world, but beyond it."

Hallelujah.

"For that we shall know his name is *God*, and have a name to call in our wilderness. Our wildness. A living light that doth shine on, never doused!"

Amen.

When the preacher opened his eyes, Rory was standing before him. On a folding card table in the corner stood a line of lard cans and wooden boxes, brought here weekly by the congregants, should the Spirit move them so. Rory was holding the can that said ORNIAS. It purred like a motor in his hands. Something atomic, no need for pistons or gears. Pure energy, encapsulate.

There was a momentary lull in the ocean of sighs and shrieks, and Rory saw a flicker of something in the pastor's living eye: fear. But just as quick it was gone, and the man was grinning wildly, like a fiend, both eyes expectant, welcoming this new evil into the room. This new test. The spirit surged around them, and Christ was doubly exalted in shouted tongues.

Rory pulled off the lid.

The serpent lay coiled and writhing like a giant possessed rope. Rory slid his hand beneath it and let the can fall away; it rang on the floor like a shot. The snake hung draped upon his upturned palms. It was swelled like a man's arm, that well girthed, and black diamonds jeweled its olive back, an elaborate mosaic of scales that looked like art and wasn't. When it rattled, the entire body hummed, the blood quickened and racing within the scaled hide. Here was death, alive and sentient in the room, presented before all those who bore witness with tear-streaked faces. They were fainting now, collapsing into one another's arms, struck down as if by the living weapon he held before them. Rory lifted the serpent yet higher, high above his head, and he was still as a tree, and as strong, and death moved slowly through his branchlike hands, calm.

Below him, the reverend's eyes had gone to happy slits, and his smile was encompassing, his face all rounded and bright, like a small sun. He no longer clapped. He was quiet, breathing slowly through his nose, deeply, like a monk in trance. His hands were clasped in front of his chest, against his sternum, as if holding something of great value. Christine was there, too, at the edges of Rory's vision, standing in the front row. Her eyes were not like the others'. They were red and fearful—*here*—and her mouth was open, ragged with breath. But Rory didn't look at her. At any of them. His eyes were a long way off.

Christine tried to stop him after the service. She waylaid him at the door, looking up hard-eyed from that dark fountain of hair. A hexagonal hatbox sat on the chair beside her, tied up with a satin black bow. She had one hand on it, as if holding down the lid.

"Rory Docherty," she said. "That was dumb as hell."

Rory looked straight ahead. He knew he could not look at her, or his resolve would weaken. The words seemed so hard to find, to prize from his lungs.

"I'm sorry," he said. "For what I said the other night."

She paused, her fingers tapping the top of the hatbox. Deciding.

"You didn't have to pick up a damn rattlesnake to prove it."

He swallowed. It felt like something had hold of his throat.

"It wasn't like that," he said.

"How was it?"

He wanted to tell her but couldn't. He was lock-jawed, dumb.

Christine watched him, her face softening. Her hand touched his arm.

"Rory," she said. "Are you okay?"

He pushed past her for the door; her fingers sang across his belly like a knife. Then he was into the darkness, his breath ghosting from his mouth. He did not look back. Couldn't. He walked between the worshipers' cars, dusty rattletraps the mills afforded. People stood in small knots, their eyes tracking him, bright with pride. This new star in their ken. This serpent handler. He rounded his shoulders, as if to protect himself from their looks. As if the steely glints of their eyes could burn through his flesh, finding the black hollows of his heart.

There was Maybelline, sitting high-tailed in the grass, still wearing her race tires. Rory came around the trunk and stopped. Before him stood Christine's little brother, Clyde, the one he'd seen floating in the window of her house. The boy was standing beside his driver's door, his face white and round as the moon. In his hands, a handmade serpent box, gable-roofed with twin lids. It was not like the others that Rory had seen. This box was twice the size, metal-screened and brass-latched, scrolled with signs and verses unreadable in the dark.

The boy lifted the box toward Rory.

"Ornias," he said.

Rory looked at him.

"I didn't know you talked."

"Only to them that's righteous."

"You ought not be talking to me, then."

Rory started past him. The boy sidestepped, blocking him, and held the box higher. Rory thought of Christine at the door, waylaying him with her hatbox.

"Him that handles him keep him. This is the keeper's box."

Rory looked down at the box. Someone had painted a white serpent along the spine between the lids. Inside lay the living serpent, dark-scaled, coiled like some evil twin of the one on top.

The boy's shoulders had begun to tremble from the weight. Still Rory didn't take the box. He could not have complications.

Not tonight.

But the boy would not be moved. He was quaking visibly now, and Rory looked into his eyes. They flared like blown coals, so certain that Rory relented, holding out his hands. Now the burden was his, and the boy opened the driver's door, standing aside like a chauffeur. Rory slid the box gently to the passenger side of the bench seat. The big viper didn't rattle, just curled itself tighter into one corner of the box. A starlet done for the night, ready to retreat from the crowds. Rory slid beneath the wheel and pulled the door closed, and the boy set his hands and chin on the sill. Rory looked at him, the box. He sucked his teeth and patted the hub of the steering wheel.

"You were the little gremlin, huh?"

"The what?"

"The one sabotaged my car those times."

The boy straightened, frowning and proud. An answer itself.

"Your daddy put you up to it?"

The boy only shrugged.

"You just tell him I'm sorry," said Rory.

The boy's mouth opened.

"Sorry for what?"

Rory cranked the big motor and pulled the gearshift into first. The boy stood back from the car.

"You just tell him," said Rory.

He let out the clutch and rumbled out of the lot, reaching for the shotgun behind the seat.

"The fuck you mean you ain't in the mood?"

"I mean just what I said, Eustace. I'm tiger-striped in scabs and my bones never felt so heavy."

Eustace stood looking at her, amazed, his shirt half-unbuttoned over the silver fur of his chest. She was still sitting at the dinner table, sipping her coffee.

"Your bones?"

"I fed you, didn't I? That ain't enough?"

He placed his big paws on the top rail of a kitchen chair, and she could hear the ash spindles crackling beneath him as he leaned toward her.

"It ain't my fault you went running through the woods like a damn old crazy woman."

Granny cut her eyes at him.

"Ain't it? Years now, people been saying you reigned over this mountain. Nothing happens on it less you will it to. Any stranger steps foot here, they got to answer to you. How come I got sons of bitches screaming on my roof, burning down my chicken coop?"

"I was a little busy that evening, saving your boy ratted me out to them federals."

"Saving your own ass, more like it. He near froze to death, the way you left him in that creek. Ain't been the same since. Somebody's put a snake in his head, one with jaws enough to swallow him up. Before long he'll be all hollowed out."

"Ain't no fault of mine."

"That boy's been to hell and back."

"He ain't the only one."

"He didn't let it turn him like you."

Eustace smiled. "I wouldn't be so sure."

"The hell does that mean?"

"Means you might not know as much as you think you do."

Granny sat back in her chair, cocking her head.

"One thing I do know. If there's no more of him, there's no more of me."

"There's other women hereabouts."

"Not like me, there isn't."

By his eyes she knew she was right.

He sniffed. "This Muldoon trouble, your boy brought it on his own self."

"Maybe, Eustace. Or maybe you just ain't what you used to be. Maybe you been slipping, letting these Muldoon sons of bitches walk all over you."

He leaned closer toward her. The chair protested beneath him, an ashwood skeleton quivering to break, and she could smell him. That wild, beasting blood.

"You don't know what it took to raise this mountain against the world. A hundred years of fallen timbers and huts, people chased out by Indians and panthers and hunger, and now it's a place where even the ghosts fear to tread. A place where badges ain't but nickel-bought stars, and fear rolls same as whiskey. Cabins up and down this mountain sprung as if of my own seed. My own blood. A world its own, where you can sit on your little porch the day long and damn the lower world to hell. So maybe you ought to rethink what you're in the mood for tonight."

Granny finished the last of her coffee and canted the mug toward the light, to see what new signs she might read in the grounds. It was the same symbol as before, a serpent coiled in bitter silt. She sniffed, cutting her eyes at Eustace.

"You know what?"

"What?"

"Sometimes I don't even know who you are no more."

A smile slunk across the big man's face. He began to unbutton his fly.

"Let me reacquaint you, then."

The white Oldsmobile was parked at the top of the road, the exhaust pipes smoking in the grass. Rory rolled down his window, snugging the shotgun against his right leg. The barrels were cold, loaded with double-aught buck. His breath was short, steady as an engine. He spoke to Ornias, the words wisping from his mouth.

"There has to be a reckoning," he said. "Evil has to be put out of the world, lest it come after whatever you love."

The smoke lay coiled and silent, as if listening.

"It don't matter if I want to do it," he said. "It has to be done."

They were nearing the Olds. Rory thumbed back the first hammer, the second, and squinted. Only one shadow inside the car. He wheeled the Ford off the road, bouncing slightly over the rough ground, and pulled up broadside to the other car, as if to say hello.

He began to raise the shotgun.

The driver smiled out of the gloom of the car's interior.

"Hidy," he said.

A deputy.

Rory froze, the shotgun wedged awkwardly beneath the steering wheel.

"Hey." He swallowed.

"Can I help you?"

Rory cleared his throat. "Sheriff around?"

The man's lower lip was pouched with chaw. He leaned further out the window and spat. There was a dark streak down the side of the door where his aim had been untrue.

"Sick," he said.

"What?"

"Sheriff's sick. Come down with a cold, he said. Scratchy throat. Went home early."

"And he let you take out the Olds?"

"Drove him home in it. Thought I might take the long way back to the station."

"Oh."

The man's face darkened.

"You aren't gonna go telling him, are you?"

Rory looked down at the double hammers of the shotgun, cocked like rabbit ears under a hawk.

"Nuh-uh. That ain't what I got to tell him."

The moon was high and round, cradled in the dark claws of the trees. Its light spilled like shattered glass on the hood. Rory drove out of End-of-the-Road, toward town, his headlights painting the road white. He knew the Sheriff lived in one of the lakefront houses on the far side of the dam, built mainly for the big men from the mills. He looked at Ornias. The snake lay like a spring in the box, its tongue forking the air again, again.

"We'll go high up in the mountains after," he said. "Just like Eustace done, living in caves and sleeping on leaves. It's a whole kingdom up there, up in the wind and trees."

They circled the square, the headlights flashing the darkened storefronts, and turned for the dam. Rory reached out and touched the box, spreading his fingers against the screen. His palm glowed.

"Don't worry," he told the snake. "I'm a-mind to set you free."

The Gumtree Dam loomed before them, a behemoth of stone. A line of white waterfalls ran down its face, the valley held flooded against its brink like a threat. The wheels hopped the joint and the sound changed, the tires whirring over concrete. On the far shore, the yellow-lit windows of waterfront houses danced through the trees, like the campfires of some powerful lake tribe. Rory thought of the little lords lodged heavy-bellied in their sitting rooms, smoking cigars, drinking bottled whiskey from across the ocean.

He was more than halfway across the span when he saw the blockade, the cars parked nose-to-nose at the end of the dam. They were covered in camouflage netting. A lick of panic through his gut. He flicked the wheel slightly one way, then hard the other, downshifting and dumping the clutch. The rear tires broke loose, bawling beneath him, and the car reversed direction, scrawling black hooks of rubber in the road. He was already accelerating the opposite way, fleeing back toward town, when his headlights lit up the broadside of a bread truck. It had been pulled across the foot of the dam, boxing him in.

"Shit."

He pulled another bootleg turn, stopping this time at the very midpoint of the dam. Smoke fumed from under the car. He was bookended, caught, and he could think only of the lights in the trees, the Sheriff so safe in the whiskey-glow of his room. Thumbing the brim of a fancy rabbit-felt hat. Drinking rock and rye for his throat. A tin-stamped star pinned to the lapel of his coat, allowing him to take, take, take.

Rory revved the engine and dropped the clutch. The tires barked, the nose jumping skyward. He roared for the roadblock, the needles swinging erect, the wheel shuddering with power. The flash of a muzzle in the distance, like sparked flint, then another and another. Rory ducked, looking through the hoop of the steering wheel. Slugs rattled the chassis like hail. A white spider lurched across the windshield and burst, a cloud of blown glass that tore across his cheek. A round slammed the seat alongside him.

Rory mashed the brakes.

The car squalled and skidded, stopping slightly sidewise in the road, blue smoke uncoiling from the tires. He flashed the highbeams in surrender. Soon he could hear the boots of men, their hard heels clapping across the concrete. His head was down, his face burned. He put the car in neutral and clasped his hands behind his head, waiting. The machine clinked and rattled a chorus of broken glass, loose metal. A side-mirror fell off.

Then they were on him, a flurry of arms ripping him from the seat. They had Winchester self-loading rifles instead of shotguns. They'd learned after the night on the mountain. One rammed the butt of his weapon into Rory's temple, knocking him flat at their feet, pain ringing through his skull. His grandfather's bowler hat, upended, spun a drunken circle in the road.

"Take his leg," said Kingman.

Hands yanked and twisted, wrenching the leg from his stump. The straps and buckles tore his flesh as they went. Rory sat up, grabbing for his lost limb, only to watch the agent swing the calf into his face like a bat. He heard his nose break, a liquid crack, and the blood came scoring through his sinuses. His eyes flooded with tears. He tried to blink them away from the men watching him and couldn't. The agent knelt over him. His face shone warped and leering through Rory's tears, and he lifted the leg high like an ax. The blow glanced off Rory's head and struck his collarbone, driving him to the ground. He curled into a ball. The blows struck his kidneys, his short-ribs and spine.

Again, again.

He could feel his cells bursting, his muscles torn. Blood booming against the blows, clouding his skin. He yelped at the crack of a rib. A sharp blow to the kidney, a vision of his urine shot red in the bowl. He would not ask them to stop. He would not.

"Stop kicking yourself," said the one wielding the leg. "Stop kicking yourself."

"Enough," said Kingman.

Rory opened his eyes. Kingman's mustache frowned over him. There was no hate in the man's eyes. No sympathy.

"Give me the leg."

The agent handed it over. Kingman looked into the stump socket, examined the buckles and straps. He lifted the bootheel, eyed the pistol sunk in the inlay. He sighted down the calf like a pool cue, frowning, as if unsatisfied with its trueness, then turned and slung the leg from the dam. Rory watched that part of himself go spinning over the guardrail, the leather straps trailing like remnant sinew. He felt lighter somehow, watching it go. Stronger. Bloody here in the road, dismembered. So much lost, there was only one thing left. Everything was that.

He looked at the Ford. Idling, the door open. The men looking love-eyed at Kingman, like they would a football captain or big-league slugger. Their rifles hung loose from their shoulders, their quarry already caught. Rory rose up to his knees and jumped to his foot, lurching for the car. It took him three hops to reach the door and every hop he thought he was dead. He reached for the shotgun still lying on the floor, pushing the barrels through the open window as he slammed home the door.

The men froze. Even Kingman, with one hand over his heart, his fingers checked just short of the pistol under his arm.

"Don't," said Rory.

He looked from one of them to the next. He could cut them down where they stood, all four of them in two barrels of shot. He thought of them bright-wrecked in the road, ghastly in remainder. Unmade.

So easy.

He looked into Kingman's face. The man looked almost amused at this turn of events. This one-legged hillbilly had bested him. He looked almost proud.

Rory spat.

"A pox on the hangman," he said.

He pulled the shotgun inside the car and rammed the stock down hard on the clutch, yanking the shifter into first. He raced the engine and let the pedal pop. The car bucked forward, squealing. It almost stalled but didn't. It roared. The revenuers' cars were parked nose-to-nose at the end of the dam. There was a gap between each and the guardrail, slightly too narrow for his car. Rory aimed for the trunk of the rightmost machine. The gas tank was under there. He thought of fire, his body burning like those chickens in the night.

He banged into second gear, again using the shotgun against the clutch, then angled the barrels away from his face. He buckled his lap-belt at the last moment and braced, hitting the quarter panel of the government car at speed. Metal screamed, his chest slammed the wheel. He tasted blood in his mouth and couldn't breathe, his lungs punched flat. He clung to the wheel like a man drowning.

Maybelline pushed him gently back into the seat. She blew cold air through the shattered windshield, into his open mouth. She crossed the foot of the dam with a little jolt, then started up the road on the far side.

Rory squinted out over the mangled hood, the night skirling coldly about his face. Kingman and the others would think he'd fled for home. The mountain.

Not yet.

He turned onto the road that wound toward the lake, slow, so they wouldn't hear the motor through the trees. The cold felt good on his busted face, his broken nose, and there was warmth in his chest. Blood shunted toward a darkening, growing bruise, throbbing like a second heart.

Soon he could see the lake through the trees, shining under the moon like hammered tin. He was watching the restless glimmer of the surface when he remembered the snake. His eyes went casting about for the box. There it was in the passenger footwell, upended. One of the hinges was busted, the door ajar. The serpent gone. Rory felt it before he saw it, looking down. The snake lay coiled on the floor at his foot. Fear shot through him, cold, as if he were seeing some part of his insides fallen ropy and slick from his gut, and he reached without thought.

"Ornias," he said.

The snake struck fast from the floor, mindless and elongate, the pink mouth glistening like a woman's sex. The fangs snapped into the web of his left hand. He screamed, swerving, drawing the hand to his chest like a wounded rabbit. The car lurched from the road, thundering over the shoulder, trees thudding past like giant ribs. He swerved back toward the blacktop, too hard, and the tires caught edgewise and the car rolled airborne, slamming down hard on the passenger side. A burst of glass and sparks, the scream of rent metal.

Darkness.

Rory opened his eyes. His head was heavy. He was hanging by his seatbelt, his world overturned. Out the window, he saw a blacktop sky, starry with broken glass. Maybelline lay on her roof in the road, ticking and hissing. There came a rattle, rising like the very sound of death, and Rory saw Ornias coiled in a bed of glass just inches from his hanging head. The viper's rattle was poised, trembling like a tiny grenade. His body snarled and kinked, some letter in a language Rory didn't know. Slowly the viper unwound himself. Rory watched the creature zig through the gleaming slivers of wreckage, a string of black diamonds passing between the broken teeth of the windshield and out into the splintery glass of the road. He watched the serpent skate off into the darkness, a whisper along the pavement.

Gone.

Rory realized that he was holding his arm out, as if to grasp the fugitive. Now he drew the arm back to himself, looking at his hand. Twin punctures in the belly of muscle between thumb and forefinger. Red bubbles the size of rabbit's eyes stood atop the wounds. Rory unbuckled himself, crashing against the headliner. He took a shard of glass and cut an X into each fang wound and raised the bloody marks to his mouth, sucking in the red tang of himself and spitting it out. Again, again. He looked at the foamy blood, looking for the viper's venom yellowing its fringes. Too dark to tell. Now he crawled through the shattered windshield, careful of the remnant glass.

He knelt in the road, breathing hard. Before him lay Maybelline, riddled and smoking, her mazed undercarriage turned up to the sky. She was black-eyed, her headlights shot out. Her body dented, her black paint torn in silver streaks. She was bleeding oil in the road, steaming. This machine that had made him fast and strong, cutting across whole counties in under an hour, boring the dark with big glowing eyes. Rory crawled back to the car, searching for the shotgun among the scrap and glass.

The pain came hard and fast. A swarm of fire ants, entering through the twin tunnels of the wounds. They came marching up his arm, firing his veins, coursing against the hard dam of his throat. He gritted his teeth against a wail. He was lurching his way down the road, one-legged, using the butt of the shotgun for a cane. He was making for the lake. The Sheriff's place.

The flesh of his hand was ballooning, as if pumped full of air. Or ants. Blood bubbled from the X-cut wounds. He tried not to look. He didn't want to see what might be squirming in the red fluid that drove him. He looked to the moon instead. It looked sick and yellow to him. A jaundiced bulb, warped on the vine. Pain shot through his gut, sharp and knifelike, like he'd eaten that shattered glass in the road.

He clung to the first mailbox on the road and vomited, a yellowy heave. He wiped his mouth with the back of his hand. Thick ropes of saliva laced him hand to chin. His spit was chewy between his teeth, his gums dry and sore. His breath came ragged, sawing against his throat. The venom, the venom. Pain and plague and madness distilled into a liquid, injected like a curse. They said the bite of a diamondback could kill a man in under an hour.

He had to hurry.

He lifted his eyes to the house before him. It looked small from the front, the windows dark, like he imagined the valley cabin where they killed the boy that was his father. Where they stole his mother's voice.

Rory spat and started again down the road.

Clouds shrouded the moon. He thought he wouldn't be able to see, but he could. He could see the edges of things glowing faintly, gilded in trace threads of golden light. The trees, the houses. As if touched by the glow of a distant fire. Faint but there. He blinked and blinked again. Still there. He thought he might be beginning to die.

He kept on.

The Sheriff's house. White with green trim. A low porch and

metal roof, a small front yard with a curl of white pavers to the porch. The window blinds were drawn, slits of yellow light shining through the cracks. Rory leaned on the mailbox, no one around. The people here had dogs that lived in their houses, slept on their beds. Some ate food from the table. The nearest house was far through the trees, hardly visible.

He steadied the shotgun on the mailbox and thumbed the breech. The barrels fell open. He checked the shells, seated snug in their chambers, and tried to blink away the weblike tendrils in his eyes. The corners of his vision were fracturing. Scaling. The night he saw was like those blinded windows, light leaking through the edges. He slid the shotgun from the top of the mailbox, jerked home the barrels, then bent and retched. Nothing but dry heaves now, long ropes of spit.

He made the porch, slid to the nearest window and listened. Nothing. He pushed himself up, flattening himself against the wall beside the door. He held the shotgun in the crook of his arm and tried the knob. It turned, unlocked. If he walked through it, he could never walk out. The hinges didn't wince. He ducked into the house, dropping to his knees as he leveled the shotgun.

No one.

A den with an overstuffed leather chair, wrinkled and creased like an old man's face. Fishing photos on the walls. Big river cats in black and white, a younger Sheriff who smiled hefting his trophies. The smell of remnant cigars and bay rum. On a side table, the pearl butt of the man's service weapon curled from the looped morass of his shoulder holster.

Rory stuffed the gun in his belt.

The floors were varnished pine. He worked his way room to room on the bony knobs of his knees, a carnival midget with an outsize gun. He pushed open doors with the heel of his snakebit hand, trying not to look at what it had become: a balloon of swollen flesh, the fingers fat as a giant's. A dark storm brewing over the knuckles, blooming up his arm. His very death on march.

He didn't find the Sheriff in the kitchen or the bedrooms or the study. Not even in the bathroom, where Rory thought surely he would find him, sick, voiding into the porcelain by one end or the other. Not anywhere.

Rory tried the back porch, the door grinding along its metal rail. Empty. A long dock stretched over the moonless void of the lake. Rory squinted. There was someone out there at the end. He descended the stairs, the shotgun cradled against his chest, and the steps seemed to be coiling beneath him, making him retch. He went crawling down the dock on knees and hand and elbow, his stump skidding for traction on the planks, the shotgun tucked under his snake-bit arm. He grimaced and bled, hardly getting his breath. He was reduced to this. Belly-crawler, dust-licker. A broken thing, bellying through the darkness.

Rory found the Sheriff in a store-bought lounge chair, asleep. One hand lay over the armrest, the fingers dangling over a half-empty bottle of bonded Scotch. His rabbit-felt hat sat crooked over his eyes. His chest rose, fell, his breath whistling through an open mouth.

"Sick, my ass."

He came around the front of the man and prodded his shoulder with the shotgun.

"Up, you. Up!"

The Sheriff stirred. He pointed up the brim of his hat, squinting one eye against the world, finding the twin bores of a shotgun in his face.

"You got to be shitting me, Docherty."

"I know it was you."

The Sheriff straightened slightly, easing his hands toward his lap.

"The hell you talking about, son?"

Rory pushed the barrels closer to the man's face.

"I'm talking about the Gaston boy." Rory paused. "I'm talking about my mother."

The Sheriff looked down at Rory's swollen hand, up at his brighted eyes.

"You snakebit, boy? You got that venom wilding in your brain?"

"You needn't worry about that. What you got to worry is how a load of this double-aught is gonna suit you." He hooked one swollen finger through the trigger guard of the revolver in his belt. It would hardly fit. He hung the weapon upside down between them, his face twisting with pain. He had to be fast now.

"I was planning just to shoot you. That was my original plan. But then I had a better idea. The two of us are gonna duel it out, right here on this dock. Ten paces or whatever the fancies used to do. Then, when I shoot you dead, I'll know I given God the chance to stop me."

The Sheriff thumbed one of the rootlike veins that climbed his neck, his other hand sitting on his thigh. His eyes cut past Rory, watching for movement in the trees.

"I never touched him, Rory. Neither him nor your mama."

"Don't you worry now, Sheriff. I won't use the buck. I brought along a deer-slug in case I had to take you from a distance. Ought to make it sporting."

The Sheriff watched him.

"Who put you up to this? Eustace?"

Rory said nothing. This was going on too long. He could feel himself growing weak. His leg was jellied, quivering. His hand the paw of an ogre or troll.

"Course it was," said the Sheriff. "I should of known."

"You should of known this day was coming."

The Sheriff's chin rose slightly.

"That boy they killed, that mill boss's son? You know your mama was sweet on him. A secret. They were sweet on each other."

Rory squinted at him. He could see worms of gold buried in the creases of the man's face. They pulsed. His hand seemed higher on his thigh than before, closer to his hip.

"Ain't many believe that," said Rory. "Most think she wasn't but a whore."

"Why else you think she sat so long in that boy's blood, not leaving his side?"

"She went dumb."

"She loved him."

Rory's eyes seared.

The Sheriff nodded, speaking as if to himself.

"That boy's daddy, he was the one funding us that were fighting the government dam. He owned half the valley. Nearly every shot-house and nip-joint rented from him. And his boy kept telling him there was some bird down along the river, some parrot thought to be extinct. Some parakeet. Said it might keep the government from coming in. Said he was writing to the Museum of Natural History, in Washington. All he needed was proof. Then those nightriders come through the valley, cutting us down. One night they caught the Gaston boy in the valley. Made sure he never did find any bird."

"It's some story you made up, just to keep me from killing you."

"I wished it was."

"Then how come you never did nothing?"

"Evidence, son. We didn't have it."

"Didn't?"

The Sheriff took off his hat with one hand, set it upturned in his lap.

"The warden down at Dix Hill, I told him to send word if your mama ever said or did something that might be a clue to what happened." He reached into the black well of the hat, bringing out a folded square of paper. "We never did find what she used to take that man's eye, you know. The one we found in her pocket. It was the investigator said a cat's paw, but we never found it." He tapped the paper against the hat brim. "This come today, express from Raleigh." He leaned forward, holding it out, his other hand nearly in shadow.

Rory looked at the man, at the note. It quivered in the space between them, light as a wing. Rory lowered the shotgun slightly, snatching the paper from the outstretched hand.

The Sheriff leaned back.

"Warden said your mama started drawing them after you come to see her last Sunday, slipping them to the nurses and orderlies." He pointed. "This is what she drew."

Rory began unfolding the paper.

"My brother, the pastor, he'll tell you he lost his eye in a timber accident," said the Sheriff. He scoffed. "A lie. One of those nightriders took it. And what you think he done it with?"

Rory looked at the shape dark-slashed across the folds.

A long handle, a round head forked like a tongue.

A tined spoon.

"Must of been the first thing your mama could get her hands on," said the Sheriff. "When she come at them."

"No," said Rory.

The Sheriff nodded.

"With the valley flooded, there wasn't no whiskey but his."

The word broke like a stone from Rory's throat.

"Eustace."

"How you think he raised that mountain like he did?"

Rory hopped backward a step, lost his balance. He fell flat on his rump, the weapons clattering around him. He looked down at his monstrous hand, his missing leg, then out at the flooded valley of the lake. The moon was breaking free of the clouds, jags of light racing across the surface like slicks of burning oil, and for a moment he could see into the very depths of this place. An underworld of drowned cabins and bright-glowing bones, a vision seen as if from mountain height.

Now darkness.

CHAPTER 28

*H*e was on a horse, descending through moonlight. He could feel the
air cooling, the road falling into the valley, the horse a machine of
muscle between his heels. He should have hit the edge of the lake by now,
but the road kept on, crooking ever deeper into the pines. In the distance,
the rumble of water over stone.

The river, not yet dammed.

*He stood before a small cabin, unpainted. Oaks crowded the place,
black and gnarled on every side, and he knew Bonni was inside. She had
snuck out from the white castle of the bawdyhouse to meet him. She was
still young, milk-smooth in her nakedness, and she was waiting for him.
He was going to hear her voice.*

*He stepped onto the porch, into darkness deeper than the surrounding
night. He heard the planks creak, felt them shift under his feet. Someone
was there. He turned to look.*

Too late.

*He was punched in the gut, hard. He dropped to his knees, no breath
to scream, and they wrenched his arms behind his back, lifting him loose-
kneed from the planks. They were wearing sack hoods, the eyeholes cut
ragged, the sack corners flat and pointed like animal ears. The burlap was
sucked up against their mouths as they breathed, darkened in vents and*

leers. They carried ax-handles and clubs. A silver medal, three-tined, shone on the bib of one.

You think some bird can stop what's coming? Some parrot?

They drove him through the door. A girl came flying toward them, her black hair wild as a mane. She scraped and pawed at their chests. One of the nightriders drove her back against a sawhorse table, his right hand forking her throat.

Best say your good-byes, said the big man. He thumped his ax-handle against Rory's chest. You mightn't not talk so good after we done.

Rory was looking only at the girl. Something silver winked in her hand. Now a flash of light wheeled from the end of her arm and the man above her screamed. He staggered backward, dropping his club, palming the bloody socket where his left eye used to be.

Rory wrenched loose his arm and spun on the balls of his feet, delivering a left hook into the leering mask of the big man standing beside him. Like hitting stone, his knuckles shattering against the point of the man's jaw. Now a club fell heavy across his back, thumping the breath from his lungs, and he was on his knees. Now another and another, the hickory handles falling bone-white in the room, shattering his ribs, and he was crawling across the planks, trying to reach her.

He had to hear her voice.

One word.

Any.

He crawled into her arms. She opened her mouth, as if to speak, and a green bird lifted from the hollow of her throat. He followed the creature out the nearest window, through the black clutches of the trees. Together they rose out of the valley, light as a song, pulled toward the moon.

CHAPTER 29

Granny May sat in her rocker, watching dusk come through the valleys. The sun was dying red in the west, and the world before her was the color of blood and smoke. The purple ridges rippled into the distance like eroded ramparts, the valleys between them dark as fractures in the earth. The blue twist of the woodstove stung in the cold air, in her nostrils, and she breathed deeply and liked the sting.

It was going to be a cold winter. She could tell. She could feel it in her bones. But the woodpile was stacked high with split oak and maple. The smokehouse was full and her boy was home. He was back there in his room, sleeping. Healing beneath the curling wings of his mother's paintings. The town doctors had kept him a week, feeding vials of antivenin into his blood. They said he would regain full use of his hand. Likely he would. They said the snake carried enough venom to kill five men and wasn't he lucky.

Granny knew it was more than luck. When Eli arrived at her porch, telling her Rory had been bitten, she was not surprised, given the signs of late. Her snakebite herbs were sitting in a small burlap purse on the shelfboard, readied for just such circumstance. That first night, while the duty nurse patrolled the halls, Granny chewed ribwort leaves—mountain plantain—applying a spit poultice of the macerated substance to the boy's wounds, packing it hard with her thumb. This weed brought toxins to the surface, drawing venom from the blood. She followed with poultices of purple coneflower, such as the Cherokee used for rattlesnake bites, and osha and yellowroot. Cold, bitter herbs that fought sepsis and poison. She applied these night after night, when the doctors were home in bed.

At intervals, she forced the boy, half-conscious, to hold lumps of ground echinacea root under his tongue, letting the medicine absorb. She did not want to risk him choking. In the days that followed, she would give him milk thistle and nettle to support his liver, and potions decocted of turmeric and sarsaparilla and oak, alternating with spoons of activated charcoal to absorb any remnant venom from his gut.

She sat by his hospital bed for a week, never sleeping, subsisting on a bag of roasted chestnuts and hard candy she brought down from the mountain, her temples rumbling as she chewed. She refused the town-food that Eli tried to bring her. She left the room only when nature forced her. She watched every doctor and nurse with one eye squinted, as if sighting them down. As soon as they were gone, she opened her herb purse, applying her own medicines to the task.

The first morning, returning from the ladies' room, she found a dark-haired girl sitting at the bedside, holding her boy's hand while he slept. A white hatbox, black-bowed, sat on the side table, waiting to be opened. The girl stood.

"You must be Granny May," she said. "I'm Christine Adderholt."

Granny growled.

"God ain't meant to live in no box," she said, "and neither is a rattlesnake."

But the girl came every day after her shift, sure as clockwork. Her brow set, her back straight. She didn't care that Granny would hardly speak to her, that the two of them would sit silent on either side of his bed, chewing lips or snacks. She kept coming, undaunted, steady as a stream that cuts stone.

At the end of the third day, Granny's jaws groaned open.

"Some hat," she said, jutting her chin toward the flat-crowned beauty the girl was wearing, colored the pale pink of a kitten's paw. "Mail-ordered?"

"I made it," said the girl. "I got my own business making them."

Granny straightened.

"Say you do?"

"Yes, ma'am. Got newspaper ads going up in Charlotte, Raleigh. I'll be out the mill soon, keeps going the way it is. I hate the kitchen, but I can make a pillbox hat pretty enough to eat."

Granny nodded. "I see that." Now she leaned back, reaching into her sweater for her pipe. "Tell you what, girl. You come for a visit on the mountain once the boy is home. I never been anything special in the kitchen, neither, but I can bake a mean stackcake." She scratched a match, winked over the flame. "And not just in the Presbyterian fashion."

Granny was alone the day the government man showed up. He was square-faced with a handlebar mustache. He wasn't from around here, didn't say much. He stood there at the foot of the bed, working his lips back and forth across his teeth. He held Rory's black bowler hat in his hands—the one her own dead husband had worn. There was a deep dent in the crown.

"You raise him?" he asked.

"That's right."

"He's a tough little knot."

"Born hard."

The man nodded, setting the hat at the foot of the bed.

"He wakes up, you tell him he gets one pass," he said. "For what he could've done on that dam and didn't. For surprising me. And that's all he gets."

Granny nodded, her tongue coiled against the side of her mouth. The man turned on his heel and walked out, his boots clopping down the hallway, growing faint. She took up the old bowler hat, rubbing her thumb along the edge of the brim, so tatty it felt serrated. She had never been good at letting go of things, be they goods or ghosts. She eyed the white hatbox on the table, still unopened, and dumped the old bowler in the wastebasket.

When Rory could speak, she was ready. She was sitting alongside his bed, thumbing a green wad into the bowl of her pipe. He blinked at her, watching the smoke uncoil from the side of her mouth.

"I don't think you can smoke in here."

"You see me doing it."

The boy looked down at his white-mounded form, at the tubes feeding him who knew what. He raised his bitten hand, ugly but there. She bent toward him.

"You do know pit vipers don't make much for pets."

"So I learned."

"Well, you best be thanking that snake."

"How's that?"

"Sheriff said he might of shot you, you hadn't been snakebit. You hadn't passed out."

Rory lifted his head, as if checking the bedrails for handcuffs. None.

"He the one that brought me in here?"

"That's right. Him and that brother of his."

"He tell you why I come at him?"

"Said he'd leave that part to you."

Rory nodded, swallowed.

"I'm tired," he said. "Maybe I ought to tell you later."

Granny licked her thumb and stove it into the bowl of the pipe. The ash hissed.

"Nuh-uh, boy. You gonna tell me now."

Granny leaned back in her rocker, the valleys welling beneath her. Her pipe lay cold on the side table, unused. There was the faint sound of Rory snoring in his room. The dusk deepened, the world bluing toward dark. She was watching her breath smoke from her throat when a pair of white headlights flared at the bottom of the drive. She watched them come bouncing up the grade, jaunty almost, the first dust of snow swirling through their beams. It was the big six-wheeled truck.

Eustace.

He parked beneath the lone chestnut, there where Maybelline used to sit, and stepped down from the cab. He had on a furry cap with earflaps, a leather vest over a flannel shirt. Bits of snow flecked the mountains of his shoulders, caught in his beard. He approached the porch, labored up the steps. He scratched his chin with a thumb.

"Come to see the boy," he said. "Brought him a jar of my very best." He patted his pocket, a square bulge. "This here is barley scotch, good for toddies."

"That's very sweet of you. He'll like that. He's back in his room."

He started for the door.

"*Eustace.*"

The big man stopped.

"You forgetting the toll?" She cocked the flat of her cheek toward him, smiling. "Give us a kiss."

Eustace took off his hat and rolled it between his hands. He tried to smile. He came down the porch. Bent over her. Kissed her.

Her hand had slipped beneath the blanket in her lap.

He never saw the blade.

It was a bone-handled straight razor, the same she'd carried in her working days. She'd stropped it bright-edged the day her boy came home.

She laid him open at the throat, deep and fast, like she would a hog. The blade winked through his flesh as through a hunk of dough, that easy, and his blood came in a bright flourish into the blued-out world. He clutched the wound with both hands, as if he might hold it together, but the blood pumped helter-skelter through his knuckles, over his fingers and down his shirt. He stepped backward once, twice. He fell off the porch, hitting the earth with a bony crack, like an ax-felled tree.

Granny stood, the razor held open-angled in her hand. Dripping. She stepped down from the porch, carefully, and stood over him, his thrashing bulk. His eyes were wide, white-bulbed, like he was seeing everything for the first time, and maybe he was. His screams were caught gurgling in the new mess of his throat. The blood bubbled through his fingers. It was like he wanted to scream, to say something, but it was the wound that kept talking instead.

She couldn't believe he'd deceived her so long.

She should have known.

She knelt beside him. He started to reach for her but didn't want to take a hand from his throat. He clung to it like something that could save him. She touched a palm to his forehead, holding the razor over his face.

"Who were the others done it with you?" she asked. "Whose eye is in the jar?"

He tried to tell her. Tried and tried. Really seemed to want to. But his words flecked and spat shapelessly from his cut throat.

"Oh honey," she said. "I'd kill you twice if I could."

She took the jar of whiskey from his pocket. Unscrewed the lid and poured it out, then sniffed. Beneath the round sting of barley there was something else. Something chemical.

Strychnine.

Just as she thought.

She screwed the lid back on the jar, leaned over him.

"Christ's father let him die on that cross," she said. "I understand why he done it." She leaned closer, whispering in his ear: "But Christ never had no granny like me."

CHAPTER 30

They buried him high on Howl Mountain at first light, up among the towers of red spruce and fir where the wind never slept, where it was always cold. They dragged him there on the mule-sled, no sound save the murmuring of ancient trees, the stomp of hooves, the slash of iron skids. They followed old paths that twisted through understories of witch hobble and purple laurel, snow-dusted, their breath and the breath of the mule throbbing in the gray. The paths grew ever narrower as they ascended, dark and sinewy veins tread by hoof and claw, the furred bloodlines of the mountain. Beneath them the valleys lay flooded in white seas of mist, the ridgelines ghostly and unreal, the world lightly powdered.

Near the summit a thick carpet of moss covered the ground, a wooly green cap that covered the bones of the fallen, the graves of beasts and men. They found a wind-thrown spruce, uprooted, the earth cratered beneath the snarled mass of roots.

Here was the place.

They dug together, unspeaking, and their breath clouded the shafts of light lancing slantwise through the trees. Rory had to lay aside his crutch and lean against the edge of the hole to keep his balance. Granny stood in the very center of it, in her tall man-boots, and her arms were streaked black as she worked. They rolled his body into the ground wordlessly, without ceremony, shoveling the black dirt over his shrouded form. The mountain would do the rest for one of its own. Reclaim him, the roots of the high forest driving his bones ever deeper through the black earth, toward the stony heart of the mountain.

They turned to find the sun dawning before them, borne white and complete over the eastern serrations. Rory rode atop the mule, having no new leg yet made, and Granny led them from the burial summit, clucking and coaxing by turn. They were nearing the edge of the high woods when a wind rose moaning as from the ground itself. Rory watched as the leaves and needles rose fluttering from the forest floor, swirling about Granny's knees, whispering around the gray cannons of the mule. He watched with yet greater awe as Granny's hair rose swirling above her head, a crown of whitening fire.

EPILOGUE

The mountain blazed with snow, fallen from the black maw of the previous night. The sun hung high and white, the sky a cold blue. A sound came throbbing through the naked twists of trees, whumping like a heart, and a crimson coupe turned the bottom of the drive. Eli was at the wheel. He parked beneath the wide crown of the chestnut tree and stepped to the porch. He seemed older than he used to, taller. His beard was combed, straight as the blade of an ax. He cocked his head toward Eustace's six-wheeled truck, white-ledged with snow.

"Is it done?"

Granny nodded. "It's done."

"Nobody's gonna hear from him?"

"There's few with ears that big."

"Good."

He climbed the porch and stood before Rory, holding out his up-turned hand. In the flat blade of his palm lay the keys to the coupe in the yard, joined by a metal ring.

"Maybelline II," he said. "It's the least I could do."

Rory rose, still getting used to his new leg.

"It isn't your fault," he said. "None of it."

"He was blood."

"There's blood blood," said Rory. "And there's family."

Granny nodded, packing her pipe.

"You said you needed a car today," said Eli, putting the keys in Rory's hand. "See if you want to give her back."

Rory closed the keys in his fist and squeezed his friend's shoulder, hard. Then he limped to the edge of the porch steps, staring out. There sat the coupe, blood-bright against the snow. Above this stood the spirit tree, bone-pale against the sky, the great crown of antlers studded with noonday glints. A hundred tiny ghosts sighing in the wind. He wondered if Eustace was one of them now, trapped there, moaning through the glass mouth of a bottle. Wordless. Just another sound, another wind on the mountain. The tree seemed to twist slightly, as if by muscular shift, and Rory closed his eyes. There it stood, pulsing in the black night behind his eyes, a white bolt of power erupted jaglike from the earth. A tree made purely of light.

He opened his eyes, setting his new hat on his head. A fedora, midnight-black, risen from the white castle of a hatbox. He was going into town today to pick up Christine. She was coming with him to Raleigh, to meet his mother. Already he could see the twin lamps of his mother's eyes, as if she were looking, for the first time, upon a creature she had birthed. She would shine, he knew. Her ribs swelled like the bones for wings, her heart too full for the narrow path of the tongue.

Eli leaned against a porch post, crossing his arms.

"What you want to tell the rest of the mountain when Eustace don't turn up?"

Granny's rocker creaked.

"Tell them it's gonna be a hard winter," she said. "But come spring we'll have something new for them to haul. Something the law ain't even caught on to it yet."

"What's that?"

Like an answer: the spark of a match.

ACKNOWLEDGMENTS

To my parents, Janet and Rick Brown, who have remained a well of strength and faith during the rockier legs of this journey. You have always believed in me, which is the greatest gift any parent could give their child. May other sons and daughters be so fortunate.

To Christopher Rhodes, who is not only my phenomenal agent but also my steadfast friend and confidant. I am so grateful for your kindness, wisdom, savvy, taste, and love. May our meditations be consistent and fruitful.

To Jason Frye, my first and oldest writer-friend, whose mentorship and faith, along with his keen eye and steady hand, were integral to the creation of this book. Search him out for manuscript services, you writers. May my secret weapon be yours.

To a dog named Waylon, who lived with me in the mountains and who brought such constant joy and light to the darker moments of a young writer's story. May you always run. And may your mother's heart heal around your loss.

To my team at St. Martin's, including George Witte, Sara Thwaite, Jessica Lawrence, Courtney Reed, Karen Richardson, and so many more. Thank you so much for welcoming me into the family. I am honored and thrilled to work with you sweet and fierce and brilliant people. May I do you proud (and sell lots of copies).

To Lauren Miller, witch woman and trauma worker, who first took me root-digging and whose expertise in herbs and tinctures and potions proved invaluable in the writing of this book. May you always find your hawthorn grove.

To Wiley Cash, who has been so incredibly generous with his time, direction, and wisdom. May our trunks long be full of ARCs.

To David Joy, who writes of contemporary Appalachia with such sweet and bloody power, and who has been so kind to my work. May we bark at the moon one of these nights.

To Steph Post, whose support and encouragement mean so much to me. May the foxes grant our wishes.

To Ashley Warlick, whose insight and wisdom always seem to arrive at the most crucial of moments, and to my whole Greenville family. May our cocktail napkins always be so fruitful.

To Katy Simpson Smith, Matthew Griffin, and Kent Wascom, who write books of such unbelievable power and majesty and who make New Orleans so special to me. I am awed and grateful, every day, to call you my friends, and I get such a thrill every time I see your names in the bookstore. May our next meal be sooner rather than later.

To the crew at Bespoke Coffee and Dry Goods, who let me keep working even as the brooms come out and the chairs go up on the tables. It means more than you know. May I long be your bodyguard.

To the Southern Independent Booksellers Alliance (SIBA) and all of the booksellers across the nation, who have been kind enough to read and recommend my work. I can call so many of you my friends, and that has been the greatest unexpected gift of this whole journey. May you love Granny May as much as I do.